GRASSHOPPERS IN SUMMER

OTHER FIVE STAR TITLES BY PAUL COLT

HISTORICAL FICTION
Boots and Saddles: A Call to Glory (2013)
A Question of Bounty: The Shadow of Doubt (2014)
Bounty of Vengeance: Ty's Story (2016)
Bounty of Greed: The Lincoln County War (2017)
Sycamore Promises (2018)
Friends Call Me Bat (2019)

GREAT WESTERN DETECTIVE LEAGUE
Wanted: Sam Bass (2015)
The Bogus Bondsman (2017)
All That Glitters (2019)

Fic
Col
Western

GRASSHOPPERS IN SUMMER

PAUL COLT

FIVE STAR
A part of Gale, a Cengage Company

Copyright © 2020 by Paul Colt
Five Star Publishing, a part of Gale, a Cengage Company

ALL RIGHTS RESERVED.
This novel is a work of fiction. Names, characters, places, and incidents are either the product of the author's imagination, or, if real, used fictitiously.

No part of this work covered by the copyright herein may be reproduced or distributed in any form or by any means, except as permitted by U.S. copyright law, without the prior written permission of the copyright owner.

The publisher bears no responsibility for the quality of information provided through author or third-party Web sites and does not have any control over, nor assume any responsibility for, information contained in these sites. Providing these sites should not be construed as an endorsement or approval by the publisher of these organizations or of the positions they may take on various issues.

LIBRARY OF CONGRESS CATALOGING-IN-PUBLICATION DATA

Names: Colt, Paul, author.
Title: Grasshoppers in summer / Paul Colt.
Description: First edition. | Farmington Hills, Mich. : Five Star, A part of Gale, a Cengage Company, 2020.
Identifiers: LCCN 2019030683 | ISBN 9781432868888 (hardcover)
Subjects: LCSH: Treaty between the United States of America and different tribes of Sioux Indians (1868)—Fiction. | GSAFD: Historical fiction.
Classification: LCC PS3603.O4673 G73 2020 | DDC 813/.6—dc23
LC record available at https://lccn.loc.gov/2019030683

First Edition. First Printing: April 2020
Find us on Facebook—https://www.facebook.com/FiveStarCengage
Visit our website—http://www.gale.cengage.com/fivestar
Contact Five Star Publishing at FiveStar@cengage.com

Printed in Mexico
Print Number: 01   Print Year: 2020

They came from the land of the Great Father, as many as grasshoppers in summer . . .
—Autumn Snow, Tsitsistas (Cheyenne)

CHAPTER ONE

Fort Kearny
Dakota Territory
December 21, 1866

"Attack! Attack!" A lone trooper galloped toward the fort waving his arm and shouting at the top of his lungs. Clouds of fresh snow boiled up behind his horse's hooves, catching the sun in a shower of glittering light. Blue-coated troopers scrambled to timber and stone emplacements along the defensive perimeter. Guards leveled their rifles, sighting the rider's back trail as his horse thundered into the quadrangle. He raced across the parade ground and pulled his blown mount to a halt in front of the post commander's office. Colonel Henry B. Carrington, 18th U.S. Infantry, stood on the rough-hewn plank porch, drawn to the commotion outside. Steam frosted his mustache and beard in gray crystals. The trooper dropped from his saddle, horse and rider blowing gouts of steam in the cold winter air. He threw up a hasty salute.

"War party, sir, attacked the wood train this morning."

Carrington knit his brow. Privately he recoiled from the news. Why must the damn red hellions resist? They stood against westward expansion. Their resistance was futile. It served only to make his job more difficult.

"How many, Private?"

"No tellin' for certain, sir. Maybe a hundred."

Carrington pursed his lips in thought. "Likely a diversion

intended to draw us out of the fort," he said, as much to himself as the trooper. The assessment suited him. An engineer by training, the post commander made a reluctant warrior, which is to say no warrior at all.

"We must mount a pursuit, sir."

Carrington had scarcely noticed the arrival of his First Battalion Commander, Captain William J. Fetterman. A combat veteran, Fetterman carried the rank of Brevet Lieutenant Colonel during the war. He arrived at Kearny little more than a month ago. He'd brashly asserted his willingness to fight, telling his new commanding officer that given eighty seasoned men, he'd ride through the whole of the Sioux Nation. Fetterman knew the colonel's reputation for stockade soldiering and his reluctance to fight. Impatient with waiting for his methodical commanding officer, he drew himself up to the full measure of his stature and lifted his bearded chin toward Carrington.

"With your permission, sir."

Carrington raised a hand as though calling for a halt. "Not so fast, Captain. The hostiles would like nothing better than to draw us into an ambush."

"The reported strength is no more than a hundred, sir. Surely you cannot allow such a piddling force of savages to intimidate the whole of the eighteenth?"

"The report is an unconfirmed estimate, Captain."

"Then, if it please the colonel, two companies should prove more than decisive."

Carrington massaged the bridge of his nose. He knew of course that some of the men found him wanting when it came to a fight. "Very well, Captain, call out C and D companies and mount your pursuit. But hear me, under no circumstances are you to cross Lodge Trail Ridge. To do so would put your command beyond our ability to support you should the hostiles attack in some larger force."

Fetterman nodded with a half-hearted salute. The old man had no stomach for a fight. "Bugler, 'Boots and Saddles!' " He hurried off to the stables.

Twenty minutes later Fetterman and a relief column of seventy-nine officers and men along with two accompanying civilians splashed through the ice and crossed Piney Creek headed toward Lodge Trail Ridge.

Tashunca-uitco sat on a windswept rise below Lodge Trail Ridge accompanied by a small band of Oglala and Brule brothers. A bank of heavy gray cloud scented with snow scudded out of the north. The warriors watched as a dark spot across the white blanket of snow grew in the distance. Gray clouds of hot breath drifted into the air along the line, giving the bluecoats and their ponies the appearance of a fire-breathing snake, winding its way toward them. The young warrior known as Crazy Horse felt his medicine grow strong. His pony shifted hipshot under him, sensing the fight that would come. His dark eyes narrowed beneath a broad brow as he squinted into the distance. High rounded cheekbones tapered to a prominent jaw around a strong nose and wide mouth. He wore a beaded buckskin war shirt, bone breastplate, and heavy buffalo coat. A single eagle feather fluttered from his long black braids in the chill breeze.

"Blue Dog," Crazy Horse addressed his brother without taking his eyes from the pony soldier column. "Tell Mahpiya-luta the bluecoats come. We will lead them over the ridge into the valley. He will know what to do."

Blue Dog nodded, wheeled his pony, and galloped up the ridge.

"Hostiles, sir," the scout pointed to a dozen riders silhouetted on a low rise near the foot of Lodge Trail Ridge.

Fetterman signaled a halt. He drew his glass from a pouch

fastened to the cantle of his McClellan saddle. He extended the brass tube and fit the piece to his eye in an unbroken motion. The riders made no move. Fetterman appraised his first look at the enemy. They made a ragtag band of savages, hardly an effective fighting force. He may have overestimated his boast of the force it would take to defeat them. He swung the glass to the left and back to the right along the ridgeline. He saw no sign of a stronger force. He returned his glass to the line of warriors perched on the rise. As if knowing they were being watched two of them stood on the backs of their horses and dropped their breechclouts, baring their asses in taunting defiance.

"Sons-a-bitches," Fetterman muttered. "Let's see how cocksure they are with the length of a saber run up their arrogant asses." He turned to the bugler.

"Beggin' the captain's pardon, sir," Sergeant Major Callahan anticipated Fetterman's order. "They's behavin' like decoys." The veteran Indian fighter jerked his head in the direction of the warriors. "They want us to charge 'em. Most likely there's more of 'em we cain't see over the Lodge Trail Ridge there." Callahan made clear reference to the land feature in the hope of reminding the captain of Colonel Carrington's order.

"Good." Fetterman grinned at the Sergeant Major's caution. "That means more heathen savages are about to get a taste of our steel."

Deep gullies and ravines gashed the floor of Peno Valley on the far side of Lodge Trail Ridge. Mahpiya-luta knew them well. He hid his warriors in them, lying down beside their ponies in the center of the valley and along the valley walls to the north and south. A thin veil of steam hung over the warriors and ponies in their hiding places, the only visible sign of their presence. It gave the valley floor the eerie illusion of a simmering caldron. The pony soldiers might see it and be warned, but Red Cloud expected they would not. They would chase Crazy Horse and his brothers into the valley where Red Cloud would spring his trap.

Lean and rawboned, Red Cloud made an imposing presence. His long black hair hung loose adorned by a single eagle feather. Deep lines etched his features as though he were hewn from the red rock buttes of the Powder River country in which he fought. A long prominent nose gave his dark eyes the set of a perpetual squint. His wide mouth twisted in a tight line. He wore a bone breastplate and buckskin war shirt that counted his many coups.

Pony soldiers built forts in his people's Powder River hunting grounds to protect white settlers who traveled the Bozeman Trail. The forts and the coming of the white eyes angered Red Cloud. He led his Oglala and Lakota brothers to war along with the Cheyenne under Moquinto, known as Roman Nose, and their Arapaho brothers. Together they would drive the wasichu from the lands of the people. This day would seal his victory.

Crazy Horse listened to the pony soldier's bugle call and held his ground. He let them come, judging the distance and the speed of the charge. His pony whickered softly and pawed the frozen ground, sensing the chase. Other ponies tossed their heads, flaring their nostrils in the breeze at the scent of the iron-shod bluecoat ponies. The ground trembled with the pounding hoofbeats of the pony soldier charge. Crazy Horse let them close to the distance of a long rifle shot.

"Yeee iee iee." He wheeled his pony and galloped up Lodge Trail Ridge, leading his brothers away from the bluecoat charge. They crested the ridge and attacked the slope to the valley below.

Red Cloud watched Crazy Horse and his band sleigh and slide down the valley wall from Lodge Trail Ridge. They skidded onto the valley floor and raced toward the wash where his warriors waited. The bluecoats followed, clearing the ridge wall as they charged into the valley. At the rim of the wash Crazy Horse pulled his pony to a sliding stop. The little horse reared, trumpeting his challenge to their bluecoat pursuers. The pursued wheeled to face the oncoming charge.

The bluecoats seemed not to notice what had happened until other warriors rose up out of the ground, ghost-like apparitions behind Crazy Horse and his brothers. Red Cloud and his warriors stormed to the attack from their hiding places. Clouds of steam rose from their war cries. Other warriors appeared on the bluecoats' left and right, filling the crisp air with clouds of steam growing out of laboring horses and a chorus of war cries. Red Cloud and his warriors surged forward.

Fetterman threw up his arm, calling a halt. Assaulted by the sudden realization they were surrounded on three sides. He wheeled his horse.

"Bugler sound retreat!" He wheeled his horse and spurred to the rear. He led the formation back across the valley as the Sioux, Cheyenne, and Arapaho closed in from the rear and both flanks. Thundering hooves throbbed in his gut, his ears split with their cries. Lodge Trail Ridge loomed ahead, the face of the slope now an obstacle to climb. He felt the press of the enemy close in. Bullets and arrows rained a relentless hail of death, overtaking his command from behind. They could not outrun them at the climb. They were exposed. The enemy would cut them down. They had one choice. Turn and fight.

He called a halt at the base of the ridge.

"Form skirmish lines! Fire at will!"

Troopers jumped down from their horses and turned to fight in wild confusion. Volleys of pistol and rifle fire raked the charging warriors. They offered too little resistance, too late to blunt the attack.

The Lakota swept over the pony soldiers with the fury of a great storm. The battle raged at close quarters for only a short time. One by one the bluecoats fell to overwhelming numbers. None survived. In this last they died as warriors.

The Lakota and their allies counted much coup. This day they would celebrate a great victory. Red Cloud's victory would be celebrated in song. This greatest victory of his war won the Powder River country for his people.

Chapter Two

Office of the Commanding General
Department of the Missouri
Chicago, Illinois
December 23, 1866

Seventy-nine good men. General William Tecumseh Sherman set aside the telegraphed report from Carrington. The shear audacity of it, scarcely beyond the perimeter of the fort; he pressed clenched fists to the throbbing in his temples. Humiliation grated on Sherman. He knew how to fight. He knew how to win. This was no way to make war.

The war hero's perpetually mussed fiery cropped hair and beard showed flecks of gray, the only indication of surrender to the passing years. Physically he remained the wiry bandy rooster of his younger years. His eyes burned with the same intensity that gave no quarter to the beleaguered rebels he'd crushed in the latter stages of the war. Those eyes dominated a face furrowed by a career forged on the fields of mortal conflict. He retained by every measure the feisty disposition, giving credence to critics who thought him insane. By the end of the war those critics were effectively silenced.

War experience shaped his assessment of the Fetterman massacre. He'd forged a sixty-mile-wide path of total destruction stretching from Atlanta to Savannah in the latter stages of the war of secession. His famous march to the sea effectively cut the Confederacy in half and paved the road to Union victory.

The path to victory over the plains tribes could be no different. You couldn't win a war hiding in a fort. You had to fight with massed force. You had to destroy the enemy's ability to sustain itself as a fighting force. Once accomplished, the enemy could be crushed in the field. The crux of the Indian problem was the fact we'd not yet found the will to defeat the red man in decisive terms. The Fetterman Fight was a good example.

Fetterman and his command were lost in a token response to hostile provocation. Carrington had to be replaced with a commander who knew how to fight. He'd put the problem of replacing him to Sam. It wouldn't be easy. The postwar reductions in force seriously depleted the officer corps. Good fighting men had gone back to peaceful pursuits. Of the officer cadre that remained, too many did so owing more to political patronage than ability. That was a problem for another day. First, he needed to report the loss to Sam. Then he had seventy-nine letters to write, two days before Christmas. He shook his head.

Office of the General in Chief
Department of the Army
Washington, D.C.
December 26, 1866
Horace Porter rapped softly at the office door, "General Parker to see you, sir."

Ulysses S. Grant looked up from his morning report. He'd come into the office the day after Christmas over Julia's protest. Given the public outcry set off by news accounts of the "Fetterman massacre," Grant wasn't surprised Ely had come to see him. He removed his spectacles and rubbed the bridge of his nose between thumb and forefinger. None of this was getting any easier.

Short and slight, the war hero general projected a bearing larger than his modest stature by a force of presence. The air around him fairly crackled with command. He wore authority like a comfortable cloak. Flecks of gray showed in his neatly trimmed mustache and beard. He scratched a match and relit his ever-present cigar. "Send him in, Horace," Grant said, waving his cigar through a haze of blue smoke.

General Ely S. Parker (ret.) was known to his Seneca people as Ha Sa No An Da. He wore his heritage proudly along with the black suit, starched collar, and ribbon tie appropriate to his station in white society. Tall and lean, Parker was quiet and observant by nature. A lawyer, engineer, and former Grant aid, his lively dark eyes missed little. When he spoke the resinous tones of a deep voice gave the weight of wisdom to his words.

"Thank you for seeing me unannounced, General." Parker crossed the office expanse in long, fluid strides.

"Nonsense, Ely." Grant rose from his desk and extended his hand. "You know you're always welcome here. I only wish you were coming on a happier errand. I suspect the subject is the dreadful loss of Fetterman's command."

"I'm afraid it is, sir."

"Please sit down," Grant gestured to one of the wing chairs drawn up in front of his desk. "It isn't going to help the Commission's work, is it?"

Parker shook his head as he folded his frame into a chair that would seem too large for a lesser man. "It couldn't have come at a worse time, General."

"You're a civilian now, Ely. Please, Sam will do."

"Thank you, sir. The commission is already badly divided. This can do nothing but add to the vengeful sentiments of those predisposed to see the plains tribes as adversaries."

"You're right of course, though I'd be hard-pressed to argue our side of the point given the bloody accounts the other side has been given to feed on." Grant pressed his fingertips to a steeple, touching them to his lips in thought. "You've been on the ground out there, Ely," he said quietly. "Setting the commissioner's biases aside for the moment, what's the answer?"

Parker furrowed his brow. "I'm not sure, Sam. I've asked myself that question more times than I can count. Enough to know there is no simple answer. It has to start with trust. We've a history with the red man that goes back to Andy Jackson and beyond. Time and again we've made promises only to break them the moment they become the least bit inconvenient to our national aspirations. Time and again we uproot the people from their ancestral homes and force them out of our way. We'll have no peace until we put a stop to the endless succession of broken promises."

Grant puffed another cloud of smoke. "Are you suggesting another treaty?"

Parker paused again. "Yes," he said at length, "I suppose I am. But one with integrity this time, a treaty we mean to keep."

"What do you propose to offer the tribes to end the hostilities?" That was the thorny question. Grant respected Parker's understanding of Indian culture. If he had an idea, it'd be worth hearing.

Parker didn't hesitate long. He'd clearly given the question thought on his own account. "Give them what they are fighting for. Red Cloud is fighting the Bozeman Trail to protect the Paha Sapa and the Sioux and Cheyenne hunting grounds in the Powder River country."

"Paha Sapa?"

"The Black Hills. The Sioux believe those lands are the sacred center of their nation. The birthplace of their people is home to their ancestors."

"Small wonder they fight to protect it." Grant released a veil of smoke with his words. "Such has been a source of conflict down through the ages."

Parker frowned. "Western expansion may seem destiny to

some. For the plains tribes it upsets the natural order. Surely a land of such vast abundance can sustain our expansion, while preserving the plains tribes' way of life." Parker's passion warmed to the problem. "As a practical matter, we won't need the Bozeman to make our way west much longer. The transcontinental railroad travels a more southerly route. It will be completed in the next year or so. Once it is, who will want to make the journey west by overland trail? Even now you'd have to question the wisdom of starting an overland journey west rather than waiting for the railroad to complete its work. If we could end hostilities by ceding the tribes the Black Hills and their Powder River hunting grounds, our westward expansion could proceed unopposed."

"You make a good point as usual, Ely. Can you get the commissioners to go along with a plan like that?"

"I believe I might with your help, Sam."

Grant narrowed his eyes behind his spectacles, concentrating on Parker. He knew where this was going. "With my help you say?"

"General, you may be the only one who can bring General Sherman around to support such a treaty. If Cump agreed with the policy, opposition within the commission would fold up like so much dirty laundry."

Grant smiled at the notion the stuffed shirt commissioners might have something in common with soiled linen. Serious again, he sat back in his chair, gazing at some distant point through another cloud of smoke. "Cump has pretty strong convictions when it comes to such matters." He mused as if speaking to himself.

"More than that, General, he respects you." The lawyer in Parker rested his case.

Grant dusted a long white ash in the crystal tray at his elbow and pondered the task his friend set before him. He and Cump had been through a lot together. He was commanding officer, though in this case he respected the man too much to pull rank. "I'll see what I can do, Ely. I can't promise more than that."

"Thanks, Sam."

The two men rose and shook hands. Grant watched Parker take his leave. Ely was right of course. Achieving a peaceful resolution to the dispute called for an enlightened policy, one that put integrity behind the commitment to peace.

The Indian problem was one among many facing the nation in postwar reconstruction. The war had been fought for more than a dispute over states' rights. The real achievement of the war was the establishment of human dignity and the rights of citizenship for all as guaranteed by the constitution. In that, the war was not over. Hostilities may have ceased, but sentiment in the south remained unrepentant. The rights of freedmen were as much in jeopardy as the plains tribes' way of life. He would face all this if he heeded the Republican voices urging him to seek the party's nomination. Johnson, they argued, could not be trusted to his own term. He'd already put Lincoln's war legacy at risk by pandering to elements in the south that resisted reconstruction. The Republican appeals were beginning to reach his sense of duty. If he accepted, he would surely make the welfare of, how did Ely phrase it? "The original inhabitants of the land," yes, that was it. He would surely make Indian peace policy a pillar of his administration. Persuading Cump to support Ely's plan seemed a worthy means of trying on the mantle of those responsibilities.

CHAPTER THREE

Washita River Agency
Oklahoma Territory
April 1867

The village comprised some fifty tipi, forming a loose ellipse along the north bank of the Washita River. Bluffs north of the village created a natural windbreak to shelter the camp in winter. Grassy flatlands to the east and west provided ample grazing for the pony herd. Black Kettle's lodge dominated the center of the village, flying the Stars and Stripes along with a white flag of peace from the tallest lodge poles.

In late afternoon women put aside their sewing and washing and turned to the cookfires. Children ran here and there in the noisy company of the camp dogs or knotted in groups laughing at play in hoop and ball games. Braves returned to the village from the day's hunting or fishing, one by one or in groups. Quiet settled over the village as late afternoon faded into early evening.

Near sunset a lone rider splashed across the sun-fired surface of the river and galloped into the village. A noisy pack of howling camp dogs charged the intruder, yapping at the heels of the brave's flashy Appaloosa war pony. Around the village the people looked up from their evening meals or where they sat at their lodge fires, their eyes drawn to the arrival of a suitor by the commotion of the dogs. He drew his pony to a stop in front of a lodge near Black Kettle's and leaped down. He pulled a buffalo robe from the saddle and folded it in his arms across his chest.

Spotted Hawk stood before the tipi in the proud bearing of a warrior, tall and powerfully built in the wiry muscled way of his people. Three eagle feathers hung in his long black braids, twisting on a gentle evening breeze. His eyes were bright black pits that glittered in the dim light of early evening below a prominent brow and hooked nose. He wore a bone breastplate over a broad chest, buckskin leggings, and a simple breechclout.

"Autumn Snow." Her Cheyenne name rang clear and strong on the cool spring evening.

She emerged from the lodge, a tall maiden, her beauty quiet and still like drifted snow. Wide-set dark eyes pooled deep and thoughtful like a mountain lake. She wore her long black hair gathered at her shoulders, framing the smooth copper planes of her cheeks. A simple buckskin dress cinched at the waist revealed a willowy frame.

Spotted Hawk unfolded the buffalo robe. She inclined her head to his as he draped the robe over them. According to custom, the pair could declare their feelings for one another in private while standing in full view of the village and posing no risk to the maiden's virtue. Time passed. Neither partner seemed to notice a mangy rust-colored camp dog curiously sniffing at their heels.

When at length they emerged from beneath the robe, Autumn Snow returned to her lodge. Spotted Hawk threw the buffalo robe back on his pony and swung up behind it. In one fluid motion he drew a new '66 model Winchester rifle from the saddle boot. He charged the rifle into the air with a triumphant whoop, spun the big App on its heels, and lit out the way he'd come. When the dogs were satisfied they'd run off the intruder, the camp fell quiet again.

Chapter Four

Washington, D.C.
April 1867

A touch of warmth in the spring breeze felt good. So did the bay gelding, Grant thought, jogging up Fifteenth Street. He could have ordered a carriage and driver. Most people in this town did. But there was nothing like the feel of a good horse to take a man away from the paper pressures of the War Department and remind him that he was still a soldier. Garrison duty had never suited him. The War Department was a palace of a garrison, but a garrison nonetheless. General in Chief of the Army qualified for the ultimate in garrison duty. The Army's top job involved too much politicking and too little soldiering. Now there's a twist of irony he thought, looking off to his left at the White House and the choice that loomed over his next meeting.

He crossed Pennsylvania Avenue and drew rein in front of the Hotel Washington. Interesting choice for the meeting, he thought as he stepped down from the saddle. The place to be seen in the District these days was the newer Willard Hotel around the corner on Pennsylvania Avenue. Insiders had begun to refer to the city as *the District* courtesy of the Reconstruction Act electoral allocations. In another touch of irony those same Reconstruction Acts gave rise to the point of this meeting. The choice of the Washington Hotel insured the meeting would take place in privacy.

A doorman dressed in a military-looking dark green tunic and striped trousers stepped forward to take his horse. The brass buttons and bright gold braid of the doorman's uniform caught the late afternoon sun in subtle contrast to the less polished brass and braid worn by the General in Chief of the Army. Grant handed the man his reins with a nod and climbed the stone steps where another attendant held a heavy, carved wooden door for him. He crossed the marble lobby, skirting the registration counter on his way to the bar. The bar was dim and quiet in the late afternoon. It smelled of cigar smoke and wood polish. The only patron greeted him with a wave from a back corner table. He smiled, striding to the table and a hearty handshake. "Eli, good to see you."

"And you too, Sam. Thank you for coming."

Elihu Washburne was an old friend and trusted confidant from his home in Galena, Illinois. A lawyer by training Washburne was a founding force in the Republican Party. At fifty-seven he was ten years Grant's senior and a head taller. His thick features gave him a fatherly appearance, made prominent by graying hair combed back from a broad forehead. His dark blue suit, starched collar, and tie could have been those of half the bureaucrats and politicians in the city.

Grant settled himself in an empty chair. He glanced around the deserted room, turning to his old friend with an amused look in his eye. "One wonders what nefarious purpose reduces us to skulking about deserted saloons in the middle of the afternoon."

Washburne smiled, signaled the bartender, and ignored the question. A waiter in a starched white jacket appeared to take their order. "Two whiskies," he ordered, well acquainted with Grant's preferences. "How is Julia, Sam?"

"She is doing quite well, Eli. Thank you for asking. And how is your family?"

"Everyone is doing well. We have much to be thankful for, at least on the home front." The waiter arrived with the drinks and departed, leaving the men to their conversation. "I wish we could say as much for the country," Washburne said, coming to the point of the meeting. "Johnson's continued obstruction to southern reconstruction has become an intolerable embarrassment to the party."

Grant nodded agreement and sipped his drink. "His behavior truly is a disgrace to the office. I'd not say it to any but you, Eli, but at times I wonder if he may have his own hood and a sheet, hanging in some White House closet."

Washburne chuckled at the suggestion of the president parading about in the middle of the night burning crosses, though he conceded the humor might not stray too far from the truth.

"Johnson was added to Abe's ticket as a gesture of unity to the south. No one foresaw the president's untimely death. Now we suffer the consequences of an ill-considered political choice, which is precisely why I asked to see you, Sam."

Grant drew a cigar from his breast pocket and bit off the tip. Eli was coming to the point speculated in newspapers all across the country.

"Sam, a number of us within the party have come to the conclusion that we could have no better standard bearer in the next election than you. We are prepared to raise the money and build the necessary support to win the nomination for you. I've been asked to see if you are willing to seek the highest office in service to the nation."

Grant struck a match and lit his cigar, filling the pause awaiting his answer. He furrowed his brow as he released a fragrant cloud of smoke. He'd known this was coming. He'd weighed the possibility without coming to any definitive judgment.

"I'm flattered, Eli. I'm a soldier, not a politician. I despise all that mealy-mouthed equivocation politics imply."

"It's not flattery, Sam. You're a leader. It's what's best for the country. The country is at a crossroads. Reconstruction is needed to preserve the achievements of the war, lest all that's been paid for in blood be lost to flawed policy and political abuse. Much work remains to be done in settling this great land of ours. The transcontinental railroad will change the face of the nation within a year or so. We are poised for unprecedented greatness, but we must have strong leadership to realize that promise. Johnson's abysmal performance gives testimony to the need for a leader with the vision to realize the great promise of our nation for future generations. Many of us who have come to this conclusion bare responsibility for our current predicament. That said, we can correct our failure by putting forward a man of your character and ability. The nation is calling you, Sam. Will you serve her again?"

Grant leveled his gaze. This of course was the nub of the matter, one of those decisions in life of which futures are made. He'd considered it as best he could. Here the future appeared clouded in cigar smoke. Eli said it best. Much remained to be done. Was he up to it? Who could say? Surely there were those who questioned his appointment to commanding general during the war. He'd had enough of his own doubts at the time. Still he'd answered the call. History accounted no time for doubt. The record stood. Those Eli spoke for knew the stakes. He knew the stakes, as best frail humankind might divine the future. What more could he do?

"You know an old soldier too well, Eli. Put like that, we can do naught but our duty."

Washburne grinned broadly. "I knew we could count on you, Sam. Waiter, bring us another round." Privately he turned to Grant. "I want to be the first to toast the next President of the United States."

CHAPTER FIVE

Oklahoma Agency
Fort Larned, Kansas
May 1867

Roscoe Denton filled his mouth with a forkful of apple pie. He supplied the ingredients and paid the post cook to bake for him. Nothing like pie to help a man pass the time between lunch and dinner. He closed his fleshy eyes to savor the sweet tart taste of cinnamon touched apple. He smacked his generous lips.

He shifted his girth in the confines of the barrel-backed chair straining to contain his bulk. Not overly tall, he indulged his appetites for food and drink to corpulent excess. He'd grown so large he waddled when he walked on short bowed legs. He traveled by buggy when he needed to travel. He reasoned the mounting and dismounting of a horse a physical undertaking beyond the dignity of a man of his stature. His face was a mass of ruddy jowls framed by bushy unkempt sideburns, his only distinguishing feature cold dark eyes near lost in fleshy folds and bushy brows. His suits were generally black, baggy, and rumpled. His badly sweat-stained linen seemed always in need of a washtub. He wore a wide brimmed slouch hat that might have been mistaken for a fire and brimstone preacher, though Denton's associations would have far more in common with the other side in a fire and brimstone debate. A knock at the door caught him with a forkful of pie halfway to his mouth.

"Afternoon, Roscoe," Luther Hatch drawled, amused at the dribble of apple juice running at the corner of the fat agent's mouth. Crumbs of pie crust spilled down the front of his shirt from his open-mouthed chewing. The red and white checkered napkin spread over his belly gave him the appearance of an unmade bed.

A rangy, weathered small-time rancher, Hatch had clotted gray hair that hung to his shoulders. Watery blue eyes were set in a near perpetual squint under an explosion of bushy brows. His droopy mustache was badly in need of a trim. In the cramped quarters of the small office, it became clear the rest of him was in equal need of a bath.

The fat man only nodded, continuing to chew, his mouth overfull with pie. He put down his fork to inspect the paper Hatch dropped on his desk. Money was about the only thing likely to take his attention away from food. In this case it was a bill of sale for the purchase of one hundred head of cattle at a price of sixty dollars a head along with two thousand dollars in gold certificates, the difference between the voucher Denton had given him and the actual cost of the herd. Expenses for inflating the bill of sale and hiring the crew accounted for four hundred dollars. The actual cost of the herd was thirty-six dollars a head.

"Hmm, very well, Mr. Hatch. This all appears to be in good order."

"Sure it is, Denton. You couldn't find a more honest thief than me. Now gimme my money and I'll be on my way."

Denton counted out five one-hundred-dollar gold certificates from the pile and passed them across the desk.

Hatch scooped up the notes and stuffed them in his coat pocket.

Lieutenant Colonel George Armstrong Custer admired his

reflection in the dusty windowpane darkened by a heavy gray cloud bank that threatened a storm. He smoothed a lank lock of dirty blond hair off the shoulder of his fringed buckskin jacket. The tunic wasn't regulation, but it served him well in the field. Very little about Custer met Army regulation. He cut a dashing figure by his own estimation. Of course, the look would be far more impressive if his colonel's pips were replaced by the general's stars he so richly deserved. He still bridled at the demotion occasioned by the postwar reductions in general staff. It had come as a bitter pill, a blow to his pride he could never assuage. It couldn't be justified. His war record should have counted for more.

Custer squinted across the parade ground through the small dirty office window. He pulled at his mustache, watching the bent scarecrow rancher Luther Hatch collect a rawboned bay at the hitch rack in front of the Indian Agent's office. "Hatch and Denton," he mumbled. "You can smell corruption from here."

"Sir?" Sergeant Major Kane looked up expectantly from his desk in the corner.

Custer set his jaw, turned on his heel and strode back to his desk. "Nothing, Sergeant Major, I was talking to myself about Denton's visitor."

"Luther Hatch again, sir?"

"Why, yes, Sergeant Major, how did you know?"

"That pair is thick as thieves."

"I was thinking along those lines myself, Sergeant Major." Custer picked up the filigree framed picture of his lovely Libbie.

"You must miss her, sir."

"I do, Sergeant Major. Three months is a long time for a man to be parted from his wife. I believe I might take a short leave to visit her at Fort Riley."

Kane cocked his head. "Grant your own leave, sir?"

"Yes, Sergeant Major, I believe I just might."

Fort Riley, Kansas
June, 1867

A single lamp created an island of light in the corner of the small parlor. Elizabeth Bacon Custer drew her legs up beside her on the thread-worn settee. She arranged the hem of her dress to cover her shapely ankles. She adjusted her book to light the bottom of the page, a delicate finger poised at the corner. The familiar verses soothed her, becalming her spirit to the prospect of sleep. Fine featured and delicate, the dark-eyed beauty captured the heart and fell madly in love with the dashing young war hero they called "the Boy General." Her father, a prominent Michigan judge, disapproved of the match, Custer being of low station and dim prospects by her father's estimation. He'd grudgingly acceded to his daughter's persistence, following her beau's promotion to Brigadier General. She'd known the life demands of an Army wife at the time of their marriage. She undertook these obligations fully and freely, though nothing could truly prepare one for the long days of separation when one's husband was in the field. Her eyes drooped. Her chin nodded. She came back to a comforting passage.

A boot scraped the front porch step. She paused mid-couplet. Now who could this be? She glanced at the clock, too late for respectable callers. The instinctive concern of a military wife caught in the back of her throat. Had something happened to George? A soft tap at the door punctuated the worry. She set the worn volume on the settee, straightened her skirt, and went to the door.

"Who is it?"

"Your fair prince, m' lady."

"Autie!" She threw open the door. A trail-dusted blue tunic blur swept her into his arms. He found her lips with his. A long cold winter of denial melted in the moment. Dry cracked desire moistened, a trickle, a splash, a stream. *But why, how?* She needed to breathe. Joy welled in her eyes. "This is so unexpected. Have you been recalled for something?"

"No, my darling, just a few days' leave to see my girl."

She knit her brow. "A leave then, why didn't you let me know you were coming?"

"There wasn't time. I only decided to come a few days ago."

"Autie, you must have known. These things take time."

"Not this time." He smiled.

"But your leave?"

He kissed her.

"Granted it myself."

Her eyes went wide. "Can you do that?"

"I just did. Now hush and kiss your husband. It's been a long hard ride and I'm parched for the feel of you."

She surrendered to crushing force and devouring hunger.

Chapter Six

Western Kansas
September 1867

Spotted Hawk lay hidden in tall prairie grass on a low ridge overlooking a shallow valley. His broad shoulders and back reflected a light sheen in the soft twilight. His eagle feathers rustled on the evening breeze. A wisp of gray smoke from the chimney of a small ranch house touched blue haze descending from painted hilltops off to the west. He studied the pony herd milling around in the corral behind the house. The small herd numbered ten or twelve sturdy ponies, the leader a flashy white stallion. Get a loop on the stallion and the herd would follow.

Young Bull and She Bear waited with the ponies at the base of the ridge. Spotted Hawk drew back from the crest and rejoined his brothers. He pointed south around the base of the rise.

"Spotted Hawk circle there." He turned north. "Young Bull and She Bear circle there. Cover white man's lodge. Spotted Hawk run ponies off there." He pointed south. "If white men fight, kill them."

Young Bull and She Bear nodded. They mounted their ponies. She Bear took Spotted Hawk's pony on his lead. They rode north along the grassy ridge out of sight of the ranch house.

Spotted Hawk took his rope and turned south at a jog. When the ranch house came into view around the south slope he dropped to his belly and melted into the prairie grasses. He worked his way patiently toward the corral. Brother Sun spent his last light by the time he reached the bottom rail of the corral. He took care to make his approach downwind of the pony herd. His movement must be quiet and sure. Stir up the herd and the white men would come with guns. He must get his loop on the stallion first.

The herd stood quiet in the north end of the corral between Spotted Hawk and the ranch house. He would use this to his advantage. The moon scudded in and out of a low running cloud cover. He waited for its pale light to darken before crawling under the rail into the corral. He did not attempt to conceal himself. He squatted on his haunches near the center of the corral and held very still. He watched the stallion through the veil of his loose hair. He muted his breathing, giving no scent of excitement. The herd stood quiet. They accepted his presence. The greatest risk of ruining the raid passed without incident.

The white sensed him at once. He pricked up his ears with a snort. The shadow did not move. The stallion fixed his attention on the intruder. The shadow held still. He did not see the eyes of a predator. It gave no sense of alarm. Slowly his curiosity roused. He lowered his nose to the dirt and pawed at the ground. The visitor did not move. He tossed his head, flaring his nostrils to the night breeze. It gave no scent of danger. The shadow did not stir. The stallion took his first cautious step toward this new curiosity.

Spotted Hawk sensed victory. He need only wait. The stallion took another cautious step toward him.

Cutting a small cattle ranch out of no-man's-land northeast of Indian territory was a solitary, risky business. Luther Hatch knew that. He also knew that the coming of the railroad meant he could get his cattle to market without the cost and risks of a long trail drive. Hatch and his partner, Cody Tull, had held their own for two years now. They had a small market selling cattle to the Union Pacific crews. That along with the occasional business opportunity provided by the Indian Agent Denton brought in what little cash money they needed. The herd was growing nicely on the lush prairie grass. On a quiet night like tonight after a hard day's work and a decent meal, a man could take some satisfaction in what he'd accomplished.

Both men dozed by the small fireplace, not yet ready to turn in but not fully awake either. A horse whinnied out in the corral. Hatch snapped awake. He listened for only a moment. He heard horses moving.

"Cody, wake up! We got trouble." Hatch bolted to the door of the rough-cut clapboard and sod ranch house. He grabbed his Winchester from the rack beside the door and dashed out to the porch. He ran toward the corral. The moon flashed free of the clouds, lighting the dust rising behind the remuda. He could see his white stallion hightailing it through the corral gate, the black shadow of a lone rider hunched over his back. The herd followed the stallion south. *Injuns,* he thought. He jacked a round into the chamber and shouldered the rifle. He fired at the dark rider, risking his horse with the shot. Muzzle flash flared. Powder smoke plumed against the night sky.

Whoops sounded out of the darkness off to the north. Cody's boots clumped onto the porch, framing the rancher in the lighted doorway. Unseen horses galloped past the house. Muzzle flashes pricked the darkness, angry fireflies chased by loud reports. Cody grunted, slowly dropping to his knees followed by the clatter of his rifle hitting the porch. Hatch spun to his left and dropped to his knee, lighting up dark shadowed raiders racing by in the dim light. Return fire bit a chunk out of a porch beam off his right shoulder. A second round thumped a plank to his left.

The shooting fell silent almost as suddenly as it had begun.

Luther Hatch stood alone, fuming to the fading beat of his horses galloping away.

Spotted Hawk rode into Black Kettle's village at midday, leading a string of five ponies, the lead a flashy white stallion. Villagers paused the affairs of the day, recognizing the arrival of a suitor with a handsome bride price. A curious crowd gathered to follow the proud warrior to the lodge of the favored maiden. From the customs of courtship, there was little need to speculate on the warrior's intentions. Many ran ahead to the lodge of Autumn Snow's family. All agreed, the young warrior stated a strong heart with such a handsome dowry.

Autumn Snow saw him enter the village and hurried to her father's lodge. Her heart pounded with joy. Spotted Hawk knew the feeling she held for him in her heart. His bride price would bring her father great honor.

Spotted Hawk rode through the village slowly, aware of the crowd gathering behind him. He let the villagers admire the prize he would pay for his bride. It marked him as a warrior who would provide handsomely for his family. He would make his offer of marriage before all the people. Autumn Snow's father, Bear Claw, could not refuse such a dowry as this for his daughter.

Bear Claw came out to greet his visitor. Tall like his daughter, he folded his arms across his bare chest as he studied the pony string the young warrior brought to his lodge. A warm autumn breeze played at the eagle feathers in the loose plaits of his hair and the fringes of his leggings. He smiled inwardly, honored that such a handsome bride price would be offered for his daughter. Few among the village fathers could claim such honor.

Spotted Hawk drew his war pony to a halt before Bear Claw. He held the lead of the ponies on his string. He watched Bear Claw study the quality of the horses with pride. He had chosen carefully. The stallion alone would give him many fine ponies.

"Spotted Hawk brings Bear Claw these ponies as bride price for his daughter, Autumn Snow."

Inside the lodge, Snow held her breath. Her heart hammered at her breast, excitement caught in her throat. Surely her father must accept such a fine bride price. Time stood still as he slowly inspected first one pony, then the next. Only the buzz of a fly broke silence in the tipi. The air grew thick and hot with waiting. Snow did not think it possible her father could refuse. Or could he? The white stallion stamped the ground, raising a small cloud of dust as though he shared her impatience. He tossed his head and flared his nostrils as Bear Claw stepped up to his withers. At last he turned to Spotted Hawk with a nod and accepted the stallion's lead. Autumn Snow's heart leaped for joy at the back of her throat.

The people gathered at sunset; drawn up in facing ranks they created a path to the banks of the Washita. The venerable shaman Standing Elk stood with his back to the river framed in setting sun, glittering on the rippled surface of the waters. Bear Claw stood beside him. A single lodge waited to receive the new man and wife.

Spotted Hawk waited for his bride at the beginning of the line of villagers. He stood proud and tall, the full measure of a warrior. The eagle feathers in his braids danced on the evening breeze, giving the only indication he might be other than a statue.

Autumn Snow walked out of the village followed by her mother leading her pony. She wore a beautifully beaded dress of white elk draped in fringes worked with beads. The beads spoke of the sky and summer grass in blues and greens. Yellows and browns represented Brother Sun shining on Earth Mother. Her hair hung unbraided over her shoulders, gathered in beaded bands. Whispers of breeze ruffled her hair and fringes of her dress as she came to him.

Spotted Hawk took her hand in his for the walk to the river in the presence of the people.

Standing Elk offered the wedding chant. It brought light to Snow's eyes in the golden rays of the setting sun. When the chant finished, the shaman offered them a traditional vase. The clay vessel filled with water had two spouts. They drank from the vase together as one, each nourishing the other by the drinking.

They turned to the people. Spotted Hawk spoke the heart of the new couple. "It is good." He drew his tomahawk and broke the vase that no other might break the bond between them.

Bear Claw nodded his approval.

Later they danced in the circle of the people before retiring to the lodge prepared to receive them. In this they came together as one in the deepest expression of all. As he held this most beautiful creature in the crook of his arm, Spotted Hawk knew the feeling of home. Home would follow their heart, wherever they spread their blanket.

Chapter Seven

Washita River Reservation
Oklahoma Territory
October 1867

Black Kettle turned tired eyes to the north. Three riders splashed across the river. Spotted Hawk, Kicking Pony, and Broken Knife returned from the hunt. They hunted as they did, for they were young men. This day they returned with nothing as they did most often. The old chief knew the difficulty of controlling young warriors who grew restless on empty bellies. They had women and young ones to feed. The wild ones would soon lose patience. When they did, they would leave the reservation. In this they risked angering the whites by stealing cattle or horses, or simply frightening some white man into a fight. Always these things led to a fight with the pony soldiers and still more bloodshed and suffering for the people.

Black Kettle moved his Cheyenne people to the Washita River reservation in the belief that here they might at last live in peace with the whites. He flew the white man's flag from his lodge to show the whites his people lived in peace. They gave up their hunting grounds in Kansas and Colorado to accept treaty terms the whites offered at the Arkansas River. In return, the treaty promised beef cattle to feed the people. He believed in peace for his people. He believed the words of the white man's treaty. In the year since they moved to the banks of the Washita, the words that promised cattle remained hollow. Black Kettle took his complaint to the Indian Agent Denton at the pony soldier fort. The fat agent's words proved empty. He would find some excuse for the broken promise and a new promise to right the one just broken.

The hunting party rode through the village to the picket line where women and children gathered prairie grass for the ponies. They dismounted and picketed their ponies. No one spoke the disappointment of another failed hunt.

Spotted Hawk came to the reservation when he took Autumn Snow for his bride. Discouraged and weary of fighting the whites, he gave up the warpath after the death of Moquinto, the war chief known to the whites as Roman Nose. The whites were strong. They were as many as leaves on the aspens. They came like a river no man could turn back. Defeat did not rest easy on the proud warrior. The routines of reservation life grated on a spirit that longed for the freedom of the old ways.

Autumn Snow looked up from her sewing as he approached the lodge. She had no need to ask his success at the hunt. Failure lined his face. He dropped to his knees beside her. She locked her eyes in his. He shook his head.

"Winter will be hard if we do not find game. We came to the white man's reservation to live in peace. People living in peace should not die of hunger."

Snow held her husband's eyes, "The white treaty promises cattle to feed the people. Black Kettle believes these words."

"Where are these cattle?" Anger lit his eyes. "We have only empty promises and lies to fill our bellies. Once we had great buffalo herds, a river of life to feed and clothe the people. Now the wasichu send us to live where there are no buffalo. White hunters slaughter the herds. They kill the great shaggy ones for their hides. The old ways lay in waste, rotting with the carcasses of the dead strewn across the land. The people die with them. My brothers say it is better to die a warrior than to starve as the white man's camp dog. We must find game or we will not survive the winter."

The truth of his words lay heavy on Autumn Snow's heart. Winter came hard and cold and closer with each passing moon. The cattle did not come. The young men grew angry and restless. The women feared for the winter. They feared for their men and for their children. She remembered Sand Creek. She was younger then. No more than a child. She remembered the bluecoats coming. She remembered the people who died all around her. The reservation promised peace. Black Kettle and the other peace chiefs agreed to words of peace for the people. Winter made a harsh judge of these words with their empty promises.

CHAPTER EIGHT

War Department
Office of the General in Chief
January 1868

"General Sherman to see you, sir," Porter announced.

Grant looked up from the report he was reading. "Send him in, Horace." He set aside the tedious logistics report from Charleston. Damned expensive police force, he thought, reflecting on the military presence required to maintain orderly reconstruction of the south. The secessionists might have been defeated on the battlefield, but that didn't stop them from venting their anger by attempting to suppress the rights of the south's freedmen. They'd only traded rebel gray for bedsheets and hoods. Local authorities looked the other way, either because their sympathies were tainted by old prejudice or, in the case of northern-bred administrators, they were too busy looting the jurisdictions they'd been sent to administer. That left the Army to enforce the Reconstruction Acts. As a result, relations between the War Department and President Johnson's southern sympathies became strained to the breaking point. And that was before any rumors of presidential ambition on his part.

Grant rose, stepped around from behind his desk, and extended his hand, disdaining the formality of a salute. "Cump, it's good to see you. Thank you for coming."

Sherman took his hand, "It's good to see you too, Sam. As

for coming, when the General in Chief of the Army calls you to a meeting, good soldiers report for duty. What's on your mind?" Sherman knew Grant too well to beat around the bush with social amenities. Sam had something he wanted of him. He'd been trying to puzzle it out on the long train ride from his Department of the Missouri headquarters in Chicago.

"Sit down, Cump." Grant gestured to two wing chairs and a simple settee arranged around a low table at the side of the office. He drew a gold pocket watch from his uniform sash and flicked open the face. Four-thirty he read, close enough. "Care for a drink?"

"After a long train ride that would go down mighty good, Sam."

"Horace, if you please," Grant called to his aid.

Sherman and Grant took facing wing chairs. Grant drew a fresh cigar from the breast pocket of his tunic, bit the tip, and stuck a match in one practiced motion. He puffed out a great cloud of smoke as Horace set two generous glasses of Kentucky bourbon on the table and withdrew.

"OK, Sam, out with it. You called me in here for more than just drinks."

Cump had a way of cutting to the quick of the matter. Grant liked that about him as a field commander. Here a little conversation might have softened the news he had to deliver. The veteran line officer would not be pleased at the purpose of the meeting.

"I've got a new assignment for you, Cump."

Sherman shook his head. "I was afraid of that. Is something wrong?"

"Nothing of your doing, it's the president."

Sherman scowled. He lifted his glass, "I think I'll take a little fortification. I have a feeling I'm not going to like this."

Grant nodded and took a pull from his glass. "The president

has requested your assignment to a commission that is to negotiate a treaty ending Indian hostilities on the Bozeman Trail. I don't need to tell you the forts we built out there to protect the settlers moving west are the reason Red Cloud and his people are all riled up. Frankly, with the Pacific railroad scheduled to complete next year, the value of the Bozeman Trail won't justify the cost of maintaining our presence there. If we pull back and offer an attractive reservation in the Dakotas and Powder River country, we think Red Cloud will make peace."

"Maybe so, Sam, but what has that got to do with me? You need a field commander over the Department of the Missouri. If the president wants a commission to make peace, why not appoint Al Terry? He's a lawyer and much better suited to treaty making than I'll ever be."

"General Terry's being assigned to the commission too, but the president wants a field officer present so we don't give the appearance of surrender."

"So he says. Sam, you know better than that. Stand up to him, man, everyone knows you're about to this year."

Grant drew on his cigar, letting the smoke mask his eyes. "I'm walking something of a fine line here, Cump. The president regards me as a political threat. He's trying to get me to take an appointment as Secretary of War to get me out of this job. He can't come out and say it in so many words but his sympathies oppose reconstruction. He knows that without the support of the Army, there'd be no one to enforce the Reconstruction Acts. He can't order us to stand down, but he's a southerner. There is no support for freedmen's rights or suffrage in the south. The achievements we won on the battlefield must now be preserved by martial law or all that blood will have been spilled in vain. Johnson would like nothing better than to have a yes-man in uniform sitting in this office. It's up to me to see that doesn't happen."

"So what does that have to do with my being assigned to window-dress some fool peace commission? There are lots of field commanders around who could do that."

"Few with your reputation, Cump. The president knows that. He also knows that if I were to take the War Department job, you'd be my choice to succeed me in this command. He knows you and I think alike on reconstruction. He wouldn't be any better off with you in this office than he is with me. I can't fight him every step of the way. Political differences notwithstanding, he is Commander in Chief."

"So for that I'm to give up a line assignment to go sweat my ass off in some god-forsaken treaty negotiation." Sherman shook his head and tossed back his drink.

"Horace," Grant called, knocking back his own glass. "The general needs another round of fortification here." Grant lowered his voice, "I'll make it up to you, Cump, once this damn election is over."

"I know you will, Sam, it just pisses me off the way the Reb in the White House is running the show."

"You know you might not like this chair when you get it. Army command makes life simple. This town is all politics. Politics is like making sausage, Cump."

Sherman puzzled over the rim of his glass. "Sausage?"

"There are some things you'd just rather not know."

Horace appeared with a crystal decanter and refilled their glasses. He left the decanter on the table and slipped back to his desk.

"Now about your replacement in Chicago, any thoughts come to mind?"

"Only one, Sam, it's got to be Phil."

Grant relit the cigar gone cold in the brass tray on the table. "Phil's a fighting man for sure and a good one." Grant turned the idea over in his mind, not completely comfortable with the notion. "He's also holding down a key reconstruction assignment in New Orleans." Grant's voice trailed off in his misgivings.

"You need a fighting man in the Department of the Missouri, Sam. Let's say we do get a peace treaty. Red Cloud goes off to the reservation and violence on the Bozeman stops. Don't think for a minute that Red Cloud speaks for the whole of the Lakota nation, let alone the Cheyenne and the Arapaho. You've still got a railroad to build and a steady flow of settlers moving west. Who is going to protect those people from the bands who don't sign on to the treaty and move to a reservation? You know as well as I, there'll be some who won't."

Grant studied the lengthening white ash at the tip of his cigar. Cump had a point. Sheridan was a good soldier and a cavalry commander to boot. He'd respect his orders, but he'd be prepared to act should the situation warrant. He needed a good man to look after the Department of the Missouri. Heaven only knew he wasn't going to have time to do it. "Point well made, Cump. I'll think about it. Now what say we head over to the Willard for some dinner?"

Chapter Nine

Washita River Reservation
Oklahoma Territory
February 1868

Snow crunched beneath his moccasins. Spotted Hawk hunched his shoulders against the cold, returning to the village in the gray light of late afternoon. The snare had done its work for the first time in many days. The thin rabbit had used much of its winter fat. Still, it was game, if only a small addition to their meager stores. Hunting had been poor through the summer and fall. Winter hunting offered even less. Deep snow and bitter cold made it dangerous to venture too far from the warmth of the lodge fire. A good hunt might produce a rabbit such as this one. Little more could be expected. Their winter stores, too little at the coming of the snows, grew smaller with each passing day.

Icy wind swept out of the north, covering the land in a thick blanket of heavy gray cloud. Snow swirled across the ridge top stinging Spotted Hawk's eyes and blurring the dark silhouette of the village on the banks of the steel gray river below. The wind raced down the face of the ridge. Snow drifted behind the lodges, passing between them where it would. Drifts swirled away from the village, running in white waves to the river. Beyond the riverbanks wind sculpted a white desert broken only by the rocks and crags of a harsh landscape.

The village tipi stood firm, backs to the wind in grim defiance of the cold. The feeble glow of lodge fires within dotted the village in lanterns of amber light, giving the only sign people survived a land frozen in desolation. Smoke from the fires rose through smoke holes. Thin wisps flattened in the wind and disappeared, chasing dancing snow snakes to the riverbank.

Spotted Hawk reached their lodge. Stooping low, he ducked through the hide, covering the entrance. Autumn Snow looked up, her dark eyes visible in shadow beyond the lodge fire. Spotted Hawk leaned his rifle against a lodge pole and shook the snow from his buffalo coat. Snow came to him and took the rabbit already gone stiff with the cold.

"The Great One Above smiles on us." Her words floated in whispered steam.

"Small comfort," Spotted Hawk grunted, sitting down to warm himself at the fire.

She spread a square of tanned deerskin on the lodge floor beside the fire where the rabbit would warm for skinning and cleaning. She set her sheath knife to the task, her fingers cold in spite of the fire. She skinned and gutted the small carcass. One haunch to roast this day, she planned, another for the next. The rest would make stock for the cook pot. If they ate sparingly it might sustain them three, maybe four days. Perhaps the Great One would favor them with another snare by then.

Snow roasted the rabbit haunch for their meal. She wrapped the remaining rabbit in the deerskin and set it in the snow at the edge of the lodge. They shared their simple meal listening to the wind howl fury at the darkness outside.

Later they huddled together in the warmth of heavy buffalo robes close by the small lodge fire. Smoke mingled with thin traces of their breath as it climbed toward the smoke hole. Spotted Hawk held Snow close, giving her body his warmth. She slept lightly, breathing softly, her hunger muted by sleep. Spotted Hawk's hunger burned hollow in his belly and hot in his heart. The rabbit had done little to fill him. Winter was never an easy time. Winter without food weakened the people to the punishments of wind and cold and endless night. They were fortunate. They did not have little ones to care for. For them ever-present hunger was yet another enemy to survive like the relentless cold. Little ones did not understand such things. They knew only cold and hunger. One day, with the blessing of the Great One Above, they would have little ones. Starving on the white man's reservation seemed no life to give them.

CHAPTER TEN

Office of the Commanding General
Department of the Missouri
Chicago, Illinois
April 1868

Lieutenant General Philip Henry Sheridan paced his comfortably appointed office, absorbed in the flood of briefing papers he'd received since taking his temporary assignment. His gold braided blue tunic draped casually over the back of the desk chair, he wore his blouse open at the collar. His braces hung in loops at his trouser legs. Known as "Fighting Phil," Sheridan established the reputation of a ferocious warrior during the war. He shared Sherman's belief in total war, total destruction of the enemy's ability to sustain itself as a fighting force. He meant to bring that belief to his new assignment. He'd earned his spurs and stars as an aggressive cavalry commander. He served under Grant and Sherman in battles that included Chickamauga, Missionary Ridge, and Lookout Mountain. He'd whipped the Confederacy's fabled young cavalry commander J.E.B. Stuart in the battle of Cedar Creek, contributing to a decisive victory that drove General Early's command out of the Shenandoah Valley. Sheridan cut off Lee's retreat from Appomattox Court House, effectively ringing down the curtain on the War of Secession.

Small of stature Sheridan was a bull of a man with a barrel chest and long arms that overpowered his short, bowed legs. Now in his middle years, his hairline receded, and a small paunch gathered over his britches. He had full coarse features, a broad nose, and full mustaches that bristled over a weak chin, belying the true timbre of the man. His eyes radiated a calculated intensity that missed little in assessing a tactical situation. He directed that intensity to his new assignment as he paced.

Cump and the Peace Commission were on their way to Fort Laramie. That should quiet hostilities in the area for so long as the talks proceed. The real threat ran from western Kansas and eastern Colorado south to Texas. Roving bands of Cheyenne, Comanche, and Kiowa terrorized settlers there and harassed the crews building railroads to serve the region. He needed a strong hand to contain that situation, which was the point of his next meeting. He'd have the strong hand all right. The problem would be controlling it. He needed to make that point in no uncertain terms.

The orderly's knock sounded at the door.

"Colonel Custer to see you, sir."

"Very good, Bates, send him in."

An uncharacteristically subdued George Custer stepped past the sergeant major and came to attention, his salute nearly crisp.

"Colonel Custer reporting as ordered, sir."

"At ease, George." Sheridan extended his hand. "We've too many campaigns behind us to stand on such formality. Have a seat." He motioned to a grouping of wing chairs surrounding a low table.

"Thank you, Phil. I just felt that under the circumstances . . ." The rest of the thought unspoken, they took their seats.

"Yes, well let's clear the air of those circumstances before we get down to business." Sheridan scowled. He meant that Custer should not miss the gravity of the situation for the familiarity of their friendship. They'd served together a long time. They thought alike on aggressive tactics. George could be counted on to carry the fight to the enemy. Sheridan appreciated that. He could also be impulsive and careless of regulations. Some flaws could be overlooked for the results the man got, though since the war ended, Custer had near tried his patience to the limit. He'd mentored the flamboyant officer, smoothing over the rough spots in his career. The most recent incident involved an inexcusable absence without leave.

"I persuaded Sam to reinstate you as part of my taking this assignment, George. I don't mind telling you that I spent some personal capital to do it and not for the first time."

"I know, Phil. Thank you. I've always appreciated your support."

"I don't want your damn gratitude, George! I want you to keep your boots clean for a change."

Custer studied the creases in his trousers.

"Libbie's a lovely girl, George. Lord knows I'd be tempted to go AWOL for her myself, but I wouldn't do it. Certainly not after the flap over those deserters you executed. What the hell were you thinking?"

"Sir, I . . ."

"You weren't thinking, George. That's the point."

Custer hung his head, chastened by his respect for the general.

"That's two strikes, George. You'd best make the next pitch count. I don't know that I've got enough draw left with Sam to bail your ass out of another foul ball."

"You won't need to, sir."

"See that I don't. Is that clear?"

"Yes, sir."

"Good." Sheridan allowed his demeanor to soften. "Now about your new assignment. I'm sending you to Fort Larned to take command of the Seventh."

Custer brightened at the mention of his beloved unit.

"I want you to establish a forward supply camp in western Kansas to provide security for the settlers and railroad crews in the area. Cheyenne renegades play hell with folks in Kansas and Colorado. Then they sneak back to the reservations in Oklahoma like nothing happened. We need to put up a deterrent presence to stop it."

"Count on the Seventh, General. If I may, sir, what should we expect from the treaty negotiations at Laramie?"

Sheridan shrugged. "Time will tell. If the hostiles go to the reservation and stay there that could settle quite a bit of trouble. The transcontinental line construction should then proceed without disruption. When the railroad is finished, people will have a fast, safe, comfortable way west. We will no longer need the Bozeman Trail. The question is, will the hostiles go to the reservation and stay there?"

"Given what you've told me of the situation in Kansas and Colorado I have my doubts." Custer smoothed his mustache, his customary self-assured bravado visibly restored.

"I share your doubts there myself. Frankly, I don't think the Indian problem can be resolved by treaty. The notion that it can makes eastern politicians feel good. It provides sufficient moral satisfaction to justify their actions. Truth is, it will take a decisive and total military victory to fully resolve the problem."

"Is that how I am to proceed in Kansas and Colorado, Phil?"

"Where force is necessitated, George, you'll have to use your own judgment. You know my position. The only good Indian is a dead Indian."

Custer met the general's eyes and nodded.

Sheridan rose, bringing the meeting to a close. "When will you leave?"

"No more than a day or two."

"Will Libbie accompany you?"

Custer hesitated, "Only as far as Fort Riley."

"Give her my compliments if you please."

Custer relaxed. "I shall, sir," he said, turning to go.

Sheridan caught him at the door, "One more thing, George." Custer paused. "Keep it in your britches until you're granted leave to visit her."

Custer clenched his jaw in a hard line and nodded.

CHAPTER ELEVEN

Fort Laramie
Wyoming Territory
April 1868

Fort Laramie looked more like a well-planned town than a military installation. It sat on the north bank of the Laramie River surrounded by broad sweeping plains. The fort had no stockade or visible defensive perimeter. Neat rows of log and clapboard buildings clustered around a central quadrangle that served as a parade ground.

A large canvas tent top beyond the eastern perimeter of the compound provided shade for the Peace Commission. Discrete rows of two-man tents flanked the rear of the commission canopy to the north and south. They concealed the post batteries and Gatling guns, arrayed to deliver a steel wall of enfilade fire should defensive action be required.

Tribes attending the peace talks camped east of the fort. Three or four hundred tipi spread across the plain.

Commissioners Ely Parker, General Alfred Howe Terry, and General William Tecumseh Sherman gathered in the parlor of the post commander's quarters. They huddled around four camp tables arranged to serve as one large conference table. The room was warm in spite of a spring breeze stirring the lace curtains in the open windows. Coats and tunics hung on chairs, formality sacrificed to some measure of relief from the heat. Sherman sat at the end of the table idly drumming his fingers as he gazed out the window. Parker paced the floor, reading Terry's latest draft of the treaty articles.

A lawyer by training, Terry had been given the task of drafting terms of the treaty. As commander of the Department of the Dakota he was closest to the situation. He understood Indian sentiment and what might be required to pacify them. Quiet and thoughtful, Terry wore his dark brown hair and beard neatly trimmed. He had a lean frame of average height. His deep-set brown eyes remained alert despite tired dark circles. He sat with his back to the table, legs stretched, one boot crossed over the other at the ankle, watching Parker read as he paced.

At length Parker paused his pacing and turned to Terry. "On balance this is a good start, General, though I'm troubled by a couple of points." He crossed to the table and bent over a large map. He studied the map for a moment and reread a portion of the document. Parker's Seneca blood made him an effective advocate for the Indian and an influential voice in Washington on their behalf. In these matters his own legal training also held him in good stead.

"Firstly, it's the description of the reservation boundaries in Article Two. I'm concerned the area is too small. The boundaries are based on an allocation of arable acreage in relation to the population. That strikes me as flawed in two respects. One is the small size of the allocation per person."

Terry pressed his fingertips together at the point of his chin. "My purpose was to offer a meaningful allocation of land without making the grant excessive."

"The size of the grant is less important than the fundamental notion the tribes will take up farming. These people are hunters. They follow the buffalo herds. We base our position on the presumption that they will settle in one place and live like white men."

Sherman glanced up. He had a dog in this particular hunt after all. "The point of this treaty is to confine the tribes to a reservation. Hunting is the way they sustain themselves in the old ways. Those are the ways we need to change. General Terry's farming acreage seems a reasonable way to accomplish that purpose."

Parker braced himself. The military view Sherman expressed underscored a fundamental flaw in the white man's approach to treaty making with the Indian. "We're here to make peace, General, not change the tribes' way of life."

"You can't seriously believe we'll have meaningful peace without the Indian changing his ways."

"How the Indian lives is not our concern, General. Our only concern is that we live in peace. That means striking a treaty both sides can live with. In this case that does not include confining, to use your term, the Indian to a farm."

"Your military judgment eludes you, Commissioner."

Terry held up his hand. "Gentlemen, gentlemen, please. I see your point, Ely. Let's look at the positives and work from there. The reservation includes the Black Hills, land the Lakota call Paha Sapa. It is a rather desolate region not suited to most white purposes, but regarded as sacred by the Sioux. I believe that by including it, we will satisfy a large measure of Indian expectation at small cost to the nation."

"General, we say in Article One that these lands are ceded to the tribes in perpetuity. They have to be able to live on the lands they are given."

"What would you have me do short of giving them the whole of the country between here and California?"

Parker bent over the map again. "The key may be taken from my second problem with Article Two." He tapped an index finger to pursed lips, composing his thoughts.

"And what would that be?" Terry turned to the map at

Parker's elbow.

"I'm sure the survey references are precise, but measures like 'the forty-sixth parallel of north latitude' and 'the one hundred and fourth degree of longitude west from Greenwich,' have no meaning to the tribes." Parker read quoting from the document. He set the document aside and bent over the map. "Perhaps we can draw a distinction between reservation land and hunting grounds that would be more meaningful to the tribes and sufficient to sustain life."

"How would you propose to do that?"

"Describe the reservation as land west of the Missouri River to the Paha Sapa," Parker continued tracing the area with his finger. "We need to define additional landmarks to boundary the reservation on the south and west. Hunting grounds could extend south to the North Platte and west to the Powder River country east of the Bighorn Mountains."

"I see what you have in mind, Ely. Let me insert that concept as Article Sixteen." Terry scratched notes in the margin of his draft.

Sherman glanced at the map. His mind seethed. *What the hell am I doing here? I serve no more useful purpose than giving Andy Johnson political cover. Why bother to negotiate a treaty at all. The Sioux needn't represent themselves so long as they have Commissioner Parker to do it for them.*

May 25, 1868

Terry rose from the camp table. His gaze wandered the etched copper features of the assembled Oglala headmen and chiefs. The canvas tent top flapped gently in the spring breeze warmed with canvas scent. He raised the treaty documents.

"Article One: From this day forward all war between the parties shall forever cease." He read slowly pausing to allow the scout, Albion Baker Brown, to translate. "The Government of the United States desires peace, and its honor is hereby pledged to keep it."

Parker too studied the tribal leaders as the reading and translating droned on. Perspiration gathered at the base of his neck and trickled down his chest unseen under his blouse. He listened again to the agreement he'd helped draw in seventeen articles. He took satisfaction from it. It was a good agreement. He hoped these leaders would see that. More importantly he hoped the people would follow their lead. The headmen nodded when they heard the talking paper speak to the Paha Sapa, the Black Hills translated into reserved land.

"Shall be set apart for the absolute and undisturbed use and occupation of the Indians herein named."

This would be the cornerstone of the agreement for the Lakota. That land of barren rock and pine forests was sacred to the Sioux. It was also ill-suited to white purposes such as farming or ranching. It gave him some comfort that this treaty might be different from the others. This treaty might indeed stand in perpetuity as it was written. His greatest satisfaction, though, came from the provision of hunting grounds in sufficient abundance to sustain life. Here the buffalo would thrive to feed the tribes for generations to come.

Man Afraid of His Horses sat with his brothers. He listened to the pony soldier speak the words of the talking papers. They came to hear these words as their Brule brothers had come before them. Iron Shell told him the words pleased the Brule. The Oglala would hear for themselves. Man Afraid of His Horses listened carefully. He would be asked to set the example when the words were finished. He would be asked to make his mark. The wasichu made much of these marks. They did not understand the people. Many would follow the men who made these marks. Others would not. The most important mark would be that of Red Cloud. Red Cloud did not come to hear these words. He waited for the pony soldiers to leave the forts in the lands promised by these talking papers.

"And it is hereby expressly stipulated that each Indian over the age of four years, who shall have moved to and settled permanently upon said reservation and complied with the stipulations of this treaty, shall be entitled to receive from the United States, for the period of four years after he shall have settled upon said reservation, one pound of meat and one pound of flour per day,"

Man Afraid of His Horses had heard these words before. Their Cheyenne brothers listened to these words when they accepted a reservation where the hunting was poor. They found the winters hard on empty bellies when cattle and flour did not come.

Sherman sat at the end of the commission table listening to the reading of a document he could now recite from memory out of boredom. He had little confidence in the enduring effect of the treaty Parker and Terry found so hopeful. One had only to look at the troubles of reconstructing an unrepentant confederacy. They'd been totally defeated and still there were problems. What might have happened if they'd sued for terms after Atlanta fell? They'd have been given, of course. But to what effect? A temporary truce, allowing an undefeated enemy to refit and rearm before the next outbreak of hostilities. Total defeat had come only after they burned their way to the sea. Tight lines formed at the corners of his eyes. He inspected the stony features of the assembled headmen. This enemy was not defeated. This enemy was being given pause, a temporary truce, time to rearm and rebuild. He didn't know how or when, but he knew with the keen instincts of a veteran campaigner, this conflict would not end. Not until they achieved final, decisive,

Grasshoppers in Summer

total defeat.

"Article Sixteen: The United States hereby agrees and stipulates that the country north of the North Platte River and east of the summits of the Bighorn Mountains shall be held and considered to be unseeded Indian territory." As instructed, Brown translated the words *unseeded, hunting grounds.*

Man Afraid of His Horses nodded. Here were the hunting grounds that would feed the people when the other promises were broken.

"It is further agreed by the United States that within ninety days after the conclusion of peace with all the bands of the Sioux Nation, the military posts now established in the territory in this article named shall be abandoned, and that the road leading to them and by them to the settlements in the Territory of Montana shall be closed."

If these words were true, Man Afraid of His Horses knew Red Cloud would make his mark.

"In testimony to all of which, we, the said commissioners, and we, the chiefs and headmen of the Oglala band of the Sioux Nation, have hereunto set our hands and seals at Fort Laramie, Dakota Territory, this twenty fifth day of May, in the year of our Lord one-thousand-eight-hundred and sixty-eight. Now I ask that each of you come forward to make his mark with your Brule brothers." Terry placed the document on the camp table in front of him and took his seat.

Man Afraid of His Horses studied the white men sent by the Great Father. Why should he trust the words of these talking papers any more than the others? Only time could answer this question. This time, the wasichu offered hunting grounds to feed the people. They offered the Paha Sapa. Red Cloud has won. He will make his mark. Man Afraid of His Horses will make his mark in honor of Red Cloud's victory. The people seldom defeated the whites. In this treaty Red Cloud took the Paha Sapa and Powder River country for the people. This victory is good. He rose and walked to the commission table. His brothers rose and followed, forming a line.

"State your name and make your mark," the interpreter said.

"Tah-Shun-Ka-Co-Qui-Pah." He made his mark.

"Man Afraid of His Horses," the interpreter said.

And so they came, shuffling forward in the dust each in his turn to make his mark.

"Sha-Ton-Skah."

"White Hawk, makes his mark."

"Oh-Wah-She-Cha."

"Bad Wound, makes his mark."

"Wah-Non Sah-Che-Geh."

"Ghost Heart, makes his mark."

Parker watched and listened as the headmen and chiefs were announced. They'd made a good treaty, one these proud people could live with. He'd seen to that. He offered a prayer to his own Great Spirit; that white man and Indian alike should be guided by it and in that, at last, find peace.

CHAPTER TWELVE

Washita River Agency
Oklahoma Territory
June 1868

The lodge fire burned low, dimly lighting the tipi. Spotted Hawk lay in the buffalo robes cloaked in shadow. He stared at the stars through the wisp of smoke in the darkened smoke hole. Hunger fed his anger. This night they had a small corn cake to share. They had no meat. Cattle did not come. Soon summer would grow long. The hard days of winter would come again. The people would starve without a good hunt.

Autumn Snow parted the lodge flap and stepped in. She carried a freshly filled waterskin to the buffalo robes. Low light covered her in shadow as she knelt to offer him the skin.

"Drink, my husband. It will ease your hunger."

Spotted Hawk sat up to drink. He saw hunger in her eyes. It hurt worse than his own. The water cooled his thirst. He passed the skin back to her and held the hand that accepted it. She set the skin aside and touched her forehead to his.

"I must hunt." Determination gave a hard edge to his tenderness.

"Will you leave the reservation?" It was a foolish question. She knew the answer, even as she feared it.

"I must. There is no game here." They sat silent for a time. "Black Kettle cannot feed the people on the lies of the fat agent Denton. I have spoken with Kicking Pony and some others. We are men. We cannot live like camp dogs."

She sat back on her heels and looked deep into his eyes. "It is dangerous to leave the reservation."

"It is death to let winter find us with no food."

She nodded. "Then hunt, my husband, but do not raid the whites. Do not fight the pony soldiers. My heart will be empty until you return to our lodge."

Spotted Hawk lay back in the robes.

Autumn Snow stood in the ember glow of the lodge fire. She pulled her buckskin dress over her head. She lay the dress aside and shook out her hair.

The sight of her willowy body never failed to stir him. He felt her soft swells and warm copper folds in his mind. His manhood grew with want. She crawled under the buffalo robe and put her head on his breast. He held her tightly to him. Her fingers trailed lightly down his chest to the thong binding his breechclout. She released him to her need. She made him a man again, a man who would hunt, a man who would feed her.

They rode southwest in search of buffalo. Spotted Hawk, Kicking Pony, Gray Wolf. and Broken Knife left the reservation to hunt lands where few white people went. They rode for days without seeing sign of the great ones. Late one afternoon they climbed a ridge. Spotted Hawk drew a halt. Red rock and scrub stretched away south and west to the end of the sky. They saw no sign of the great ones. Spotted Hawk spoke.

"We come far to find no buffalo. We must ride north." North would take them back toward the lands of the whites along the iron horse trail. If they didn't find buffalo to hunt, they might find stray cattle. North raised the risk of confronting white men. Spotted Hawk saw no other way.

Kicking Pony nodded. The others agreed in turn. Spotted

Hawk wheeled his pony and picked up a lope to the north.

They rode north many days before they saw buffalo sign. It lifted their hearts to ride on. On a bright sunny afternoon, they heard shots coming from the far side of a low ridge. They galloped up the ridge and drew rein below the crest. Spotted Hawk slipped down from his pony. He crouched low and ran forward. Dropping to his belly he crawled through the prairie grass to the crest of the ridge. White hunters supplying meat to the railroad crews had taken four shaggy ones from a small herd in the valley below. Spotted Hawk counted three hunters. His blood ran hot with anger. Now they would hunt.

He ran back to his brothers. "White hunters kill buffalo. We run off hunters and take the meat they have killed."

They mounted their ponies and rode to the crest of the ridge. They ranged across the skyline plainly visible to the hunters below. One of the hunters pointed at them. The shooting stopped. They retreated to the wagon they used to haul hides and took cover there.

The warriors started down the ridge wall at a walk. The hunters let them come. A puff of smoke announced the report of a fifty caliber Sharps rifle. The heavy bullet struck Gray Wolf's pony in the chest. The pony bellowed its death song and dropped to its knees. Gray Wolf leaped into the prairie grass and disappeared.

Spotted Hawk wheeled his pony west and kicked up a gallop circling the wagon below the ridgeline. Kicking Pony dropped from his pony and disappeared in the prairie grass. Broken Knife galloped east, drawing fire from the hunters. He reached a position flanking the wagon and dropped into the long grass.

The shooting fell silent. The hunters had no targets. They had become the hunted. Time passed. Silence disturbed only by buffalo lowing and flies buzzing around the carcasses of the fallen. Overhead, buzzards gathered, riding currents of summer breeze in lazy circles. The hunters hid behind their wagon nervously searching the waving grass sea for their attackers.

Spotted Hawk worked his way around behind the wagon to a clear shot at the hunters. He cooed the call of a dove. Broken Knife answered. He had a shot from the far side of the wagon. A third call said Kicking Pony or Gray Wolf was close to the wagon.

Spotted Hawk shouldered his rifle. He chose the hunter on lookout to the rear of the wagon for his target. Wind would not matter at this range. He had only to allow for the bullet to strike slightly below the point of his aim. The man wore a shabby slouch hat with red whiskers and shoulder-length hair. The scalp would make a fine prize. He set his sights for the top of the man's left shoulder. From there the bullet would fall to his heart. He breathed, slowing his own heart. His finger pressed the trigger lightly. The Winchester bucked hard. The bullet slammed the hunter back against the wagon. Spotted Hawk ducked low as the second hunter swung his Sharps on line to him.

Broken Knife's shot dropped the man before he could discharge his rifle. The third hunter turned to the rear of the wagon. Gray Wolf leaped over the wagon behind him with a war whoop and buried his tomahawk in the back of the man's head.

The brothers rushed the wagon, whooping in victory. Spotted Hawk stood over the dead hunter with the red hair. He drew his knife and dropped to his knees. He took the red scalp with a clean slice and shook it in the air, lifting his voice in a victory cry. Blood spattered his cheek and chest. It ran down his arm as a mark of his coup.

He walked toward the herd milling about the wounded lead cow. *This is how the white man hunt. They hunt for hides, leaving the rest of the great one's life-giving gifts to rot. They slaughter as many as they wish with no thought to the needs of* the people. Spotted Hawk showed the great shaggy ones the scalp he and his brothers had taken in vengeance for them. These dead would feed his people, not the white men building the iron horse trail.

He shook his head sadly at the wounded cow. His sorrow only deepened by what more he must do. He raised his rifle and shot the wounded great one in the head. She died with a groan. The new lead cow came forward. She sniffed the body of her fallen sister and bellowed to the herd. Slowly the great ones drifted off to the west.

They found salt in the wagon to cure the meat. They spent the rest of the day skinning, butchering, and jerking fresh killed buffalo. That night they ate the heart of the lead cow at their campfire. They roasted the hump and filled their bellies for the first time in more than a moon. They defeated the hunters and found food for the people. This night Spotted Hawk felt more like a man than he had in many moons.

The next day they filled the wagon with meat. It would not feed the people through the winter, but they would have food for a time with more time to hunt. On the third day they set out to return to the village. Spotted Hawk scouted ahead to avoid any whites who might see them with a stolen wagon loaded with meat and hides. Gray Wolf rode one of the mules that pulled the wagon. Broken Knife and Kicking Pony trailed behind, brushing away wagon sign as they wound their way southeast to the Washita.

CHAPTER THIRTEEN

Washita River Agency
Oklahoma Territory
July 1868

Autumn Snow sat among her sisters sifting cornmeal, searching for worms in the agency ration. A hot summer breeze licked at loose tendrils, escaped from her braids. Dust swirled along the cracked parched riverbank.

Running Fawn flicked the dry husk of a dark brown worm into the red dirt where she sat. "We are like a worm in the white man's flour."

Autumn Snow considered the dead worm in the red dirt. Her sister's words rang with truth. She did not like them. This truth burned Spotted Hawk's heart. The white man's treaty took away the people's pride. It broke the circle of life in the old ways. She tilted her chin toward the worm. "This is our place in the white man's world. This place weighs heavy on the heart of a warrior."

Fawn nodded. She too saw her own husband's troubled spirit.

"Spotted Hawk is a warrior. He would rather hunt to provide for his lodge than accept the white man's cattle or the lies they tell us when the cattle do not come. He fears this place will make him father to sons who will never be warriors. Proud warriors do not live on white man's beef and flour with worms." She felt his pain in her words. "Spotted Hawk cannot live the life the whites give us."

Fawn nodded. "My sister is wise."

The hunting party galloped the last quarter mile into the village, announcing their victory with war whoops. Gray Wolf lumbered along behind, riding a mule pulling the wagon loaded with meat and hides. They pulled their ponies to a stop in front of Black Kettle's lodge.

Black Kettle fixed the young warriors with a careworn gaze. They hunted off the reservation. It troubled him, but he could do nothing to stop them. Empty bellies spoke louder than words. Cattle meant little to warriors who would be free. The young men knew Denton lied. They had no reason to believe him. A few cattle would not persuade them. Now they returned with a wagon. This meant more than a hunt. Black Kettle watched Spotted Hawk slip down from his pony. A fresh red scalp hung from his belt.

"You killed a white man." The accusation hung hot with anger and concern for the story they would tell.

"We found no buffalo to the south and west," Spotted Hawk began as a crowd of villagers gathered. Autumn Snow stood among the women, relieved her man had returned.

"We rode north. We found iron horse hunters killing a herd. We rode in to stop them. They fired on us. We killed them and took their wagon. It is filled with the meat from their kill. There will be meat for a time in the village."

Black Kettle shook his head. "If pony soldiers find what you have done, they will punish all the people."

"Better to die a warrior's death than starve as the fat agent's camp dog."

"You wish for a warrior's death, Spotted Hawk, but what of our women and children? Would you take them to your warrior's death?"

Spotted Hawk darkened. Black Kettle spoke like an old woman. "Better that than see them starve in the snows."

"You forget the death songs of Sand Creek. You bring great danger to the people. This is a bad thing, Spotted Hawk."

"We must hunt or we will starve on white lies." His deep voice held a determined edge. "We will hunt again."

Black Kettle's eyes grew sad. "Killing whites is not hunting. The next time it may be their cattle you hunt. Then Pony soldiers come."

"Cattle make Tsitsistas white man's camp dog." Spotted Hawk said. He turned in defiance and led his pony to the picket line.

"Unload the wagon and burn it. If the Great One Above is with us, the Pony soldiers may never know."

Broken Knife and Gray Wolf burned the wagon as Black Kettle ordered. The village women divided the buffalo among the people. They had meat at their lodge fires that evening. Later, Autumn Snow sat quietly beside Spotted Hawk as he smoked his pipe.

"There is wisdom in Black Kettle's words," she said softly.

Spotted Hawk fixed her with a sharp look. "Black Kettle speaks like an old woman."

"Those are words of the old ways. You cannot bring them back. The white men are here. They are many and they are strong. War in the old way has not held them back."

He let a wisp of sweet tobacco cover his eyes. "Would you have me wait for Black Kettle and the fat agent's lies to feed you? We would starve."

She dropped her eyes. "I know you are a warrior. You bring honor to our lodge. I do not wish you a warrior's death. Hunt if you must, but do not fight the whites. Killing means only more killing."

He let her words speak to his heart. He nodded and set his pipe aside. "For you I will do this."

She rose to her knees and touched her forehead to his. The buffalo robes would welcome him home this night.

The herd came to the village as a rising cloud of dust on the horizon followed by a low bawling moan in the distance. Black Kettle stood before his lodge greeting the sight and sound with great relief. The cattle would feed his people through the coming winter. In this the white men kept their word. With cattle he could keep the young men on the reservation and preserve the peace for yet another season. Without these cattle he would never be able to hold the wild ones to the peace.

Spotted Hawk saw the cattle as scraps, fallen from the white man's table. Scraps they might feed a dog. It would feed the people in the coming winter if their hunting did not. He saw no honor in this. It made him less than a man. He remembered the day they took buffalo from the white hunters. That day he again lived as a warrior. That day he lived like a man. They took what they needed from the great shaggy ones. They let the rest go to feed them in the days to come. Left to their ways, the whites would have killed them all. They would take what they could use and leave the rest to rot. The urge to hunt ran deep in a warrior's heart. How would he teach this to sons who grew to manhood feeding at the foot of the white man's table? Hunger counted much in the circle of life. Feeding it brought honor to the hunter. Feeding it like a dog did not.

Autumn Snow, like many of the other women, felt relieved. Her husband and the other warriors may not welcome this, but these animals would feed the people in the coming snows. Cattle would feed the cookfires; they would not warm the hearts of men denied the pride of the hunt. The fear of starvation would pass for this winter. Perhaps the whites would keep the words of their treaty this time.

Custer drew the column to a halt on a grassy ridge overlooking a shallow valley below. He squinted against the glare of the sun as he studied the scene. Little remained to mark the site of the hunt and the fight that interrupted it.

"Let's go in for a look," he said, as much to himself as to his adjutant, Lieutenant Cooke.

"Forward ho!"

The column jogged down the grassy ridge to the valley floor. Coyotes and vultures had done their work on what little remained of the butchered buffalo.

"Call a halt and dismount, Lieutenant," Custer ordered over his shoulder.

Cooke raised his right arm and barked, "Company halt!" The column drew to a halt.

"Dismount!"

The troopers stepped down to a jangle of bridles, sabers, and the creak of saddle leather.

"There." The Crow scout Curly pointed to something lying in the prairie grass that did not appear to be remnant of a buffalo carcass.

Custer paced the area inspecting the bodies. Three dead hunters, two shot, one with his head caved in by a tomahawk blow. They'd all been scalped before the scavengers did their grisly work.

"Sergeant Major Kane, burial detail front and center." He turned on his heel as the burial detail went to work. He watched the scout Curly work his way around the killing field searching for sign.

"What do you make of it, sir?" Cooke said.

"Looks like Indians took offense to the hunt. If Curly can

figure out who's responsible, I expect the Seventh will be handing out retribution."

"You think General Sheridan will authorize such an action?"

"Already has. I'm to keep the peace by the exercise of such means and measures as may be reasonable in my judgment," Custer repeated Sheridan's self-assured instructions. "General Sherman himself is concerned about Indian provocations in spite of all the treaty making up north." Custer twisted his mustache on this last and spit as if ridding himself of a sour taste.

Reasonable means and measures in Iron Butt's judgment, Cooke thought. *That would be whatever it took to turn them light colonel's pips into stars.*

Curly trotted up to Custer. The Crow scout was known for the wavy black hair that topped his braids. His handsome features were chiseled in dark copper. He had high wide cheekbones, alert dark eyes, and full lips. He spoke from deep in his chest.

"Cruly find tracks. Four warriors take meat in hunter wagon. Dead pony on hill is marked Cheyenne."

"Which way did they go?"

Curly shook his head, "Maybe south. Trail swept clean."

Custer rubbed his chin, looking off in the direction the scout indicated. "Black Kettle, I'll wager."

Cooke could hear the bugle call.

Chapter Fourteen

Western Kansas
September 1868

Luther Hatch pitched a forkful of hay into the corral from the loft door. He rested an elbow on the fork and wiped sweat from his eyes with a soiled bandanna. A thin cloud of dust wound its way up the road in the distance, growing larger as it drew near. A buckboard emerged from the dust cloud. Denton, the fact the agent had driven out here likely meant a herd had arrived down on the Washita. He climbed down from the loft to greet his visitor in the dusty yard.

The sun burned hot in a cloudless blue sky. A light breeze swirled small dust devils across the corral. Flies buzzed around piles of fresh horse droppings. Hatch rested a bootheel on the low fence rail and leaned against a post. He pushed his hat back to dry sweat-matted hair as Denton drew the buckboard to a halt in the yard. The fat man did not exert himself to get down. He never did.

"Good day to you, Luther."

"It is a good day, Denton. I expect you're here to tell me there are longhorns down on the Washita."

"Very perceptive. As a matter a fact there are. If your prescient powers were any better it might save me this tedious drive."

"My what powers?"

Denton wiped sweat from his brow with a handkerchief gone wet with the work. "Pre . . . never mind. The market for feedin' railroad crews has gone up some with winter comin' on. A man might make forty-five or fifty dollars a head these days."

Hatch cracked a crooked half grin. "Usual split?"

"Usual split."

"Me and the boys'll take care of it."

"Come see me when you're done."

"Sure. Be there before the snow flies."

Denton managed a bland smile. "Good day then, Luther."

"Good day, Roscoe."

"Hey up there!" Reins slapped the sturdy bay into a wide turn. The agent headed back the way he'd come.

Washita River

Easy pickin's was about the only way Luther Hatch could describe what it took to run off some sixty head of longhorns. He and his boys rode down to the Washita on a crisp September morning. The Indians were hunters not herders. They turned their cattle loose north of their village where the grass was plentiful. They relied on the fact the herd wouldn't stray too far from water. When they needed meat, it was easy enough to hunt up the herd, take what they needed, and leave the rest to take care of itself. It was almost like hunting buffalo. As a result, there weren't any guards for Hatch and his men to contend with. It was simply a matter of rounding them up and driving them north to his ranch.

Spotted Hawk watched them go. Fury built a slow fire in his chest. The white rancher Hatch stole the herd the fat agent sent them. The words of the treaty meant nothing to white people. Spotted Hawk's people would starve in the snows without this food. He would not allow this to happen. He leaped to the back of his pony and raced back to the village.

The App slid to a stop in front of Black Kettle's lodge in a cloud of dust prancing and circling in a swirl of yapping camp dogs. Black Kettle stepped out, summoned by the ruckus as Spotted Hawk jumped down.

"White men steal cattle."

Black Kettle felt a knot tighten in his chest. This was the sort of trouble he had hoped to avoid. It was hard enough to hold the wild ones to the reservation without this. To do it in the face of treachery might be more than he could hope.

"Spotted Hawk take warriors. Bring cattle back."

Rage glinted in the young warrior's eyes. Anger fired his words. Black Kettle found little he could say. He knew the threat of starvation. Still he could not risk letting the warriors ride off the reservation on such a raid. White man's law protected only the white man.

The chief drew strength and force of will from his inner spirit. "Spotted Hawk must not pursue the white men. Black Kettle will go to pony soldier fort. He will make words with Indian Agent. Let pony soldiers return cattle back to Tsitsistas."

Spotted Hawk turned sour. "Always with Black Kettle it was the same. More white man's words. More white man's lies. Tsitsistas can not fill our bellies with words when the snows come."

Black Kettle heard the anger in Spotted Hawk's words. He remembered his own hot blood as a young warrior. "Pony soldiers bring cattle back. It must be so."

The next morning, Black Kettle, Lone Bull, and a delegation of the tribal elders rode out to Fort Larned. He'd convinced Spotted Hawk and the young warriors to let him try to persuade the Indian Agent Denton and the pony soldiers to return their cattle. *If they would.* Doubt haunted him as they rode. The fat agent would tell them what they wanted to hear, but would the pony soldiers return the cattle? They must. Words alone would not stop warriors whose families faced starvation.

Grasshoppers in Summer

Days later Black Kettle and Lone Bull waited under a white flag of truce at the gates of Fort Larned. A sentry opened the gates and escorted them across the parade ground to the Indian Agent's office. Black Kettle and Lone Bull dismounted. They stood on the dusty parade ground waiting to see the fat Agent Denton. Dust swirled around them, eagle feathers and fringe ruffled on the breeze. The sentry knocked on the agency door and announced their arrival. Denton waddled out on the porch. He stood owlishly blinking back sunlight as he looked down on them.

"Black Kettle, Lone Bull, to what do I owe the honor of such a visit?"

Black Kettle doubted he truly spoke of honor. "White rancher Hatch steal our cattle. We come to ask pony soldiers to bring cattle back to Tsitsistas."

"Why that's a serious accusation, Black Kettle. Do you have any proof?"

"Spotted Hawk see them. Hatch has Tsitsistas' cattle. That proof."

"If that's true, why, yes I suppose it is proof. We'd have to check the brands to be sure of course. I'll have a word with Colonel Custer and tell him of your concern."

"No. We go see long knife chief now. Ask him bring Tsitsistas' cattle back to Washita."

The old chief was savvy, Denton thought. He wasn't about to let his complaint die on the agency steps.

Black Kettle turned away from Denton. He and Lone Bull led their ponies across the parade ground toward Custer's headquarters with the sentry trailing behind. Denton waddled after them perspiring in the dust and midday heat. *Damn nuisance having to deal with such matters in this heat.* He wondered what the colonel would make of this. Hatch better have changed those brands.

The sentry climbed the step to the commandant's office and knocked.

A muffled "Enter," sounded through the door.

The sentry stepped through the door, snapped to attention, and picked up his salute. "Sir, the Cheyenne chiefs Black Kettle and Lone Bull are here to see you, sir."

"Send them over to see Denton. Can't you see I'm busy here?"

"Sir, they've already been to see Mr. Denton. He's accompanying them now."

Custer scowled. "Very well then. Damn it." He rose from his desk. "Dismissed, Corporal."

"Thank you, sir." The sentry hurried back to his post.

Custer stepped out of his office onto the sunlit porch. He cut his usual stylish figure with a fringed buckskin jacket over his uniform blouse and red-striped blue trousers. His hat cocked at a rakish angle with the left side of the brim pinned up. His boots gleamed fresh with his orderly's polish.

"What the hell's goin on here, Denton?"

"Black Kettle alleges Luther Hatch stole some of his cattle. He wants you to call out a troop to take them back to the Washita."

"Oh, he does, does he? That's a pretty serious charge, Black Kettle. It's a hangin' offense if it's true. The cattle probably just strayed off. Why don't you go round 'em up yourself?"

"Cattle no stray. Cattle driven away. Spotted Hawk see Hatch and his men take them. If our warriors take cattle, white man's law protect white man."

Custer studied the determined old chief. Black Kettle was one of the peace chiefs who kept the young bucks in check most of the time. He suspected renegade Cheyenne were responsible for killing the buffalo hunters he'd seen on patrol. Sheridan hadn't seen that as sufficient provocation to action, lacking more than suspicion for proof. Hatch was an old reprobate. It would come as no surprise if Black Kettle's story was true. For all the rancher's dealings with Denton the two of them might well be involved in some plot to cheat the Cheyenne out of their cattle ration. If that was the game, Hatch would certainly be smart enough to change the brands on the agency cattle. He didn't think much of turning Seventh Cavalry troopers into cowboys. They'd ride out to Hatch's place only to have him deny any knowledge of the agency herd. If he did nothing, the Cheyenne just might take matters into their own hands and that might well result in all the "provocation" he needed.

"All right, Black Kettle. I'll send a detail over to the Hatch place to have a look. If there are any cattle there that don't belong to him, we'll see that they get back to you."

Black Kettle heard the long knife chief's words. They weighed heavy on his heart. He would carry the burden of unshakable knowing back to the Washita. *White man's law protects only the white man.*

Chapter Fifteen

Washita River Agency
Oklahoma Territory
October 1868

The first signs of winter came early that fall. Spotted Hawk and Autumn Snow huddled together for warmth under a heavy covering of buffalo robes. Outside the lodge, a white crystal frost spread over the land foretelling the long sleeping season that would soon be here. They had seen no sign the pony soldiers would return the stolen cattle.

Spotted Hawk lay awake staring into the dark smoke hole at the top of the tipi. Autumn Snow sensed his unrest. She felt the anger that burned in his breast where she rested her head. She knew without lifting her head that he lay awake. The hollow rumblings of hunger in the pit of his stomach spoke of the stolen cattle. Soon the warriors would wait no longer. Black Kettle's words of warning fell on ears and hearts turned to stone.

"My husband is troubled."

Spotted Hawk turned to her. "Black Kettle and Lone Bull go to the white man's fort. They make words with the Indian Agent, Denton, and the long knife chief, Custer. They say pony soldiers bring back our cattle. They lie. Tsitsistas have no cattle. The people will starve in the coming snows. White man's law does not protect Tsitsistas. White man's law protects only the white man. Winter is coming. Cattle will return only if Dog Soldiers bring them back."

Resolve stiffened in him. It frightened her. What would they do if the pony soldiers came? She shut her eyes and her ears against childhood memories of Sand Creek. They never spoke of it. Still the memories would not go away. Sand Creek was another reservation. Black Kettle led his people there when the whites made a treaty to take gold stones from Tsitsistas' lands in Colorado. In the years when the whites made war between their own tribes, food did not come to the reservation. She was a child at the time, too young to understand. Years later her mother told her. Young men went to find food. They found cattle. Pony soldiers came. This she remembered from her child's eyes. She heard the bugle and gunshots that woke them from sleep. She smelled smoke from burning lodges and gunpowder. The screams of the wounded rang in her heart with the death songs of those who would die. She closed her eyes to the vision of women keening over fallen husbands and other children crying over mutilated mothers. Many died that day. Her father crossed over to walk with the spirits. Her mother followed Black Kettle and his family to safety in the hills. She prayed she would not see these things again and yet, once again, young men would fight for cattle. Her Spotted Hawk would be among them. Tears leaked from her eyes.

Her tears fell hot against his chest. He felt her pain. Instinctively he held her tight.

"We cannot face winter without food."

His words tasted hard and bitter to her ears. Autumn Snow had no words to stop him. He knew her fear, though he could not be any other than a man. Women would carry these fears. They would hold their tears and pray to the Great One Above that they would not shed them over the bodies of their people.

Black Kettle watched them, resigned, unable to stop it. Spotted

Hawk, Kicking Pony, Gray Wolf, and Broken Knife led their ponies up from the picket line; like ghosts they appeared out of a foggy mist, rising from the river chill. They would do no more than take what belonged to them. They would do it because the white man's law held no justice for the people. Spotted Hawk paused beside his pony and met Black Kettle's eyes. Each man spoke his heart without words. Each heard the other man's heart.

Young men would do what young men must do. He had done all he could. He had no words stronger than hunger. He could only pray the Great One Above would protect his people from what might follow. He watched them swing up on their ponies.

Spotted Hawk wheeled his war pony and led his brothers out with a whoop. All who heard knew. Dog Soldiers rode to feed the people. Gray folds draped riders and horses in a dark shroud as they passed into the mist. Only the telltale drumming of hoofbeats marked their passing, slowly dying away in the distance.

Spotted Hawk and his brothers found the cattle on a crisp autumn afternoon in pastures southwest of the Hatch ranch house. Hatch and his men were nowhere in sight. They rounded up the herd and drove it south to the Washita.

Trailing the herd, Spotted Hawk felt like a warrior again. He was a man providing for his family as he once did on the buffalo hunt. In this he was not the white man's camp dog. His chest filled again with pride of purpose. One small doubt gnawed at his sense of right. *White man's law would protect the white man.*

Luther Hatch scowled at the valley pasture where he expected to find the cattle quietly waiting for him to drive them to market. His rage turned a black storm cloud. The cattle were gone. The trail told the story. They'd been driven south by four or five riders mounted on unshod horses. *Indians,* he spat. Without those cattle he had no deal with Denton. That would cost him a lot of money if he didn't do something about it. He could ride down there with the boys and steal them again, but the Indians would likely be watching the herd this time. He didn't have enough men to take on the whole tribe. There had to be another way. Hatch squinted off to the south, searching the horizon for his next move. In spite of it all, a slow smile spread over the answer. Yep, that was it.

Hatch thundered into Fort Larned. He slid his lathered horse to a stop in front of the post commander's office. He leaped down and started up the steps. The orderly on duty blocked his way.

"Luther Hatch to see Colonel Custer."

"Stand fast, Mr. Hatch. I'll see if the colonel will see you." The orderly pivoted smartly and knocked on the office door.

Hatch heard a muffled summons beyond the door.

"Mr. Hatch to see you, sir." The announcement waited a silent response.

Hatch shuffled his boots in the chill air, frustrated at the delay. A sharp autumn wind blew out of a sky heavy with leaden clouds. It whipped the brim of his hat and swirled clouds of dust across the parade ground. Hatch's horse stamped his impatience for him, snorting clouds of steam. He needed Custer to save his deal with Denton, but that didn't make it any easier to deal with the self-important bastard. Finally, he heard a chair scrape through the office door followed by some indistinct order.

"The colonel will see you now, Mr. Hatch." The orderly stepped aside at the office door.

Custer stood at a small camp desk. His buckskin jacket hung over the back of his chair. His uniform blouse was open at the collar, his suspenders hung at his sides. He smoothed his mustache as he sized his visitor, mild disinterest in his cold blue eyes.

"What seems to be the problem, Mr. Hatch?"

"Injuns stole my cattle." He rasped.

"That is a serious charge, sir. What makes you so sure?"

"I seen the tracks myself, sixty head or so bein' driven down to the Washita by riders on unshod ponies."

Custer let the words sink in. A small smile tugged at the corners of his mustache. *Provocation,* here it is a cause for action. Hatch might be a no-account low life, but his accusation had one thing in its favor. He was white. "You will keep peace and order using such means and measures as may be *reasonable in your judgment.*" Sheridan's instructions came back to him. *Use your judgment, George. What could be more reasonable than recovering stolen cattle?*

"Very well, Mr. Hatch. We shall look into your loss. If your assertion proves accurate, rest assured the Army will take appropriate action to restore your property."

"Thank you, Colonel. I'm sure I can rely on you to deal with them thievin' red bastards."

Chapter Sixteen

Fort Laramie
Wyoming Territory
November 6, 1868

They came all through that spring and summer, Brule, Oglala, Minneconjou, Yanctonais. They came in long shuffling lines to make their marks on the treaty. Parker took great satisfaction from witnessing what he believed to be historic peace making. His only nagging doubt had been Red Cloud's absence. Now, as he stood at the end of the commission table on a clear cold November morning, listening to the treaty being read yet again he felt his mission coming to a successful conclusion. The great Lakota war chief sat before the commission tent as so many of his brothers had before him.

Parker eyed Sherman seated at the end of the commission table, aloof from the proceedings as he'd been all summer. He expected this signing; this more than any other must give Sherman a bitter taste. Red Cloud had won. The disputed lands along the Bozeman Trail once again belonged to his people. The Army presence there had been withdrawn. Political appearances notwithstanding, Red Cloud had won his victory. He'd defeated his adversary. In truth, the prize Red Cloud won held greater symbolic value for his people than any value it might hold for the whites. Parker himself had argued that the Bozeman would be of little value once the transcontinental railroad was completed in the coming year. The whites could easily give it up in the name of peace. The economic and political wisdom of that was unassailable. However, none of that would make it sit any easier with the bluecoats.

Sherman rubbed his hands against the cold. The canvas tent top may have provided some relief from the summer sun, but it did little to break the cold wind blowing down from the north. He studied Red Cloud with the intensity fighting men have for their opposition. He'd steeled himself against the moment. He sat drumming his fingers, forced to witness events that could never be numbered among the Army's finest hours. The politicians believed this treaty meant lasting peace. Sherman found his sympathies grounded in more pragmatic terms. He considered it a truce, temporary at best. The illusion of peace would give the enemy time to regroup, resupply, and gain strength. He studied the dark eyes and the etched features of the war leader, listening to the terms of his adversaries' surrender. Sherman could recite these treaty terms in his sleep. His only curiosity left in the matter: *How and when would the fighting resume? How and when would the final blows be struck?*

"Mah-Pi-Ah-Lu-Tah," the interpreter announced.

Red Cloud makes his mark.

Parker eased back in his char. *I have done what I came to do. Now it is in the hands of the chiefs and the Army to keep the peace.* He prayed to his Great Spirit that would be enough. Only time would tell.

Department of the Missouri
Chicago, Illinois
Sheridan studied the telegraphed report from Custer. It represented that an Indian war party had raided a ranch north of the Washita reservation and had stolen a herd of cattle. Custer requested authority to mount an operation to recover the cattle and bring the hostiles to justice. On its merits the report seemed

a reasonable response to the provocation. Knowing Custer as he did, Sheridan suspected he would use the incident to justify the fight he was spoiling for. Custer proposed an action Sheridan favored in tactical terms. He would mount his operation on a winter camp when the hostiles would least expect it. The response would be swift, brutal, and in all likelihood, vainglorious to Custer. The Department of the Missouri could use a military action to send a message to the rest of the tribes under its supervision. Any hostilities would be met with decisive force. It was an important message for those subject to his authority, including the still dangerous Red Cloud. The Oglala war chief had only recently signed on to the Fort Laramie Treaty. He'd gone to his agency reservation. The question was, would he stay there? An exemplary military action in response to a breach of the peace would give him and his Sioux brothers something to consider.

Sheridan mulled Custer's request. Recovering stolen cattle and bringing the guilty to justice represented a reasonable response. He could justify the operation. Knowing George, the fact that he bothered to request permission at all suggested he probably had more on his mind than simply recovering some stolen cattle. He would undoubtedly exceed any authority Sheridan granted, but then his actions would be his responsibility. Sheridan scratched out his reply for the orderly to telegraph to Fort Larned.

Permission granted. Godspeed.

Chapter Seventeen

Washita River Agency
Oklahoma Territory
November 27, 1868

Custer squinted into the gray light of predawn. The sleeping village lay veiled in steam, rising from the river in the chill morning air. Some fifty lodges stood in a loose cluster along the west bank of the river. Most glowed softly from within where low-banked lodge fires lit them like lanterns. Thin gray wisps from dying embers rose through the smoke holes, mingling with leaden cloud and river mist. The village stood quiet save the occasional yap of a camp dog.

Black Kettle's lodge was easily distinguished from the others. It flew the stars and stripes from one lodge pole and a white flag of peace from another. Both pennants flapped in the chill morning breeze.

Custer's mind reached out to the prize he would take this day. The Seventh would ride to glory under his command. Newspapers would carry the accounts of this hour across the nation. He would see to it. They would toast him a national hero once more. General Sheridan would have the victory he desired thanks to his courage and daring. It would be a grand celebration, perhaps one to return him to his rightful rank and a general's star.

He drew his saber. The soft metallic scrape against the scabbard gathered the power of the charge as a conductor might tap his baton to draw the orchestra's attention. He looked left and right from the head of the column. "Major Reno, on my right, Captain Benteen, on my left"; he left Cooke to finish the order.

"Form skirmish line!"

The order disdained concern for any warning it might give the sleeping village. Troopers peeled forward left and right forming a skirmish line along the east bank of the river. Great clouds of steam marked the movement of troopers and horses along the riverbank. Weapons and tack creaked and jangled softly in the morning stillness.

The Crow scout Curly drew his sturdy paint in behind the colonel's bugler and standard bearer, flanked by Lieutenant Cooke and Sergeant Major Kane. As Custer's lead scout he welcomed this fight. The Crow had a long war history with the hated Cheyenne. This day he would count coup on his ancestral enemies. The glory would be greater if he rode at the head of a Crow war party. This fight would not be remembered in song or told in story around his family's lodge fire. Today he followed the bluecoats as they rode down on a sleeping village. No one would sing this song.

Custer swept his eyes left and right. The formation stood ready. Along the line, clouds of steam rose from the mingled breath of horses and men like some fire breathing monster prepared to strike. Six hundred strong, the formation stretched along the riverbank at the water's edge. He raised his saber.

"Bugler sound the charge!" His saber flashed forward; a silver scythe sliced the coming dawn.

"Forward, ho!" He drew out the command, the melodic sound of his power as intoxicating as vintage cognac. The bugle shattered the morning stillness. Sharp notes in bright bars summoned the line to advance. Up and down the riverbank, men and horses surged forward, splashing into the river.

★ ★ ★ ★ ★

All across the camp, sleeping villagers woke to the bugle call. The first to leave their sleeping robes stared in disbelief at the dark line of troopers charging across the river, churning white foam froth like thunderheads rolling before a storm. The pony soldiers opened fire as they splashed ashore on the west bank of the river. The village broke into a melee of panic and confusion. Women and children ran screaming in every direction. Here and there a warrior found his weapons and mounted a defense of the women scrambling to rush their children to safety.

The bugle call woke Kicking Pony from a sound sleep. He grabbed his rifle and ran from his lodge. He could see the line splashing across the river through a misty fog. He cursed the treachery of white men who attacked a winter camp. They knew no honor as warriors. He ran for the picket line south of the village. Cheyenne Dog Soldiers fought from their ponies. He paused to lever a bullet into the chamber of his rifle. He picked out the nearest trooper and dropped to his knee. His bullet struck the pony soldier in the chest. His horse reared, pawing the air before it leaped up the riverbank. The dead pony soldier splashed into the muddy ice crystals on the riverbank. Kicking Pony let out a victory whoop and ran for the picket line.

Pony soldiers rode down on him. They cut him off from the picket line. A blue wall turned on him in a line, their steel shod horses charged toward him. He could not reach his pony. He levered a round into his rifle and dropped to his knee. He fired. The rifle bucked. The recoil masked the bullet that struck him. It caught him in the leg with a force that knocked him to the ground. He willed himself back to his knee over the searing pain. He levered another round into his rifle and fired. Powder smoke plumed over the charging bluecoats. They bore down on him. He worked the lever and fired once more. The second bullet struck him in the chest. It knocked him back with the force of a pony kick. Red gouts sprouted from the gaping hole in his chest. The instinct of a warrior took possession of his body. He shouldered his rifle once more. The muzzle of the weapon refused to hold steady. He willed it to land on a blue target. He fired into darkness.

Kicking Pony hit his target, opening a wound in the trooper's left shoulder that forced him to pull up his charge. A third bullet shattered the darkness that had taken Kicking Pony's skull. He pitched forward in the mud as the pony soldier charge thundered over his lifeless body.

Gray Wolf rushed his wife and two small children, one an infant in her mother's arms, out of their lodge.

"Run!" He pointed to the hills north of the village. He watched them run, knowing he would see his loved ones no more. He turned to meet the pony soldier charge. He would cover his family's escape as best he could. They might have a chance if he could keep the pony soldiers from catching them. He fired into the charging line as it entered the village. He put himself between his family and the bluecoats and backed away slowly, keeping the soldiers in front of him.

The skirmish line dissolved among the lodges, splintering into small groups, individual combats, and pursuits. The village swarmed with soldiers. Women and children ran screaming in every direction. Gray Wolf saw Kicking Pony fight and fall. He felt his death song rise in his throat as he saw a pony soldier set out after his wife and children. He levered his rifle and shot the horse out from under the trooper. The animal screamed and pitched forward, its head between its forelegs. The trooper fell from his mount as his pony rolled up on its saddle, legs flailing the air in its death throes. Gray Wolf leveled his rifle at the fallen soldier. A dull metallic click told him the weapon was empty. He charged forward, swinging the rifle like a war club.

He struck the trooper in the side of the head as he attempted to get to his feet. A hail of bullets ripped into Gray Wolf as men of the Seventh Cavalry rallied to the defense of one of their own.

Pony soldiers overran the village. Black Kettle grabbed his wife Medicine Woman by the hand and ran for his pony. He felt again their flight from Sand Creek so many winters past. Rifle fire rained a death rattle around them as they ran. Black Kettle's heart ached for his people. He feared this for the taking of cattle. He should have stopped it. *White man's law protected only the white man.* In this last he failed his Tsitsistas family.

They reached the picket line. He cut his pony free. If the Great One Above smiled on them they might yet escape. He pulled himself up on his pony. He felt old. He could no longer spring to the saddle as he had as a young warrior. His bones grew tired. Fighting for peace sapped his strength. He was weary of losing to war. If it were not for Medicine Woman, he would welcome his death song in this battle. He pulled her up behind him and wheeled south. He urged the pony to a gallop. They raced out of the village and swung east toward the river. If they could flank the bluecoat charge, they might escape across the river to safety.

Custer saw the old chief attempting to flee. He barked his order to a nearby troop. Sergeant Crowley rallied his troopers and galloped after the chief and his squaw. They charged down on them from behind firing sidearms and carbines from the saddle.

Black Kettle felt the pony soldier pursuit. He looked over his shoulder past the wide fearful eyes of his woman. Bluecoats galloped after them. They were too many to fight. Their only chance was to run. He bent over his pony and urged him on. If they could make it across the river maybe the pony soldiers would give up the chase.

Grasshoppers in Summer

Pistol and rifle reports sounded behind them, somehow distinguished from more distant fire by the intent of their aim. Medicine Woman hugged him tightly, her arms around his belly pressing her face to his back, her body rigid with fear. She let out the barest cry at the jolt that hit her hard in the back. Her grip on his waist became rigid with the onset of death. The next volley tore through their bodies just as they reached the riverbank. Bullets fell like hammer blows, lifting them off the back of the pony. They hit the pony too. Staggering and stumbling into the river the animal bellowed death's agony. Black Kettle and Medicine Woman pitched forward and fell into the icy river shallows together. River cold hit like another bullet. Medicine Woman clung to him in her death grip. Black Kettle's death song could not reach his voice past the bullet holes in his chest. Cold turned light. Earth Mother reached out to him with arms gone soft and warm.

Crowley and his troop never stopped to examine the bodies they rode over. They simply trampled them in a sweeping turn back to the village, back to the carnage.

Broken Knife managed to get to the picket line before the pony soldier charge cut him off. He swung to the back of his pony and galloped back to the village, coming in behind the charging troopers. He saw the village; his home had become a killing field like those of the great shaggy ones. These were not buffalo to be killed for meat and skins. These were his people. As he galloped into the killing, he saw his sister Rain Water run from her lodge. She held her dress up as she ran, her copper legs pumping furiously. A pony soldier with a black beard wheeled his horse to run her down. He leveled his pistol and shot her in the back. The force of the bullet knocked Rain Water to her knees. She fell forward on her hands. Bright blood appeared in the dark crevice of her buttocks. She struggled to her knees. She could no longer run. She looked over her shoulder at her attacker, her pretty face twisted in a mask of fear and agony. She tried to crawl away from the soldier. He leveled his pistol and shot her again.

Broken Knife's war cry filled with rage. He galloped onto his sister's killer. The vision of the pony soldier, holding the smoking gun, seared his heart. He fired his rifle over the head of his galloping pony. The pony soldier screamed. His horse reared. Blood splattered the leg of his blue uniform. The bluecoat lost his saddle and fell to the ground. Broken Knife bore down on him. His vision ran red, his heart turned bad with black vengeance. He was so intent on his sister's killer he paid no attention to the soldier on the ground.

The soldier stepped into Broken Knife's path. He caught his pony's lead in a gauntleted fist and jerked the horse's head down. The pony twisted over its foreleg. The leg gave way, the pony went down, throwing Broken Knife over his head onto the hard, frozen ground. The fall stunned him. The soldier drew his long knife and advanced on the dazed warrior, struggling to get to his feet. The long knife let him rise.

Broken Knife shook his head to clear the vision of his sister's killer. He reached for his knife on unsteady legs. He could think only of avenging Rain Water's death. The bluecoat blocked his path to the killer. The pony soldier fixed him with piercing white eyes and drove the silvered length of his long knife through his belly. Broken Knife looked down in disbelief where the shining steel ran through him. His legs turned to water, heavy water. They would not hold him. He felt himself sink to his knees. The pony soldier placed a muddy boot on his chest beside the blade. He drove Broken Knife back, pulling the long blade from his belly. It made a terrible sucking sound as though Broken Knife's body fought to keep it in. Pain burned like cold fire. Thick red blood poured from the wound. The pony soldier picked up Broken Knife's rifle and knife where they had fallen and threw them away from him.

"Die slow heathen." He mounted his horse and wheeled away back into the fray.

Spotted Hawk found his weapons in an attempt to mount some measure of defense. He stood before his tipi defending his wife and his home. He levered round after round into the swirling bluecoat storm that had overtaken the village. He saw his brother Dog Soldier, Broken Knife, fall to the bluecoat long knife. Broken Knife knelt in the mud, holding the mortal wound in his belly. Spotted Hawk saw a painful death for his brother. Broken Knife turned his eyes to Spotted Hawk in an unspoken plea. Spotted Hawk swallowed bitter gorge laced with fury. He levered a bullet into his rifle. He took careful aim. The rifle charge released Broken Knife's spirit to the welcome embrace of his ancestors.

Bullets flew like a swarm of angry bees, singing the death songs of those they touched. Gun smoke hung in the morning mist, an acrid gray haze broken by towers of smoke and flame from once peaceful lodges. Smoke clawed at Spotted Hawk's throat and eyes. Here and there the pony soldiers ran among the tipi, carrying torches. Still he fought.

The first bullet struck him, a glancing tear through the soft skin of his arm. He dropped to one knee, making himself a smaller target and continued to fire until his rifle clicked empty.

Autumn Snow huddled inside their lodge staring in disbelief at what was happening. She saw the horror of Sand Creek let loose once again on a peaceful people. Why? Her gut wrenched sick. Her scream died in her throat when Spotted Hawk fell. She could not staunch the pain. She rushed from the lodge and fell on him, covering his body with hers. All around her, shooting and screaming continued. She closed her eyes in horror as a pony soldier leveled his pistol and shot two naked children fleeing the village. Such death may be a blessing. She prayed. Winter death would be cold and slow.

At last the shooting fell silent. Slowly the screaming died away to the moans of the dying and the cries of the grieving. Snow saw nothing through her tears. Soldiers tore down the lodges and set fire to the tipi. Had any survived they would find no shelter for the winter in this camp. Steam rose from the bodies where warm life escaped from their wounds. A woman shrieked somewhere on the other side of the village. She remembered the horror of the knives at Sand Creek. She wondered if these pony soldiers took scalps and body parts like the bluecoats in Colorado.

Suddenly they stood before her. Polished black stained with the muddy blood of her man. The boots gleamed before her tear-flooded eyes like some evil predator come to claim its kill.

Custer reached down and grabbed the young woman by her braids and dragged her to her feet. She was a pretty thing if one were to clean up the tears and the blood smear on her cheek. She recoiled from him in round-eyed terror. He liked that. She was ripe too by the swell of her breast. She pulled away. He didn't like that. Still she might bring warm woman's comforts to a cold camp cot.

"How are you called?"

It was an order not a question. She blinked back her tears and said nothing.

He struck her across the face with the back of a gauntlet. "How are you called?"

Her voice cracked. "Autumn Snow."

"Is this your man?" Custer gestured to the fallen warrior.

The woman closed her eyes and nodded.

"Looks like you'll be needin' another. Fortunate for you, I might take a fancy to you myself. Please me and you will be treated well. Fail me and you'll learn a new meaning for beating. Do you understand?"

She stared at him through dull lifeless eyes.

"No matter, you'll understand soon enough. Sergeant Major Kane, see that my personal prisoner accompanies us back to the fort." He pushed her at the burly soldier. "And, Sergeant, see that she isn't damaged."

Spotted Hawk heard the words of the long knife chief. He willed his body to rise and fight. It would not. The pain of his wounds raged at the edges of his body as the words of the long knife cut a searing path through his heart. He could only watch through the flicker of one eye as they led her away before he slipped into the darkness growing cold in his bones.

Curly watched as the sergeant called Kane led the woman away. His eyes swept the camp. Everywhere they lay dead and dying. The warriors fought bravely. The women and children lay fallen among their men. He had seen much blood and killing. He hated the Cheyenne. But these people lived in peace. He found no glory in this killing. He looked down at the body of the woman's man. He had seen him fight. He had seen him fall. This man fought with honor. This man was a warrior.

Then he saw it. The man's chest moved. He lived. Curly drew the tomahawk from his belt. He stood over the fallen warrior. He wore the eagle feathers of a Cheyenne Dog Soldier. His bone breastplate made no match for bullets. Still strong medicine spared his life. Curly raised his tomahawk to a worthy warrior. He counted coup with a light touch. He turned to his pony, swung up on his back, and trotted off after the yellow hair, leaving the fate of the fallen warrior in the hands of the Great Spirit.

One hundred and three died that day; warriors numbered fewer than a third.

CHAPTER EIGHTEEN

Office of the Commanding General
Department of the Missouri
Chicago, Illinois
November 30, 1868

Sheridan put down the report and drew a cigar from the box on his desk. He bit the tip and scratched a lucifer to light. He let the sulfur burn away before turning the cigar to an orange glow. He savored a mellow draw. According to Custer, one hundred three hostiles fell to the brave men of the Seventh in a firefight on the Washita River Agency. The stolen cattle were recovered and returned to their rightful owner. Custer recommended a medal of valor for one Sergeant Crowley who personally secured the fall of the renegade chief, Black Kettle. *Renegade.* Sheridan turned the word over in his mind. For some years now Black Kettle had distinguished himself as one of the peace chiefs among the Cheyenne. The term "renegade" struck him as out of character, unless of course one's purpose in using it was to justify the events of the report. Custer further recommended the Seventh for a unit citation, acknowledging the accomplishment of their mission in the face of hostile fire. Of course, all of this begged the question of his personal recognition. Sheridan would add his recommendation to the report before passing it on to General Grant at the War Department.

No doubt Custer would reap his rewards. The newspapers were already filled with glowing accounts. The stories trumpeted the heroic actions of the glorious Seventh Cavalry. They touted the Washita River battle as the finest hour in the Seventh's storied history. They lionized the Seventh's dashing commander, "Colonel" George Armstrong Custer, recalling his distinguished war record and battlefield appointment to Brigadier General. Sheridan smiled. None of the news accounts properly referenced Custer's "Lieutenant" Colonel rank. He knew why. Custer's capacity for self-promotion seemed limitless. More than likely he had newspaper reporters accompany him on the raid. His ambition was boundless to the point of ruthless. It was a character flaw. A flaw an enlightened commander could count on.

Galena, Illinois
December 1868
Morning sun filtered through leafless trees and lace curtains, pooling on the worn parlor carpet. Outside a fresh dusting of snow covered the yard and a road not yet ground to muddy ruts by the day's traffic. A cheerful fire crackled in the fireplace. The glow of firelight chased dim shadows to the corners of the room. President-elect Ulysses S. Grant sat in a comfortable wing chair across from the fire, reading a newspaper. The headline screamed, "Custer Leads Seventh to Victory." The story lead proclaimed, "103 Hostiles Fall in Washita River Battle." Grant sipped a steaming cup of coffee as he read the news account of the battle.

 The soft splash of a jogging horse and the jingle of harness brass announced the arrival of a visitor drawing rein in front of Grant's small comfortable home. He slipped his watch from his vest pocket and flipped the cover open. Ten thirty, *punctual as ever, Eli.* He set aside the paper and rose in anticipation of his visitor's rap at the door.

 "Come in, Eli." Grant greeted Congressman-elect Elihu

Washburne along with a draft of winter chill.

"Mr. President." Washburn's greeting trailed a cloud of steam in the chill morning air. "It's good to get out of the damn cold." He grumbled as he peeled off his great coat and hung it on the tree in the entry hall along with his muffler and top hat.

"Don't get carried away with that title just yet, Eli. Besides I'll always be Sam to you. Julia's just made a fresh pot of coffee. Come in and sit by the fire. That should take the chill out of you."

"Best offer I've had all morning."

They crossed to the parlor. Washburne dropped into a wing chair at the side table beside Grant's. He glanced at the paper, while Grant poured a cup of coffee from the service resting on a sideboard next to the fireplace.

"Less than a month since they signed the Fort Laramie Treaty." Washburne shook his head. "Just goes to show how fragile peaceful relations with the tribes can be."

Grant nodded, placing a steaming cup and saucer on the side table at Washburne's elbow. "Fragile, yes, but in this case I wonder if the action was warranted. George can be a loose cannon. He's spoiling to regain the general's stars he lost after the war. Even Libbie natters Phil about it."

Washburne frowned, considering the comment. "The paper says Custer was on a mission to recover stolen cattle when the fight broke out."

"That's the part that doesn't make sense," Grant said, taking his seat. "The Washita River is well within reservation territory. Why would the Cheyenne steal cattle when the treaty assures the provision of meat to feed the people?"

"Sam, you and I both know the Bureau of Indian Affairs is riddled with corruption. It's entirely possible they didn't have the beef they'd been promised."

"Yes, of course. The bureau is another problem we will have

to clean up. We've been so busy these past couple of years trying to maintain the reconstruction in the face of Johnson's obstruction, our challenges in the west have gone unattended."

"We'll be back to work soon enough. Frankly, I'm ready for one of those lovely Virginia springs."

"That does sound pleasant, though I expect I'll be too busy to enjoy it. These last weeks have been a welcome respite after the turmoil of the last few years and the strain of the campaign."

"When do you plan to return to Washington?"

"Julia would leave tomorrow if I'd agree. She's chomping at the bit to start planning the inaugural ball. I'm holding out until after the holidays."

"As long as we're on the subject, of Indian policy," Washburne said, returning to the purpose of helping the president-elect plan his administration. "What have you decided about your post at the War Department?"

"I'll appoint Cump. Militarily he's the best qualified general officer we have. Al Terry is probably closer to my position on Indian policy, but Cump went along with the Fort Laramie Treaty. He's been one of my most trusted fellow officers for a long time. I know I can count on him to do the right thing."

"So, you've given thought to your Indian policy then." Washburne's unspoken part in these informal meetings was to help Grant formulate his thoughts. The policies would be Grant's. Talking out loud helped him fashion them.

"I have given that some thought, though I can't say I've come to a firm course of action." He rose to add a log to the fire. The flames crackled, sending a shower of sparks up the chimney. "More coffee, Eli?"

Washburne nodded and held out his cup. Grant filled their cups and returned the pot to the sideboard and took his seat.

"Indian policy is not a war to be won militarily as some think. The challenge is to find ways to live in peace with our Indian neighbors. The Fort Laramie Treaty provides a framework for that. If you think about it, Eli, the transcontinental railroad makes an interesting dividing line. The land and resources south of the northern route we've chosen are abundant. Surely, they can satisfy our ambition toward westward expansion. The treaty sets aside land north of the rail line to accommodate our first American neighbors. The way Ely Parker explains it, the Sioux and their allied tribes will have the Black Hills along with hunting grounds in the Powder River country. The Black Hills are sacred to the Sioux, but it's rough country, not really suited to farming or other white purposes. It's worth more to the tribes than it is to us. The Powder River hunting grounds are large enough to sustain the plains tribes' way of life. Those accommodations can provide a lasting peace based on the rights and protections the Constitution guarantees us all."

Washburne pursed his lips on the rim of his cup, "Constitutional protections? That sounds like citizenship."

Grant paused and sipped his coffee, considering the implications of the statement. "Yes, I suppose it does. It's no different than the rights granted freedmen in the south really. I don't find a provision in the Constitution that speaks to white supremacy. It affords rights and protections to all Americans."

"That won't be a popular view with some, Sam."

"No, I suppose it won't."

"You've never been shy about a fight. You picked yourself a hell of a good one this time."

Grant pursed his lips, drawn to the crackle of the fire. *One hell of a good fight, name one that wasn't.*

Chapter Nineteen

Fort Larned, Kansas
December 1868

Autumn Snow cowered in the corner of her cell wrapped against the cold in a thin blanket. They gave her a bed of straw she shared with lice and other vermin. Her days were filled with menial kitchen tasks, subsisting on meager rations, unless she was taken to him. They did not feed her this night. They would come for her. She turned inside herself with dread. She should have died with her husband and saved herself from such punishment as this. She did not expect this. How could she have known? The yellow hair could be kind. He could also be cruel. Moons passed slowly, cold and gray, bright and dark. Winter was always a struggle to survive. Here she had food. Cold steel bars and straw gave little comfort. She missed the warmth of the lodge fire. She missed her husband. Boots crunched in the snow outside the stockade door. Her stomach lurched. Boots meant they were coming for her.

The stockade door swung open with a groan, protesting as though it felt her cold and pain. Icy wind blew in with bright white moonlight reflected on the snow outside. The sergeant called Kane came in followed by another pony soldier. Always there were two, as though she might overpower one and make her escape.

Kane took down the ring of keys from the peg beside the door. They jangled as he walked to the cell and unlocked the door. The door sang a high-pitched song, mourning her fate. The two men stepped inside.

"On your feet." Kane ordered.

She stood on leaden legs. He stripped her blanket away. They took her arms and led her out. She shivered against the cold. Rough hands drove her into cold white light. They ushered her across the parade ground toward the yellow light spilling from the window where she would endure him again. The moon cast long shadows on the snow like ghosts crossing an eerie white world. Cold cut through her buckskin dress. The yellow light meant warmth. It also meant pain. She wished she might lay down here and die of the cold. If only they would let her. They would not.

Her moccasin slipped on the icy step to the office door. Kane caught her arm and rapped the rough planks with a gloved fist.

"Enter." The muffled order sounded through the door. Her bowels turned to water at the sound of his voice.

They pushed her into the darkened office toward the pale light spilling from the open door across the room. Floorboards groaned under her feet, mocking her helpless passage.

He sat in a chair beside the bed in his small room, boots stretched out before him. She stood in the light of the doorway framed by the darkness beyond.

"That will be all, Sergeant." Boots scraped the plank floor behind her. The door closed, leaving her alone with him.

The yellow hair smoothed his mustache, devouring her with hungry wolf eyes. Pony soldiers hunted in packs like the wolf. The wolf seldom hunted alone, unless the prey were weak or wounded. In these times when they were together, the yellow hair hunted alone.

"Are you hungry?"

She closed her eyes and nodded, shutting out the sight of him, wishing she could deny the coming thing. She was always hungry when they brought her to him. She knew they would come when they did not feed her. He ordered it. It weakened her.

"Please me and you shall feed from my plate."

A tray lay on the bedside table. She could smell cooked meat. Her mouth watered over the churn in her stomach. She would please him. Pain pleased him. This she had in abundance.

"Take off your dress."

He breathed the words like the pant of a wolf, savoring its prey. This wolf would not kill her. That would be too kind. This wolf would only use her. She raised the simple buckskin dress above her head, hiding her eyes from him as long as she might. A cold draft licked her skin. The small stove in the outer office never warmed the room. Winter chill seeped through chinks in the walls and around the tiny window frame. She let the dress fall and lowered her eyes to the floor. Cold prickled her skin in the way that excited him.

"Yes, that's better, much better. Now take off my boots."

He lifted his leg for her to straddle. She stepped over the outstretched boot, wooden in obedience. She picked up the boot and bent to the task in the way he taught her. The way he liked.

"We must enjoy our time together while it lasts. The Seventh is being relieved. We leave for Fort Riley soon."

The words grew thick in his throat as she worked to free him from the polished boot. She hated his boots almost as much as his eyes. She remembered the muddy stains, Spotted Hawk's blood seen through her tears. He did not rush this night. If his need were urgent, he would use his other boot to push her to the floor, pulling the boot off with her. This night he watched her struggle. In times like these she knew he made it hard for her. He enjoyed her struggle until at last the boot came away.

His mustache lifted, his lip curled at the corner, amused. His eyes followed her beneath half lowered lids. He lifted the other boot.

"General Sheridan has a plum assignment for me to go along with the medal I'll receive for my great victory down on your Washita."

He spoke words like these more to hear the sound of his own voice than to tell her things she did not understand. His strained voice told her his pleasure was rising and that soon, very soon it would be upon her.

"We'll soon have to stop these lovely assignations. Libbie wouldn't approve of our little arrangement. You'll just have to live without me until we take the field again. But that is for later. For now . . ." He dropped his gaze to buttons bulging with demand.

It was an order.

Washita River

He survived by the blessing of the Great One Above. Or was it a rage that burned like a lodge fire to warm him when little else would? In truth it must have been some of both.

The pony soldier fires did not burn everything. He crawled to the buffalo robe he once shared with Autumn Snow. It saved him from freezing those first few nights. He drank snow and ate from a small store of pemmican overlooked amidst the ruins of their lodge.

He constructed a small shelter from unburned fragments of tipi and buffalo robes. He made fires of broken lodge poles and saddle parts of those who no longer needed them. The days deepened his rage. They filled his heart with lust for vengeance. The slaughter of his people lay in frozen piles all around him. Snow shrouds covered the dead only to thaw or blow away in the icy wind. His heart ached with the loss of his wife. The pain never left him. The long knife chief took her. Where? Unknowing ate at his heart. The pony soldier fort, he must have taken her to the pony soldier fort. Spotted Hawk prayed for life. He vowed to the Great One Above. He would kill the long knife and free his Autumn Snow.

The antelope came as a gift of the Great One. A yearling, it wandered down to the river to drink. The pony soldiers did not kill Spotted Hawk. The antelope fed him after the pemmican ran out. He took it for a sign. The Great One answered his prayer. He would survive. He would free his wife and avenge her or die in the trying.

His pony ran off with the ones that got away. It returned later sensing his master's need. When he was strong enough to ride, he rode south to a village the pony soldiers had not destroyed. His brothers took him in with what remained of his antelope. He survived. He held the memory of Autumn Snow in his heart. Washita rage ran hot in his blood. He would avenge the blood of his people and the loss of his beautiful wife. One day he would hear the long knife's death song. One day in a summer to come. The dream sustained him through the long winter night.

The scars on his body were healed by the time the snow began to melt. Warmth slowly returned to the banks of the Washita. Spotted Hawk rode upriver to the north as soon as the snows began to melt. Winter drew a gentle blanket over death and destruction in the remains of Black Kettle's village. He wished to leave the killing field behind before wildflowers paid their respects to the remains of the dead. He rode northeast to Fort Larned with enough bullets to kill the long knife chief. He would free his wife or die in the trying.

He made his plan as he rode. He would go to the fort. He would ask to speak to the long knife war chief. He would ask the yellow hair to speak with his sister Autumn Snow. He would kill the yellow hair when he brought her to him. From that they would make their escape or die together. If the yellow hair would not let him speak with her, he would kill him and find some other way to free his wife.

He rode up to the fort gates one early spring afternoon. A strong breeze whipped the eagle feathers in his braids. It gave slight chill to a day that might otherwise have found warmth. He halted at the sentry's challenge.

"Spotted Hawk make words with great long knife war chief."

"Go away. The colonel wouldn't be makin' palaver with an Injun even if he was here. The colonel's gone. The Seventh's been recalled to garrison duty back east."

The words hit Spotted Hawk like the blow of a war club. The yellow hair was gone. Did he take Autumn Snow with him? The banked rage that sustained him through the long winter flared. What was he to do now? He would need the guidance of the spirits to find his way from here.

Guidance came with the clatter of a buckboard. The Indian Agent Denton drove past Spotted Hawk with little more than a sidelong glance. He took the road east to the Pawnee River Trading Post on his weekly trip to restock his larder. Spotted Hawk watched him go. In that moment he saw the path he would take.

It was a glorious sun-drenched day for a drive. White puffs of cloud floated on a spring breeze that shifted southwest at mid-afternoon and turned warm. Denton absently occupied his mind with the inventory of his appetites and mental shopping list. He would stay the night at Pawnee River. The trading post afforded the advantage of fine cooked meals he might linger over. The beer would be cold, the port acceptable. He could almost taste it as the buckboard rocked along.

Spotted Hawk trailed the fat agent far enough from the fort to be sure he had nowhere to run. He let the miles pass by, stoking his rage. He remembered the cold hunger of the fat agent's broken promises. The agent lived in the long knife lodge. He may know what had happened to Autumn Snow. Did the long knife chief take her when he left? Could it be the pony soldiers still held her there?

The road passed along the riverbank, cutting off one path to escape. Overtaking a white man's wagon with a swift war pony would be child's work. The fat agent must be given time to fear. He must come to know his peril. Spotted Hawk would feed his rage with the satisfaction of the hunt and the kill. He kicked his war pony into his attack lope, cresting the ridge south of the road, and galloped down on the buckboard from behind.

Hoofbeats coming fast sounded above the bay's gentle gate. Denton shifted his bulk to turn in his seat. A lone rider astride a great Appaloosa sparked the first tremor of uncertainty. Not just any rider, not just any spotted horse thundered out of the hills south of the road. A war cry turned his bowels liquid with fear. The .38 pocket pistol he carried in his coat pocket offered little comfort. Suddenly here in open country it seemed less than lethal.

"Hey up!" He barked to his horse, flicking his whip for emphasis. The bay gelding responded with a surge, laboring to pick up speed under the weight of the wagon and the bulk of its passenger. Denton put up the buggy whip. He juggled his attention between driving and his pursuer as he fumbled in his pocket for the pistol. He wasn't much of a shot in the best of circumstances. The short-barreled pistol wasn't accurate beyond close range. Add bouncing over rough road in a buckboard, caught between his pursuer and the riverbank, and you had a man near defenseless. The little gun and five bullets were all that stood between him and his would-be attacker. Fear welled up inside his girth like a flood. He felt the warrior gain on him. He looked over his shoulder and blinked. The big spotted horse drew close. His hand trembled as he attempted to cock the little gun. He turned in his seat, the buggy lurched, his aim bounced. The warrior ducked behind his pony's neck. The horse cut aside. The shot went wild.

Spotted Hawk kept his distance, feigning attack with a whoop to draw a wild shot, then swinging away to avoid becoming a target. He counted the fat man's rounds. Red faced, the agent gaped round eyed with fear as he bounced heavily on the little wagon seat. His horse labored under the weight of the work. It would not be long.

The bay slowed. Denton could feel it. The brave on the Appaloosa weaved from right to left behind the buckboard, forcing him to turn this way and that to keep track of his whereabouts. Another war whoop sounded close. He turned in his seat. The warrior was almost upon him. He snapped off his third shot. The horse and rider cut away, no more damaged than the puff of powder smoke. The fatback and beans he'd had for breakfast churned a greasy ball in his gut with the realization he was in mortal danger. He clung to a thread of hope. Hope that help might find him on the trading post road. He needed to hold his fire and conserve his two remaining bullets. It was all he had to fend off the warrior's inevitable rush for the kill.

Suddenly his laboring horse stumbled. The buckboard veered left. The front wheel struck a rock on the roadside. The rim shattered with a loud crack. Denton pitched off his seat as the buckboard turned over. He hit the hardscrabble roadbed with a force that drove the breath from his body and sent his gun spinning away. He lay stunned for what seemed like long moments. Reason resolved in a long shadow. The warrior stood over him.

Spotted Hawk kicked the fat agent to roll him over on his back. He looked into the rolls of flesh around owlish eyes, blinking furiously for want of the shattered spectacles knocked askew on his face. His fat jowls quivered with fear. Sweat poured off the man's face, smearing him with mud. Blood seeped from a cut on his forehead.

"Did the yellow hair take the Tsitsistas woman, Autumn Snow, with him?"

Denton blinked, not understanding the question. The warrior dealt him a fierce kick in the side. Breath burst from his lungs. Searing pain shot through his chest, the first sign of a broken rib. Reason screamed in his addled brain. *Think!*

"Did the long knife chief take the Cheyenne woman with him?"

Custer. Cheyenne woman, yes, yes, the pieces fit. He remembered now. What became of the colonel's squaw?

"I, I don't know." He stammered between broken teeth. The warrior's features darkened in a mask of rage and frustration. How could Custer have been so foolish as to put him in such a predicament?

"You made lies of the Great Father's treaty."

The accusation boiled blood hatred. Denton retreated into his fear, fighting the urge to retch. He had no answer to satisfy his accuser.

"I have money. Yes, that's it, I have money." He fumbled in his coat pocket for the wad of gold certificates and the pouch full of coins. He held out the money. "Here, take it. Take it all. It's yours if you'll only leave me go in peace."

"Go in peace." Spotted Hawk spat. "The way you sent the pony soldiers to bring peace to my people on the Washita." He drew the tomahawk from his belt. He balanced it in his hand.

Denton fixed his gaze on the weapon. The Washita, this one must have survived. Realization dawned. His end would come to this. A dark stain spread slowly across the front of his trousers.

Spotted Hawk let the disgusting man whimper and tremble with a woman's fear. "Our women and children died with more honor than you, fat man." He raised the tomahawk. The agent's hands quivered before his face as if they might ward off the blow.

"Please, no."

Spotted Hawk's vision burned red. Where had they taken his Autumn Snow? The bodies of those who died huddled beneath their blankets of snow called out for vengeance. He filled his war cry with their death songs and drove the heavy iron blade through the fat agent's outstretched hands, shattering them like a bundle of twigs. The blow caved in the agent's skull above eyes fixed in disbelief. White bone splintered as it gave way to splatter the soft mud within. He drew back a second blow to destroy the shattered shell of the man. One death seemed not enough for this one.

He stood over the corpse. Triumph soothed the wound in his heart for only the briefest moment. He needed more white blood to feed his rage, much more. He knew that trail. That trail led north to the lodge of his sister's husband. Tashunca-uitco and his people lived the old ways in the Powder River country. He would find hope among them. As long as Crazy Horse roamed free, the Paha Sapa remained the sacred center of the people. His loved ones would walk the spirit lands among their ancestors. One day he would find Autumn Snow among them. One day when he'd spilled enough white blood to cool the flame in his heart.

CHAPTER TWENTY

White House
Washington, D.C.
May 1869

Grant sat at his desk wreathed in cigar smoke. The halo of a single lamp pooled an island of light amid gathering evening shadows. He studied Ely Parker's brief describing legislative options for reforming Indian policy. Parker sat across the desk, waiting patiently as the president read.

Grant laid the report on the desk. He removed his reading glasses and placed them on top of Parker's document. He sat back in his chair and folded his hands across his belly. "It all starts with the Fort Laramie Treaty doesn't it, Ely?"

"It does, sir. It is our best opportunity to right the travesties of past Indian policy. We've broken one treaty after another the moment they become in some way inconvenient to our presumed destiny to westward expansion. In Colorado it was the discovery of gold. Then we had to have a passage to the Pacific Northwest. Now it's a transcontinental railroad. For the Indian the story is always the same. We force them to move out of the way. We subject them to our notion of progress."

"But, Ely, surely you see the importance of the railroad. It's the reason we were in a position to make the Fort Laramie Treaty."

"I do see that, Mr. President. The treaty protects Indian hunting grounds. It does not protect the herds they hunt there. The herds remain threatened. White hunters kill them to feed the railroad construction crews. Commercial hunters are beginning to find a market for buffalo hides here in the east and abroad. The Indian depends on the treaty hunting grounds and the buffalo herds that live there. The reservation system is a disgrace. The people are plundered by corruption in the system. The treaty hunting grounds are intended to provide food, shelter, and clothing. Things the reservation system fails to provide. If white hunting pressure on the buffalo herds continues, the tribes will be unable to feed and clothe their people. I fear the consequences if that is allowed. Desperate people do desperate things."

"I'm aware of the reservation problem, Ely. I am as committed to rooting out those abuses as President Lincoln was to righting the wrongs of slavery, but as you know, undertakings of this nature can never be accomplished quickly. You've given me a good start on some options here." Grant gestured to the report. "I appreciate your thoughtful analysis. I want you to expand on this work. Take a hard look at the reservation system. Congress appropriates funds to provide for the tribal needs, but too little good comes of it. Help me make the case for real reform. We need hard facts. The Bureau of Indian Affairs has its share of political patrons. We must be very sure of ourselves before we confront those who may be corrupt. In the meantime, I do have one idea that might help.

"We may not be able to reform the bureau overnight, but we may be able to improve our oversight against abuse. I'm thinking of engaging religiously affiliated groups to oversee administration of the agencies. Principled people of goodwill on the ground at the reservations may be better able to assure the welfare of the tribes than we shall ever be able to do from here in Washington. Such people can be counted on to uphold high moral principle."

A soft knock at the door cut short the conversation. "Come in."

"Mr. President, a telegram just arrived from Colonel Dodge." Horace Porter handed him the yellow sheet of transcribed telegraphy. "I thought you'd want to see it right away, sir." Porter crossed the office and handed Grant the telegram.

"Thank you, Horace. That will be all for this evening."

"Thank you, sir." Porter let himself out as Grant read the telegram.

"Well, Ely, it seems we have a transcontinental railroad at last. The Union Pacific and Central Pacific joined their tracks today at Promontory Point in Utah." The president sat back in his chair and took a long thoughtful draw on his cigar.

"That is historic news, Mr. President." Parker held his reservation private.

"It is, Ely, it truly is. It's taken nearly six years. We've paid a dear price in blood, sweat, and national treasure to achieve it, but by any measure history will record it as a worthy investment. We may yet struggle, healing the wounds of rebellion, but this nation is now bound in a union of commerce never to be shaken again."

"A union of commerce." Parker turned the president's words over in his mind. The railroad seemed the purest expression of the oft-cited destiny to westward expansion. A ribbon of iron now stretched from sea to sea.

"Courage and sacrifice, Ely, they embody this nation's every great achievement, going back to its founding. Courage and sacrifice define the character of the people building this great nation. History shall record this railroad among her greatest achievements."

"I'm sure you have the right of that, Mr. President. I only hope our achievements spare room for our first American neighbors."

Fort Riley, Kansas
December 1869

The woman was of the hated Cheyenne. If she'd been taken to slavery by a Crow warrior, Curly could have seen honor in it. He saw no honor in this captivity. The long knife chief took her from the body of her man at the Washita. The warrior fought and fell bravely. Curly counted coup on a worthy warrior. The woman's misfortunes doubled that day when she was taken for Custer's prisoner. He took her for his woman after the Washita fight. Sergeant Major Kane held her captive when the long knife lived in the square house with his white woman. She worked in the kitchens cleaning pots and scrubbing dishes. The sergeant kept her in a cell at the back of the stockade. He did not beat her severely for fear of his chief. He made sure no other man took her.

She was always hungry. Curly would steal biscuits or jerky for her when he could. Once he stole an extra blanket. They spoke only with their eyes. Curly thought her pretty, quiet, and still like snow, deep and thoughtful like the pool of a mountain lake. This night he had a biscuit for her.

She heard his footstep in the dark beyond the barred window. Sour-smelling straw rustled under her feet as she rose and went to the window. He held a biscuit in his hand. Her fingers trembled as she accepted the biscuit from the Crow scout. Moonlight reflected gratitude in her eyes from the dark shadows of her cell. Here among the whites, the only kindness she received came from a hated enemy. The Crow and Cheyenne made war for generations. This one scouted for the pony soldiers. It spoke to the low character of the Crow people. Still many Crow held to the old ways. She found honor in that. That must explain why the handsome warrior treated her kindly.

The pony soldiers called him Curly for the wavy black hair that topped the braids falling to his shoulders. She would prefer his slavery to that of the yellow hair. The yellow hair killed her husband. He took her from his body. She lost everything that day, her husband, her home, her people. She wished she had been allowed to follow them into the spirit lands in death. Instead she'd been condemned to the possession of her husband's killer. He kept her locked up for fear she might run away. Foolish man. She had nowhere to run.

CHAPTER TWENTY-ONE

White House
Washington, D.C.
April 1870

Ely Parker listened as the president outlined the themes of his Indian peace policy and the reforms he desired in the Bureau of Indian Affairs. The president relied on him to assist in fashioning and administering Indian policy. He took his responsibilities seriously. He brought thoughtful analysis and common sense to the political and cultural realities of the problem. Indian advocacy came naturally to him. The president knew he needed an advocate. Others found it easy to look the other way when it came to matters of Indian rights. Most regarded their presence in the west as little more than an obstacle that must be overcome to advance white purposes. The Indian resisted, determined to defend their homelands. The Army was called to protect white interests. Natural hostilities developed. Accommodation would be found to one contention, only to be followed by some new dispute; and the cycle repeated.

The pressing problem at hand centered on administration of the reservations. Corruption ran rampant in the Bureau of Indian Affairs. The president determined the fastest way to deal with it was reliable oversight on the reservations. He proposed to enlist religious groups to oversee maintenance of the reservations. Good people of strong Christian principle, he reasoned, could be counted on to advocate for the rights of the tribes and provide oversight to the agent's treatment of their charges.

Josiah Bradburn, an Elder in the Maryland Society of Friends, sat across from Parker in the White House meeting. He too listened to the president. Tall and pinched with long gray hair and bushy brows, Bradburn's severe countenance suited the righteous certainty of his beliefs. Even his hazel eyes seemed oddly cold. He reminded Parker of a gnarled length of hickory. A sturdy moral rod capable of caning opposition to submission.

"So, as you can see, Friend Bradburn," the president said, "peaceful relocation of the tribes to reservation lands proceeds, though a few notable exceptions remain for diplomacy to resolve. We believe you can help us with the civilization provisions of treaty administration. The treaty provides parcels of land for the Indian to farm. It further provides subsidies in the form of seeds, farm implements, and mules or oxen to commence cultivating the land allotted to each family. The reservation Indian must be taught to farm. It is his path to productive civil society."

"Yes, Mr. President, I see that." Bradburn made his fingertips a crooked steeple. "There is somewhat more to be done, however. The Indian must be schooled. He must be educated to take his place in society. I have read the treaty and applaud the provision for schools." He stabbed the air with a crooked index finger. "Education is the first step toward enlightenment. The Indian must be taught to turn away from heathen beliefs and embrace proper Christian faith."

Grant nodded.

Parker recoiled inwardly. He shook his head unable to keep silent. "I struggle with these provisions of the treaty, Mr. President. The tribes are hunters. They have long held traditions and beliefs. Farming and Christian conversion seem harsh departures from their tribal ways. Some may embrace these opportunities for the good of their families or the dictates of their hearts, but I believe the universal enforcement of white values on Indian culture goes too far."

Bradburn straightened in his chair. "You can't be serious, Commissioner Parker. You presume to question the will of God?"

"I don't question the will of God, Mr. Bradburn, only your interpretation of it. The tribes have followed the traditions and beliefs of their grandmothers for generations. God did not seem to object."

Bradburn wagged an accusatory finger at Parker. "As have heathen of all stripes down through the ages, until the true message of Christianity came to their salvation."

Grant drew a cigar from his breast pocket, bit the tip, and scratched a match. "Gentlemen, gentlemen," he held up a hand, calling for truce around his cigar while he puffed it to light. "The truth will find itself somewhere between the two of you, I'm sure. As a practical matter, Ely, I doubt the two cultures can coexist on equal terms for very long. Look at your own experience. Your law and engineering educations have taken you far from the tribal culture of your ancestors. The plains tribes' path to prosperity must surely follow a similar course."

Bradburn nodded approvingly.

Parker fixed the president in his gaze. "It is true that I have benefited from my education and experience. Those are choices I made. Don't assume that all our people will see things as I did."

"Our people?" Bradburn's jaw dropped in disbelief.

"That's right, Friend Bradburn, my people are Seneca. We too are first American."

"First American, what a preposterous notion. Your people, should I indulge you, may aspire to be American once taught to embrace Christian civilization."

"You are wrong, sir. This nation was founded to assure

religious liberty. No one should understand that any better than a Quaker, Mr. Bradburn. You look at my suit and see a white man with dark skin. Don't assume that my tribal heritage and culture have no place in my life. Do you presume to know what is in my heart when I turn to the Great Spirit in prayer?"

The room fell uncomfortably silent. Grant filled the void.

"Yes, well at some level I suppose you have a point, Ely. That said, we've only to look to the freedmen of the south to see that the path to prosperity is American citizenship, not ancient tribal custom."

"One last matter, Friend Bradburn." Grant turned to the Quaker elder around another puff of smoke. "Your mission must also help us root out corruption in the administration of the reservations. The reservation system is a stain on our national character. You and your Friends will have the opportunity to observe abuse when it occurs. You will be able to identify those who defraud the system and deprive the tribes of their rightful benefits. I am ordering investigations into these matters, but these things take time. Any evidence you can offer would serve to speed our purpose along."

"You can count on our support in this important work, Mr. President." Bradburn offered his commitment as much for Parker's benefit as for that of the president.

"Very good, I was hoping you would say that. I think Friend Bradburn well suited to help us in the administration of the Red Cloud Agency. Don't you agree, Ely?"

Parker didn't agree. He only nodded.

Fort Riley, Kansas
April 1870

Deep shadow concealed him in the alley between the barracks and the stockade. Clouds ran through the night sky, touched by moonlight in places where they parted. Night chill seeped out of the north, riding the echo of the day's prairie wind. He stood with his back pressed against the rough-cut timber beside the darkened stockade entrance. He listened to the rise and fall of rhythmic heavy breathing in the darkness beyond.

Why do this for a hated Tsitsistas? The question haunted him for weeks from the moment he'd thought to free her. It made no sense. If they were caught, he might be shot or put in prison himself. Women captives were always taken for slaves. Some found the favor of a husband, but most served as this one. If she were a Crow captive, he would have given it no thought. She was not a Crow captive. She was a white man's captive. He saw no honor in that. He found her comely, though he did not desire to take her for his woman. Her husband was an honorable warrior. His woman deserved better than white man's slavery. For that he would free her.

He watched a thick dark cloud cover a sliver of moon. He slipped around the corner into the stockade entrance. The cloud passed. Dim moon glow spilled in behind him. The first cell door stood open; the guard's snoring came from the shadows within. Curly took a large key ring from a peg beside the door. He wrapped his hands around the heavy keys to silence them. He moved silently down the row of empty cells, feeling his way through the darkness to the far end of the stockade. He could hear her breathing in the recesses of the small cell. Moonlight touched the barred windows behind him, casting long shadows across the cell block. He fitted the key in the lock and turned. The soft "click" sounded like a gunshot in the stillness. He stood frozen, listening. He heard nothing. He eased the door open.

Metal hinges grated metal for an instant. He froze again. He heard her stir in her blanket. He slipped into the cell out of the moon glow that might expose him to the guard. Still he felt trapped between the noise of the cell door and the risk she might awake and cause some alarm. She did not use the cot in the cell, preferring instead to sleep on a pile of straw in the corner. He moved swiftly to her side and dropped to a knee. He clamped a hand over her mouth. Her eyes opened wide, white in low light. He bent to her ear.

"Quiet." He hissed. "Curly is here to help you. Do you understand?" She nodded. He released his grip on her mouth. "Follow me."

He went to the cell door. He heard no sign of movement beyond the soft rustle of the woman behind him. The passage remained dark. If the guard were disturbed, he would light a lamp. He led them into the passage. A service entrance at the back of the stockade opened to the quadrangle beyond. He would not use the stockade entrance again. He lifted the bar holding the door slowly and set it aside, careful to make no sound. He opened the door. Moonlight spilled between the running clouds. He waited for the next cover of darkness. He said nothing, only motioned for her to follow him. Outside, he softly closed the door, sealing out any telltale light. He led her quickly around to the back of the stockade where they melted into shadow. He set off at a brisk pace moving silently in the shadows past the stockade to the barracks. They followed the back wall of the barracks to the corrals and stable beyond. He waited at the back of the barracks for full cloud cover before skirting the corral to the back of the stable. A sturdy paint pony tethered there waited quietly.

"Curly's pony," he said. "Take him and return to your people."

Moonlight caught the swell of a great crystal tear coming to her eye. "Why do you do this for me?"

"There is no honor in white man's slavery, even for Tsitsistas."

"You are a good man, Curly."

"For a Crow."

"No, you are a good man." She held his eyes for a moment. She turned to the pony and swung up on its back. She found the saddle provisioned with food and water. She took one long last look at him. He stood, arms folded across his broad bare chest. Cold light frosted the great wave in his top knot. She would never forget his kindness. No more need be said. She wheeled the pony away.

CHAPTER TWENTY-TWO

Wyoming Territory
May 1870

Autumn Snow took her time. She followed a meandering trail north and west toward the Rosebud. She traveled by night at first, avoiding white roads. She skirted the farms and towns she encountered until she found her way to open country where she could safely travel by day. Many days passed. Her meager provisions ran low. She had no means to hunt. Some part of each day she foraged for berries, nuts, and roots. She survived. Broad flat plains passed into rough country. Rough country would lead her home to the mountains of the Powder River country.

She picked her way through dry washes and around jagged ridges, avoiding the skyline. Slowly, day by day, the land warmed to spring. Tender new prairie grass waved in green seas broken by rugged rock formations. Red rock walls and sentinels stained white with alkali cut the rugged landscape in centuries-old layers. Scrub sage clung to the hillsides in clumps. Tumbleweed chased the wind in dried balls. Most days the sun rose warm, the sky clear. It beat rock surfaces like an anvil that rang in shimmering waves of reflected heat. The lands of her people could be harsh. Soon she would see the gentle prairies and mountain streams she knew as a child. Game flourished there. The precious treasure of water was plentiful. The spirits walked these lands, completing the circle of life with her people. Soon she would find her way home.

The iron horse shrieked beyond the rise ahead. It did not cry the long mournful song of its coming. It raged in short angry screams as though crying out in some distress. Curious, Snow squeezed her pony into a lope up a gentle rise to its crest.

The iron horse trail cut through the valley below. The great fire breathing monster stood frozen, surrounded by a herd of buffalo. A sea of shaggy brown stretched across the dun green land as far as the eye could see. Tatanka contentedly grazed the grassy plains on both sides of the tracks. White puff balls of cloud dotted the bright blue summer sky, making faster progress flowing east on an easy breeze than the mighty iron horse.

The beauty of the sight stirred Snow's spirit. She smiled. The people could not stop the whites or their iron horse from coming, but these great shaggy ones, the life blood of the people, owned the land. They stopped the white man and his iron horse in its tracks, leaving them powerless. It spoke to the strength of the old ways in a way that warmed her heart.

The beleaguered train crawled forward, belching steam, wasting wood and water while the iron horse whistle screamed in protest. The herd paid the monster mild disinterest. Inside the conductor in his blue coat scurried up and down the train furiously mopping his brow and checking his watch. *Damn buffalo play hell with the schedules. We're runnin' later by the minute and not a damn thing to be done about it without risking a derailment.*

His anger would have amused Snow had she seen it. She would not be amused when she came to know the lengths white men would go to serve the master of the little clock and this thing they called schedule.

Snow rounded a bluff, skirting below the crest, hidden in the tree line. She drew rein overlooking a shallow valley. The scene below hit her gut like a pony kick. Skinned buffalo carcasses, rotting in the afternoon sun, stretched across the valley floor in every direction. Great shaggy heads and hooves were all that remained to identify the bloody mounds of raw meat. Vultures fed at will on carrion so plentiful they had no need to fight among themselves over it.

White hunters had set the stand to ply their commercial hunting trade. The stand made killing brutally efficient. Hunters would find a herd, identify the lead cow, and bring her down with a wounding shot. The herd would mill around their fallen matriarch in confusion. They made no attempt to flee while the hunters systematically slaughtered them. The business returned three dollars a hide at twenty-five cents a shot. A competent hunter could bring down two hundred kills or more in a day.

Eastern market demand for buffalo hides grew with the ability to ship hides by rail. The railroads encouraged the practice of hunting, for the freight the hides represented and the fact vast herds wandering the plains disrupted their schedules. The Army protected the hunters out of a belief that the surest way to drive the remaining hostiles onto the reservation was to destroy their ability to sustain life in the wild. The old ways followed the herds. Buffalo provided food, shelter, and life itself. Without the herds, they reasoned, the tribes would be forced onto the reservations. The only ones who weren't served by the arrangement were the buffalo and the tribes who depended on them.

Her stomach turned sick, not from the smell that overwhelmed even the gentle upwind breeze, but from the vast and total waste. Buffalo provided her people food, shelter, clothes, cooking utensils, sewing materials, fuel for the cookfire, and many other things. The shaggy ones were the gift of life from the Great One Above. White hunters killed for no more than skins. These great ones could have fed and clothed a large village for many winters. Her people would never have killed so many. They would never have killed the cows and calves that would feed them in the winters to come. Snow had heard of these hunts, but words could not prepare her for the savage massacre the butchers left behind.

Her heart ached. She heard the spirits of the land cry out in anger and wailing death songs. The great shaggy ones were a brown river of life flowing to her people. They roamed the land in herds too vast to number. The people hunted them out of respect for a gift of the Great One Above. Now the whites killed the great shaggy ones and with them they killed the ways of her people. Many would die from the death of this life. Even her pony dropped his head and pawed the ground as though he sensed the moment. She wiped at her eyes and squeezed her pony forward into the valley desecrated by death.

Water scent told her the banks of the Rosebud were near. At midday a village emerged, the lodges shimmering in the haze along a glittering creek bank. Her eyes and heart filled with a feeling of home, in spite of the emptiness that came from knowing she would not find her family there.

She squeezed up an easy lope, splashing across the river. A swarm of children greeted her, running amid noisy yapping camp dogs. She drew rein beside a group of women washing clothes on the rocks at the riverbank. Women roused from their work to take note of her arrival.

"Where is the lodge of Tashunca-uitco?" she asked.

A heavy woman with a round moon face pointed north. "The Oglala camp near Sitting Bull's Hunkpapa."

Snow sat her pony, her expression an enforced calm. Would she be welcomed? Would she be accepted? Doubt weighed on her heart as she nudged her pony through the village.

Just then joyous whoops announced the arrival of a small band of warriors, returning to the village from the northeast. Nearly a mile to the north they wheeled into the river across from where the woman said she would find the Oglala and Hunkpapa camps. The warriors splashed across the river, sparkling water catching the sun. They whooped and shook rifles and tomahawks in the air with celebration. Villagers began to move toward the center of the village. The arrival signaled some great news.

From the manner of their return, Snow knew they must have songs to sing and stories to tell of some victory or successful hunt. It stirred her heart to hear her people's joy after so many moons among the whites. At a distance she noticed the warrior with the spotted war shirt waiting to greet the returning warriors. Crazy Horse stood before his lodge. The circle of the people spread around him waiting to greet the returning braves.

Snow guided her pony through the village throng, hurrying toward the returning warriors. As she drew closer, she could see Cheyenne warriors among the Sioux. Her heart lifted. Looking over the heads of the crowd her eyes shot wide. Her heart jumped in her breast. Her breath caught in her throat. *It must be a ghost.* She blinked, but the ghost vision remained. She sat her pony, wide eyed. The ghost vision clouded. Her eyes filled with tears. It could not be so. The hand pressed to her mouth trembled. Tears spilled down her cheeks, glistening in the sun. Still the ghost sat the spotted horse.

She leaped down from her pony. The press of the people swallowed her. She tried to run. The crowd held her back. She could only wiggle her way past one body, then the next. Her mind seethed with the questions. How could this be? Her husband was dead. The yellow hair took her from his body. Could this warrior be Spotted Hawk or only one who looked like him? Could her husband truly live? Her heart grasped at the hope. If it were not true it would be the cruelest trick of the prankster.

Suddenly, she came free at the head of the crowd standing a respectful distance from Crazy Horse. Snow ran to the Cheyenne brave riding Spotted Hawk's pony. She stopped at his side and stood looking up at him frozen in time but for the tears of joy streaming down her cheeks.

Spotted Hawk looked down at the woman and blinked. His eyes filled with unasked questions and thanks. He leaped from the back of his pony and swept her up in his arms. He held her to his chest, unbelieving that all he had lost had been found. He said nothing. The time for questions would come. For that moment each needed only the comfort of the other's arms.

They sat in the circle of firelight, Snow beside Spotted Hawk, Crazy Horse with his wife, Spotted Hawk's sister, Black Shawl. They celebrated the return of Autumn Snow with roast buffalo hump, a rare feast in these days of lost herds. As the moon rose full and bright in the eastern sky, Spotted Hawk told the story of watching the long knife chief take his wife, unable to fight for his wounds.

Crazy Horse listened intently to his wife's brother. Lean and powerful, his red granite cheekbones, square set chin, and chiseled features made a mask of light and shadow in the reflected firelight.

"The Great One Above gave Spotted Hawk new life. A buffalo robe that did not burn kept me from dying of the cold. The antelope that came to the river to drink fed my body. Anger and hate for the long knife fed my heart. In the spring Spotted Hawk went to the pony soldier fort to find Autumn Snow and kill the long knife. Spotted Hawk did not find her there. He could only kill the white agent Denton and ride north to join his brother Tashunco-uitco." He fell silent to the soft crackle and pop of the fire. He returned the painful memories to a place in his heart he would visit again for his vow to kill the yellow hair.

"Today I give thanks to the Great One. My Autumn Snow is here." He circled her with a protective arm. "Did the long knife hurt you?"

Darkness touched Snow's eyes at the memory.

Black Shawl read her pain. "Let Autumn Snow tell what she wills to your ears alone."

Spotted Hawk understood. He nodded. He knew in his heart. It kindled new rage. "How did you escape? How did you find me?"

Snow straightened her back. "A Crow scout helped me."

"Crow dog," Crazy Horse spat.

Snow straightened her back defiant. "The Crow scout called Curly is not a dog. He is a good man. He stole a blanket for Autumn Snow. He stole food for me. No white man showed kindness to Autumn Snow, only the Crow scout. He helped me escape. He gave me his pony to ride to the dances in the moon of making fat. Here joy returned to my heart in the gift my husband lives."

Chapter Twenty-Three

Red Cloud Agency
North Platte River
Wyoming Territory
July 1870

Avery McSerley pawed a small stack of blankets in the wagon bed. A hot summer breeze ruffled the wide brim of his black slouch hat. He pushed smudged spectacles up the bridge of his nose and checked the freighter's tally. "Looks like a hundred, give or take seventy-five." He suppressed a crooked grin.

The freighter, Tobias Wood, a lanky scarecrow in dirty buckskins, chuckled and spat a stream of tobacco juice into the dust beside the wagon wheel. The inflated lading and receipts would pay him handsomely for his load even after McSerley pocketed more than half the voucher.

McSerley's boots scraped the rough-cut log step to the agency office as he hoisted his black clad frame to the boardwalk. He paused at the office door, stopping Wood at his shoulder. Up and down the dirt road leading to the agency, women shuffled through wind-whipped dust swirls to receive their monthly allotment. Some were accompanied by children. Others came with dogs pulling travois to carry their shares. A line formed at the storehouse window. Those waiting stood in wooden silence, staring vacantly as their numbers grew.

McSerley led the way into the office. He sat behind a cluttered desk while Wood waited impatiently, shifting his weight from one boot to the other. He scanned the bill of lading and wrote out a receipt in the amount of one thousand dollars. He passed the receipt across the desk to Wood. The freighter half smiled at the figure and scratched his mark at the bottom. McSerley picked up the receipt and set it aside with the bill of lading. He drew a steel box from his desk and opened it. He removed a stack of bills, counted out one thousand dollars in hundred-dollar gold certificates. He passed four bills to Wood and pocketed the rest.

"Pleasure doing business with you, Mr. Wood." McSerley half smiled. "I expect I'll need another shipment in a few weeks. It seems I'm already in short supply."

Wood nodded and turned to go. He paused at the door. "Looks like you've got company, McSerley." He stepped aside. Red Cloud stood in the bright sunlit road beside the wagon, holding a flour sack.

McSerley scraped his chair away from the desk, stretched his frame, and straightened his coat. He stepped to the doorway in the shade of the porch and looked down at the chief of his agency charges.

Red Cloud stood tall and impassive. He ignored the flies buzzing around the wagon. He glared at the agent and said nothing.

"The line for the monthly allotment forms at the warehouse." McSerley jerked his thumb toward the line of women.

Red Cloud stepped forward, reaching into the flour sack. He drew out a pinch. Flour coated his red granite fingers. He tossed the brown husk of a worm on the plank at the agent's boot.

"This is the meat promised by the white man's treaty?" The accusation hung between them, buffeted by the wind. "My people get too little flour, too many worms, not enough meat."

McSerley braced his chin. "Your complaint will be duly noted in my report to the commissioner. Now go along about your business."

"White hunters kill the buffalo. Lakota find little to hunt. Artic-al Ten," Red Cloud spoke the unfamiliar term deliberately. "Promise the people flour and meat."

"Don't turn Lakota lawyer on me, Red Cloud. It don't matter what Article Ten says, I don't have the cattle. I will notify the commissioner of your complaint. Now get in line with the rest of your people."

"The Great Father's treaty promise flour and meat. Wasichu make his mark."

"Then take your grievances to the Great Father."

War Department
Office of the General in Chief
Washington, D.C.
March 1871
What in hell is Sam thinking? Is 1600 Pennsylvania Avenue so far removed from reality the man can't recognize a state of war when he sees it?

Sherman stared in disbelief at the provisions of the Indian Appropriations Act. The president had been a soldier's soldier, an effective wartime field commander. Sherman counted it a privilege to have served under him. How the hell did he explain this?

Grant had the bill introduced into congress and signed it into law. Sherman had heard about it, but this was his first look at all of the provisions. The law acknowledged the need to insure the "welfare of Indians as individuals," the first step in a process leading to "Indian citizenship." *Citizenship! What in blue blazes was the man thinking?* The act set forth a policy designed to care for the enemy based on some misguided notion about equality with whites. It included provisions for Indian education, medical care, generous food subsidies, and financial support for the reservations. All of these molly-coddling programs formalizing treaty obligations were now institutionalized under the direction of the Interior Department, Bureau of Indian Affairs.

The Indian problem belonged to the War Department. Sherman knew without question that it would take the Army to confine the savages to reservations and keep them there. Sam's infernal Indian peace policy would come to no good. More than likely a lot of innocent people would die.

Sherman owed his appointment as Commanding General to Grant. Grant appointed him to the post shortly after his inauguration as president. The president respected Sherman as a brother officer who had served with distinction. In the latter stages of the war, Sherman took the city of Atlanta and then launched perhaps the most decisive offensive of the war, a campaign known as Sherman's March to the Sea.

In his famous march, Sherman led four corps, some 60,000 seasoned troops, from Atlanta to Savannah. He gouged a sixty-mile-wide path of total destruction through the South that effectively cut the Confederacy in two. This scorched earth strategy forever framed the fiery field commander's philosophy of total war. Destroy the enemy's ability to sustain itself as a fighting force and you destroy the enemy. Grant's Indian policy was the antithesis of Sherman's view of the problem. He knew without question the Indian must be thoroughly defeated. No amount of treaty making and misguided peace policy would ever bring final resolution to the matter. Nonetheless the president had his fool policy enacted into law. The stubborn question that vexed him: what was to be done about it?

A knock at the door momentarily broke the general's dark mood.

"General Sheridan to see you, sir."

"Show him in, Thomas." Sherman rose to meet his old friend

and comrade in arms. He'd sent for Sheridan to take an important assignment. That assignment had just become more difficult thanks to the Indian Appropriations Act.

"Phil, it's good to see you. Thank you for coming." Sherman extended his hand, dismissing of the formal courtesy of a military salute.

"It's good to see you too, Cump."

"Sit down, Phil." Sherman waived him to one of the leather covered wing chairs drawn up in front of the massive desk that dominated his spacious paneled office. The American flag stood in a standard beside the credenza. A portrait of President Grant hung over the credenza. Sherman would have preferred a portrait of General Grant but political protocols in Washington were steeped in traditions even the Army had to respect.

"So, tell me, Phil, how are things in New Orleans?"

"Honestly, Cump, reconstruction is well under way and things are pretty quiet. I haven't had much excitement since Sam sent me back there once you were done making peace treaties."

Sherman shook his head. Groveling with the enemy at the Fort Laramie Treaty table still provoked a sour taste in his mouth. "I know. That's why I thought you might be ready for a more important assignment."

"Then I'm all ears, General."

"Phil, I want you to take command of the Department of the Missouri once again. I need a good man to oversee resolution of the Indian problem."

The Department of the Missouri stretched from the Mississippi River to the Powder River country between Canada and Mexico. It encompassed territory where elements of the plains tribes stubbornly resisted the nation's westward expansion.

"The Department of the Missouri is a plum assignment for a fighting man, Cump. I'm flattered."

"Don't be, Phil. You and I think alike on the Indian problem. You're the right man for the job, but it won't be easy. I'm afraid our Commander in Chief isn't of a like mind."

Sheridan's bushy brows pinched the bridge of his nose. He sensed some new development in Sherman's demeanor. "Now what?"

"Here, take a look at this." Sherman slid the Indian Appropriations Act across his desk. He fished a cigar out of his tunic and scratched a match while Sheridan scanned the document.

"This is unbelievable! What is Sam thinking?"

"I wish I could say. Maybe the trappings of the office or the association of all those mealy-mouthed politicians has softened the general's better judgment. The facts are his Indian peace policy is at odds with everything we both know needs to be done to fully and finally resolve the problem. This isn't an easy assignment I'm asking you to take, Phil. I'll cover you as best I can, but if you do the right thing, you're likely to wind up on the wrong side of the president's policy."

Sheridan furrowed his brow. Sherman's warning was well taken. The assignment could make or break his career. For good or ill it would surely fix his place in history. Tactically he knew how to defeat Indians in the field. They lived off the land. You had to fight when the land wouldn't sustain their mobility and subsistence. That meant fighting in winter. He knew he could win and he knew how to do it, but not without running afoul of Grant's fool policy. He mulled the conundrum. *Surely there must be some way to get the job done and give himself political cover.* And then it came to him. His expression softened. His eyes crinkled at the corners.

"I'll take the assignment, Cump, on one condition."

Sherman regarded the savvy cavalry commander through a cigar smoke haze. "And what would that be, Phil?"

"Give me Custer."

A small smile creased the corners of a far-seeing look in Sherman's eye. He rose and took Sheridan's hand.

"Brilliant."

Chapter Twenty-Four

White House
Washington, D.C.
July 1871

Orville Babcock appeared at the outer door to a sun-soaked presidential office.

"Commissioner Parker to see you, sir."

Grant sat at his desk in his shirtsleeves. He set his reading glasses aside, disturbed by the assessment of the Bureau of Indian Affairs he'd been reading. He rose to greet his Commissioner of Indian Affairs. He considered putting on the coat draped over the back of his chair but waved the thought aside in deference to the sultry summer heat that hung over the capital.

"Show him in, Orville. We'll need a few minutes before the meeting. Show Secretary Delano and General Sherman to the conference room when they arrive."

"Very good, sir." Babcock stepped aside and ushered the Commissioner of Indian Affairs into the office.

"Ely, good to see you. Thank you for coming." Grant waved his guest to the settee at the side of the office. "Coffee?"

"Please, sir." Despite their occasional disagreements, Parker respected Grant's effort to reform Indian policy. The president gave him the opportunity to work on behalf of his people. Doing the right thing by the Indian wouldn't make either of them politically popular. With the president's support, he could make a difference. Without his support it would be impossible to do his job.

"Two coffees, please, Orville." The aide busied himself at the sideboard while Grant took his seat in one of the wing chairs next to the settee and launched into the substance of the meeting.

"I've just been reading your report, Ely. It makes for a pretty tough assessment of the bureau."

"I made an effort to be factual and objective, Mr. President. My personal feeling is that the state of the reservations is deplorable. The bureau's administration is a scandal. Past Indian policy is a dark stain on the moral fabric of the nation."

"Those are strong indictments, but I'm inclined to agree with you." Grant nodded. "I'm more interested in your sense of what is to be done about it."

Babcock set two bone china cups and saucers emblazoned in gold with the presidential seal before them. Aromatic steam rose from the dark rich brew. Babcock withdrew, quietly closing the door, leaving them alone.

"Corruption in reservation administration is rampant. It is a long-term problem that must be rooted out," Parker said. "Those guilty of abusing their positions must be found, prosecuted, and punished."

"I know the bureau needs to be reformed. Secretary Cox and I are committed to doing it, but it will take time to weed out the corruption. The bureau is full of political appointees with pull in this town. Point an accusing finger at one of them and you better have your facts straight or there'll be hell to pay."

"Mr. President, I don't believe we have the kind of time you and the secretary need to clean up the mess. Our most pressing problem demands action now."

"Oh, and what would that be?"

"Food, sir. Commercial hunting is killing off the buffalo herds at an alarming rate. Without the herds the tribes can't feed themselves. That leaves them dependent on cattle and grain rations provided by the reservations. My investigation suggests no more than twenty-five cents on the dollar of funds appropriated by Congress for maintenance of the tribes actually reaches the people. They are not getting the food they need to survive. Starvation is a very real threat. People faced with starvation become desperate. Desperate people do desperate things."

"What do you propose we do?"

"I can think of only one way to address the problem."

Grant paused over the rim of his cup, "And that would be?"

"Protect the buffalo herds. Let the Indians hunt. They've fed themselves for generations that way. It gets agency corruption out of the food supply and doesn't levy the cost of feeding the tribes on the taxpayer. Equally important, the Indians retain some measure of their way of life."

"But what about the provisions we've made to teach the tribes farming?"

"Mr. President, I know you mean well, but it's too slow. Farming isn't something the tribes embrace. Protect the buffalo in the Powder River hunting grounds and you'll feed the people while you clean up the mess in the bureau."

Grant nodded thoughtfully. "As usual, Ely, you make good sense."

Babcock appeared at the door. "Secretary Cox and General Sherman are waiting in the conference room, Mr. President."

"Thank you, Orville." Grant rose, relit his cigar, and picked up his coat. "Come along, Ely. Let's see if we can make some of your horse sense rub off on Secretary Delano and Cump."

Secretary of the Interior Columbus Delano waited impatiently for Grant to start the meeting. Both he and General Sherman had a stake in Grant's proposed peace policy. Delano's stake, the Bureau of Indian Affairs, wasn't one he was happy about. He'd read Parker's report, which served to confirm what he already knew. The bureau was riddled with corruption and an abject failure by any measure when it came to managing the reservation system. The abuses hadn't been created on his watch, but the problem of cleaning up the mess surely would fall on his shoulders. Proving cases of graft and fraud would be difficult enough without the fact that agency appointments had routinely been handed out to political patrons. Many of those lining their pockets at the expense of the tribes had powerful political connections. When it came to Indian rights, public opinion ran from indifferent at best in the intellectual northeast to openly antagonistic in the west. Impatient as he was, Delano wasn't looking forward to this meeting.

Footfalls and the scent of cigar smoke announced the president's arrival. Delano and Sherman rose as the president entered the conference room followed by Commissioner Parker.

"Good morning, gentlemen."

"Good morning, Mr. President," they answered in unison.

"Have a seat. Feel free to remove your coats if you wish. It's a man's only defense in this heat." Grant took his place at the head of the table. "Now let's get down to business. Have both of you read Ely's report?"

Delano and Sherman nodded.

"My policy, as you know, is to pursue peaceful coexistence with our Indian neighbors. Unfortunately, as a nation there is little to be proud of when it comes to our treatment of the tribes. We set aside one treaty after another the moment it becomes the least inconvenient to some measure of our westward expansion. It's little wonder the tribes have no faith in our word. There is nothing we can do about past policies. The best we can do is to live up to our current commitments, but even that won't be easy given the deplorable state of the bureau.

Mr. Secretary, what do you propose to do about it?"

"The bureau is a complex problem, Mr. President. It is doubtful we can correct the abuses quickly. I have had meetings with Treasury and Justice. I've asked George Boutwell to help me conduct an audit of the agency books, and I've asked Secretary Akerman to help me launch an investigation of reservation procurement practices."

Grant nodded his approval at mobilizing the resources of Boutwell's Treasury Department and the Justice Department under Ebenezer Rockwood Hoar. "Seems like a good start."

"We will have to proceed with deliberation however," Delano said. "Many of those who come under investigation will have powerful political allies."

"That, of course, is precisely the problem, Secretary Delano." Parker had little patience with bureaucratic dissembling. "While you deliberate, the tribes continue to suffer. The bureau you oversee pockets seventy-five cents of every dollar Congress appropriates to meet our treaty obligations."

"I understand your concern, Commissioner." Delano bristled. "I am not here to apologize for past patronage practices or to impugn the integrity of your report, but we need time to build cases that justify corrective action."

Grant threw up his hands. "Gentlemen, gentlemen please. I understand the need to be thorough, but as Ely points out, the problem of feeding the tribes is urgent. The tribes simply are not receiving the food supplies they need to survive. It is becoming a matter of life and death. You need to keep that urgency in mind as you direct the audits and investigations. In the meantime, Ely has an interesting proposal on how we might address the problem of the food supply in more immediate terms. Please tell General Sherman and Secretary Delano about your idea, Ely."

"It's really quite simple. Buffalo are the Indian's natural food supply. Commercial hunting is destroying the herds. We should enact legislation to protect the herds and allow the Indians to hunt. It takes the secretary's corrupt agents out of the business of cheating the tribes out of their food and it relieves the taxpayers of the burden of feeding the reservations. It also allows the tribes to maintain some measure of their way of life."

Sherman snapped to attention. He'd been passively disinterested in Delano's problem. This was a different matter. "Surely you don't take such a notion seriously, Mr. President."

"There's a lot of horse sense to what Ely proposes, Cump."

"Sam! I'm sorry. Mr. President, General Sheridan supports thinning the herds. It denies the hostiles the ability to sustain themselves as a fighting force."

Parker leaned across the table toward Sherman. "That would be the same General Sheridan who is on record as saying, if I may quote, *'The only good Indian is a dead Indian.'* "

Sherman stiffened against the unfamiliar brunt of dissent. "General Sheridan is a field commander whose record is beyond reproach. His judgment of the tactical situation in the Department of the Missouri is not a matter for bureaucratic conjecture."

Parker's dark eyes flashed. "Starvation is not conjecture, General."

Grant liked the fact Parker said his piece without backing down. It didn't matter who was on the receiving end. Sherman's ears pricked back the way they did when he was damn good and mad. The fact that the meeting hadn't dissolved into a shouting match or worse testified to the decorum that came with the presidency. Grant hadn't commanded this much restraint as General in Chief of the Army. He leveled a determined glare at his General in Chief.

"I understand Phil's assessment of the situation, as would the good people of Georgia I'm sure. This is not about a fight to defeat an enemy, Cump. This is about a path to peaceful coexistence with our neighbors. Ely is going up to the hill and find sponsors for a bill that protects the buffalo herds and he's going to do it with my full support."

Parker sat back quietly, savoring a small feeling of satisfaction.

Sherman clenched his jaw and held his tongue, his features scarlet. His mind raced. Senators and representatives in the western states would see the folly in such a law. Railroad interests probably would too. Sam was wrong on this, dead wrong! He had some sponsors of his own to find.

Fourteenth Street
Washington, D.C.
September 1871

Grant actually supported this damn fool nonsense. Sherman fumed in the back of his carriage rocking up the street toward Pennsylvania Avenue. Parker had gotten a couple of high-minded northeastern congressmen to introduce his silly "Buffalo Bill" in the House. The northeasterners were sympathetic to the Indians on misguided humanitarian sentiment. Parker persuaded them that protecting the herds would save the Indians from starvation. He also argued that it would preserve the dignity of their way of life. *Dignity be damned!* His arguments about taxpayers not bearing the burden of feeding the tribes appealed to fiscal conservatives and that just might be enough to get the damn bill passed over the weak resistance of underrepresented western interests. Sheridan would be furious. Sherman knew the feeling. He couldn't just sit idly by and let this travesty go unchallenged.

The Senate was the place to stop this nonsense. The Senate is where the thinly populated western states had their strongest voice. He could go to Grant's political arch-adversary in the

Senate for help. Carswell could be counted on to oppose anything the president supported on principle if nothing more. Tempting as that might be, Sherman couldn't be seen as taking a political position on the legislation, let alone one in opposition to the president. *Washington politics made strange bedfellows,* Sherman thought, reflecting on the former rebel officer's war sympathies. He set the thought aside. It had taken some time to figure a strategy he could use without exposing the War Department or himself to a charge of engaging in partisan politics. This meeting should make for a good start. His driver drew the carriage to a halt in the circular drive fronting the Willard Hotel.

Sherman stepped down from the carriage and bounded up the stone steps past the uniformed doorman. He crossed the elegant polished marble lobby past richly upholstered seating groups and dark polished wood furnishings. Colorful murals covered the ceiling high overhead. The back bar at the Willard was a favorite gathering place for legislators and those who sought to influence them. Grant was even known to come across Pennsylvania Avenue from the White House for a drink on occasion. That fact probably accounted for the popularity of the place with the influence peddlers and hangers-on known as lobbyists. And that was the purpose of this meeting. The company man waited at a back corner table in the dimly lit bar. He rose as Sherman approached the table.

"General Sherman," the company man extended his hand. "William Styles, Esquire of the firm Baynor, Conklin, and Styles."

Sherman took his hand. "I'm pleased to meet you, sir. Thank you for agreeing to see me."

"How could I resist when your message said you wished to discuss a matter of vital interest to my client?" They took their seats. Styles continued in a confidential tone. "Still I am puzzled to understand where the interests of the Army and the Union

Pacific come together."

A white coated waiter appeared to take their drink orders. Styles selected Kentucky bourbon, counted among the benefits of the end of the war in the north.

Sherman sized up the company man as he ordered. A sparrow-slight bespectacled man, of nervous habit he presented a polished appearance. Washington law firms made a business of representing their clients' interests in matters of congressional legislation, government policy, and political influence. It became a natural extension of their corporate and civil relationships. These were men of words. They curried favor, cultivated influence, and effectively advocated on behalf of their clients. Such men were paid well for these services. As a rule, Sherman didn't trust lawyers or politicians. They were men of slippery purpose, driven by the winds of convenience and opportunity. Like it or not, he needed this one to deal with the problem at hand. The waiter hurried off to fill their order.

Styles turned back to Sherman. "Now, where were we? Oh, yes, I was asking how the interests of the Army and the Union Pacific come together."

"We have a mutual interest in the matter of buffalo."

Styles blinked. "Buffalo? Surely you have the advantage of me, sir." His glasses drifted down the pinched bridge of his nose as he spoke. "They are a nuisance to us to be sure. They play havoc with our schedules, but the commercial buffalo trade is thinning the herds nicely and the problem grows less onerous every day." He paused to push the offending spectacles back to their intended position. "When it comes to the Army, I'm afraid I don't see the connection at all."

Sherman hunched forward across the table. "Buffalo provide the food supply that allows the plains tribes to sustain themselves as a fighting force. Keeping them on the reservations is the Army's job. That job is a lot easier when the Indians depend on the reservations to feed them."

"Yes, I can see that, but surely the commercial buffalo trade benefits the Army then as well as it benefits my client."

"It does, Mr. Styles. The problem is that legislation is afoot to restrict commercial hunting and protect the herds."

"Restrictions on commercial hunting? Why that would be, un-American."

The waiter returned with their drinks. He set the glasses on the table and withdrew. Sherman resumed the conversation.

"There's a bill to protect the buffalo herds in the House. It is gaining a following with certain easterners of humanitarian persuasion. Ely Parker got the idea going up on the Hill."

"I see." Styles made a steeple of his fingers, blinking behind his glasses. "Now that is a concern. I can see where my client's interests would not be served by such a turn of events."

Sherman took a swallow of his drink. "The Army, of course, can't take an official position on such matters particularly when the bill has the administration's support."

Styles nodded. "But railroad interests alone won't have enough influence to stop such a measure. What do you suggest?"

The man got right to the point. Sherman liked that. Maybe this unholy alliance would work better than he'd expected.

"We can't stop it in the House. The northeastern states hold a large block of votes. There are too many 'enlightened intellectuals' among them, men who believe Parker's arguments about the so-called injustices done the tribes. Fiscal conservatives sign on to the notion that if the Indians feed themselves, the treasury will not be burdened to do so. The place to look for sympathetic ears is in the Senate."

"I understand." Styles pressed his wayward glasses back into place. "Surely we can mobilize western sentiment on the security issue. Western states can be expected to mount a stiff opposition. They have significant economic interest in the unrepresented territories, but western interests represent a distinct minority." He rubbed his chin, mentally counting votes. "Unfortunately—the west alone isn't enough."

Sherman drained his glass. He motioned to the steward for another. He had the answer. "Perhaps Senator Carswell could bring along his southern colleagues. They need little encouragement to oppose the policies of this administration."

Styles had yet to touch his drink. "Senator Carswell could very well raise the votes needed to defeat the bill. The question is, will he be able to persuade his moderate and uncommitted colleagues?"

Sherman shrugged. "Defeating the bill won't be easy even in the Senate." He paused for a moment as the waiter returned with his drink. He'd considered the possibility represented by Styles's doubts. "If Senator Carswell is unable to raise the votes, we have one other card up our sleeve."

Styles's expression blanked, puzzled.

"Senator Carswell chairs the Senate Select Committee on Indian Affairs."

Realization flickered behind the railroad man's spectacles. His pinched features cracked an uncustomary attempt at a smile. "You have a flair for politics, General. Perhaps you should consider a second career when you retire from the Army."

Sherman sat back.

"To victory then." The company man raised his glass for the first time.

"To victory," Sherman echoed and bumped back his drink. *Mission accomplished.*

CHAPTER TWENTY-FIVE

Red Cloud Agency
North Platte River
Wyoming Territory
September 1871

Red Cloud rode up to the site of the schoolhouse flanked by his brothers Spotted Tail, Chief of the Brule, and Big Bear. Josiah Bradburn stood in his shirtsleeves giving orders to the men building the school. The long black coat that gave him his Indian name lay on a pile of freshly cut wood. Construction of the schoolhouse had begun almost from the moment the black preacher arrived at the agency. Rough-hewn beams rose to the blue summer sky beside the dusty road. The black preacher sent for Red Cloud and his brothers to show them the school. He turned at their approach and waved, giving the sour nod he passed for a greeting.

"Red Cloud, Spotted Tail, Big Bear, welcome, thank you for coming. Come see the fine school the Great Father is building for your children."

The chiefs slipped down from their ponies. Big Bear took the leads from Red Cloud and Spotted Tail. "You go. Big Bear hold ponies."

"Big Bear does not go to school?" Red Cloud mocked surprise. Big Bear grunted and squat in the dust, holding the pony leads.

Bradburn led Red Cloud and Spotted Tail over to the building site. "Is it not a wonderful sight? It is God's work, I tell you, God's work. With His almighty help we shall have it finished in time for classes to begin in the fall. Think of it. Here your children will be taught to read and write like white children. They will grow up to take their rightful places in civilized society. You should take great joy in this. You have much to be thankful for."

Red Cloud ignored the black preacher's prideful proclamations. "It would be better for our children if they had food for their bellies this winter."

"Yes, yes, I've spoken to Agent McSerley of your complaint. He says he made your concerns known to the commissioner."

Red Cloud spat. "These words he has said before. Still our women and children go hungry."

"That is why this school is so important. When your children are educated, they will be able to feed themselves by the work of their hands."

Spotted Tail lifted his chin to the skeleton of log beams. "This school will bring back the buffalo?"

"Spotted Tail knows that is not what I meant. This school will teach your children how to work and support themselves in the white man's world. It will teach them the true meaning of God's love."

Red Cloud turned bright eyes on the black preacher. "Wakan Tanka loves the buffalo. Wakan Tanka is not pleased white men waste the gift of the great shaggy ones."

"Yes, well I didn't summon you here to discuss food or heathen religious beliefs. I asked you here to show you the school so that you will tell your people to send their children to it when it opens. Will you do that?"

"School do no good on empty belly." Red Cloud folded his arms across his chest.

"You know I am sorry about that, but I didn't invite you here to discuss food. You must discuss that with Agent McSerley. Now about the school," Bradburn mopped his brow in frustration.

Red Cloud turned to the preacher, ignoring the school. "You say you were sent here by the Great Father to keep the words of his treaty. The Agent McSerley tells us to take our grievances to the Great Father. My brothers and I wish to go to the Great Father's house. We wish to tell our troubles to his ears. You tell him we wish to see him. You take us to the Great Father. Then we send our children to your school."

Bradburn's jaw dropped at the audacity. "Why, why that is most extraordinary. I've never heard of such a thing."

"We ride the iron horse to the Great Father's house. He will hear our words with his ears. Then our children will go to your school." Red Cloud turned on his heel and returned to his pony. Spotted Tail followed, leaving the black preacher gaping after them.

Washington, D.C.
Willard Hotel
November 1871

"To what do I owe the pleasure of your invitation, William?" Carswell stretched out his hand in greeting. The rounded baritone drawl resonated in the dark empty cavern of the Willard Hotel bar.

Styles took Carswell's hand with an unctuous smile. "My client wishes to pledge support for your reelection campaign."

"Splendid, William." Carswell beamed. The quintessential southern gentleman, Senator Thurman A. Carswell, Colonel C.S.A. (ret.) cut a lean and swarthy figure with a vigorous glow for a man advanced in his middle years. He smoothed a prematurely gray mustache. "News such as this is always welcome. Let's drink to it. Waiter!" He showed the lawyer to a back corner booth in the near deserted bar. "You know you could have dropped by the office to deliver that kind of news. What accounts for an invitation to do it over drinks at so early an hour? Could it be no one's here to see us or overhear what you have to say?" A spark of amusement lit his smoke gray eye.

Styles's stiff countenance cracked in a knowing breach to his facade. "That's what I like about you, Thurman. You don't miss much and you get right to the point."

The waiter arrived with their drinks, set them on the table, and withdrew.

Styles lifted his glass, "To a successful reelection campaign then."

"To success." Carswell took a swallow. "As always, I am grateful for your client's support. Now what's on your mind, William?"

The lawyer toyed with his glass. "There is a small matter of interest to my client that may come before your committee."

Carswell smiled. As expected, they had some business to do. "I'm listening, William."

"There's a bill making its way through the House. Some call it the Buffalo Bill."

"Hmm, I seem to recall hearing something about that."

"Ely Parker proposed the idea to the bill's sponsors with the president's support." The mention of Grant's support pricked the senator's interest. "It proposes to ban commercial buffalo hunting to protect the herds."

Carswell knit his brow. "What's the point?"

"The idea is to preserve the Indian's ability to hunt. It takes the Bureau of Indian Affairs and the reservations out of providing the tribes' sole source of food."

"Ah, the bureau, hmm, that actually makes sense."

"The bill is gaining a following with eastern Indian sympathizers. Fiscal conservatives like the idea of reducing the cost of supplying food to the reservations. The west can't muster enough opposition to defeat it."

"Defeat it. I gather you are opposed. So where does the railroad interest come in?" Carswell tossed off the last of his drink and signaled the waiter for another.

"The herds play hell with the train schedules. You get a big herd on the track and it can hold a train up for hours."

"So, what do you want me to do about it?"

Styles paused while the waiter delivered Carswell's drink. "Kill it."

"If the southern caucus voted with the west it might be close," Carswell mused, counting votes. "Practically speaking delivering the whole of the caucus on something other than a reconstruction issue is problematic. I don't know, Bill. I just don't know."

Styles met Carswell's gaze in a gesture of helpful sincerity. "We might help you raise enough votes to refer it to your committee for hearings."

Carswell paused. A half smile spread over the rim of his glass. "Oh, William, you are a devious bastard. No wonder your client's interests are always so well represented. The Buffalo Bill will never get out of committee."

Chapter Twenty-Six

Cheyenne Station
Wyoming Territory
March 1872

Cold wind denied the onset of spring. It whipped the blanket-wrapped figures standing on the platform. Red Cloud stood with his back to it, flanked by Spotted Tail and Big Bear. Behind them the new passenger lounge provided Bradburn and the other white men warm respite from the elements. The passenger lounge adjoined the smaller original station that now provided offices for the Union Pacific, Western Union, and Post Office. Beyond the passenger lounge to the east, partial walls and beams marked construction of the new Union Pacific Hotel. The new structure stairstepped toward leaden gray clouds, scudding southeast ahead of the northerly wind. The distant wail of a train whistle born on the wind reached the platform.

Spotted Tail turned toward the sound and squinted into the cutting wind. "Iron horse comes." His words were barely audible above the wind gusts.

Off to the west a dark plume of smoke grew against gray clouds where the silver ribbon of rail appeared out of a bright point of light on the prairie. *The iron horse comes.* Red Cloud repeated the words in his thoughts. The iron horse divided the land. It drove the great shaggy ones and the spirits of the people from land they once roamed freely. It confined the people to hunting grounds written on papers. The old ways passed away along the iron horse trail.

The iron horse followed its mournful whine, rumbling into Cheyenne station belching white smoke. An icy foreboding balled in the pit of Red Cloud's stomach. Many at council questioned the wisdom of traveling to meet the Great Father. His own doubts worsened as the one-eyed monster ground its brakes in a deafening scream like some great predator claiming a kill. Dirty black smoke stained even the dull gray clouds above. The spirit of the sacred buffalo recoiled before it. He heard his people cry out against the shrill call of the whistle. The fire breathing monster roiled a deep disturbance in his spirit. Soon it would swallow him and carry him away from the land of his people. It would carry him to the Great Father's house in the white man's land. Who could say what they would find in the strange land of the rising sun. The Great Father may be no better than those who broke his promises. Red Cloud prayed it would not be so. Why would the Great Father bother to make promises he did not mean to keep? If he meant to keep them, then he should know those he sent here did not.

The doors to the passenger lounge opened as the train rolled to a stop. The black preacher Bradburn led the other white passengers out to the platform. He motioned Red Cloud and his brothers to follow as he led the way down the platform toward the end of the train. The door to the last passenger coach stood open. A man in a long blue coat stood beside the step up to it. He wore a sour expression as though something beside the iron horse smelled bad.

Bradburn led the way up the steps to a path that passed between rows of stiff benches to an empty row among the handful of travelers already scattered about the car. Here and there people turned to stare at the unexpected presence of Indians among them. Some showed surprise, some outright contempt. Red Cloud had learned to look past such people. He and his brothers took seats the black preacher showed them.

They were little more than settled when the train lurched into a roll. Red Cloud fought the urge to grip the edge of the seat as though the great monster might throw him to the ground and grind him to dust between its great wheels. The car moved slowly at first, bumping the rails. It swayed unsteadily from side to side as though it might fall over. His stomach turned sour. A knot collected in his throat as the iron horse gathered speed. It passed a watering tower, leaving the east end of town behind.

Red Cloud sat straight and still, watching the lands of his people rush by as the iron horse thundered east. The white men ate and slept on the iron horse. They went forward to the next car where food was served to them at tables covered with white cloth. The black preacher and a black man in a white coat brought plates of food to Red Cloud and his brothers. Bradburn showed them where to make water. As afternoon wore into evening the rhythmic rattle of the rails lulled Red Cloud into acceptance. He would survive the iron monster that carried him ever deeper into white man's land. Land where once the people lived free.

As the miles of this trail rumbled by in the gray light of the next day, Red Cloud had a growing sense that here in the homelands of the whites he would be even more out of place than in the iron horse coach. The iron horse and the talking wires made a path for the whites. They made a path from the white villages of the rising sun to the villages of the setting sun. New villages grew up beside the iron horse trail wherever it went. Towns and cities grew in number and size and age as the iron horse traveled ever deeper into the white man's land. Red Cloud took it for a vision of what the lands of his people would become with the coming of the iron horse. The people knew the spiritual meaning of the iron horse. They saw it as a symbol for the coming of the white man. They understood some small part of it, but no one could truly see it as he saw it now. It made his heart heavy. It steeled his spirit. He would speak to the Great Father for his people. Some part of this must be stopped. Some land must be spared for the people. He prayed the Great Father would help him. He prayed the Great Father meant to keep his promises.

White House
Washington, D.C.
April 1872

Red Cloud stepped down from the carriage followed by his brothers. They stood shoulder to shoulder, looking up at the Great Father's massive white stone lodge. Red Cloud wore a dark suit and starched collar the black preacher gave him for the occasion. Spotted Tail and his brothers stood oddly out of place in their blankets, buckskins, and feathers. The black preacher hurried around the back of the coach, a chill spring breeze whipping his cloak in billows like a prairie storm cloud.

"This way," he said.

His anxious manner amused Red Cloud. They followed the preacher up stone steps from the drive to the doors of the front portico. He rapped a heavy brass knocker to the polished wood door. Moments later a white-haired black man, wearing a starched white coat, opened the door.

"Josiah Bradburn and the Red Cloud delegation, we have an appointment to see the president."

The butler stepped back, opening the door for them with a sweeping gesture to enter. A second, younger white-coated attendant stepped forward to take Bradburn's cloak. He turned to Spotted Tail, offering to take his blanket. Spotted Tail pulled the blanket tighter around his shoulders. The attendant shrugged and went off to hang Bradburn's cloak.

"This way," the older man said. He led them down a broad central corridor.

Red Cloud followed Bradburn. He held his bearing straight and strong in the presence of so much white power. His eyes darted left and right as they passed down a hall made of brightly polished stone. The hard white man's shoes tapped a hollow drum song announcing their way. No unexpected visitor or enemy would surprise the Great Father here. Gray morning light filtered through tall lace-curtained windows, gleaming against the polished floors. Blankets of many colors covered the floors of the rooms they passed on every side. Lamps of bright brass and glass hung from white painted walls and high ceilings. Pictures of dark suited white men and frilly powdered white women hung on the walls. One picture showed red coated men on horses chasing spotted dogs. Red Cloud marveled at the size of the Great Father's lodge. Who could possibly use so much?

The hallway ended in a large room lined with bookshelves and chairs. Dark suited men with shiny oiled hair sat at desks on either side of a white painted door.

"Reverend Bradburn and the Red Cloud delegation," the old black man announced to one of the dark suited men.

The man stood and nodded to Bradburn. He arched an appraising eye at Red Cloud and his brothers. "One moment." He turned to a white painted door. He knocked, opened the door, and announced, "Reverend Bradburn and the Red Cloud delegation." A muffled reply came in response. The dark suited man stepped aside, holding the door open wide.

Red Cloud and his brothers followed the black preacher into the Great Father's office. Red Cloud took it all in. The large gray lit room with its great polished desk. A soft covered bench and chairs circled a low table at the side of the room. The Great Father came out from behind his desk to greet them. He was a smaller man than Red Cloud had expected. The Oglala chief towered over him. A tall dark-skinned man in a dark suit followed at his shoulder.

"Friend Bradburn." The Great Father greeted the black preacher.

"Mr. President," the black preacher returned the Great Father's handshake. "May I present Red Cloud, Chief of the Oglala Lakota. This is Spotted Tail, Chief of the Brule Lakota, and Big Bear."

The Great Father had lively dark eyes that softened in welcome. "Chief Red Cloud," he held out his hand in the white man's greeting. Red Cloud locked the Great Father's eyes and took his forearm in a warrior's greeting. The Great Father returned his grasp.

"Let me present Commissioner Ely Parker. Commissioner Parker represents the Bureau of Indian Affairs."

Red Cloud eyed the commissioner suspiciously. Was this the man the Agent McSerley sent his complaints? Was this the man who did nothing about them? He met Red Cloud's stare with a nod. The suit was that of a white man. His eyes said he was of the people.

"Commissioner Parker." The black preacher broke the silence with a curt nod.

"Reverend."

Red Cloud sensed tension between the black preacher and the one called commissioner. Some past disagreement he thought. The black preacher built schools. A man of the people would not.

"Please be seated," The Great Father gestured to the soft covered bench.

Red Cloud, Spotted Tail, and Big Bear filed around the low table to the bench and took their seats. Red Cloud wondered at white ways. They covered the floor with thick robes only to sit on benches and chairs. This soft bench would have made a better seat on the iron horse.

"Coffee?" The Great Father smiled.

Red Cloud nodded.

"Sugar?"

The chief smiled and nodded again. The Great Father knew something of Lakota ways.

"Orville, if you please." The Great Father turned to Red Cloud. "How was your journey?"

"The iron horse comes great distances with little rest. We saw many villages. Your people are as many as blades of grass. Do your lodges all turn to stone when they become old?"

The Great Father chuckled and shook his head. "No. Only those we wish to last many years are built with stone. What did you think of New York?"

Red Cloud paused while the coffee was served in fine white cups painted with the sign of an eagle. Even the Great Father respected the power of the eagle. "The lodges cover Earth Mother in stone. The people travel in straight lines through narrow canyons. Tall lodges crowd out the sky. They hide the sun much of the day. Red Cloud wonders if these white lodges may some day crowd out the sun in the land of his people. Already they scatter the buffalo." Red Cloud brought the conversation to the matter at hand.

"White hunters kill the buffalo. Hunting is poor even in the Powder River hunting grounds given the Lakota by treaty."

"I know this problem." The Great Father nodded, fishing in his pocket for a cigar. He offered one to Red Cloud.

Red Cloud shook his head. "We smoke sacred pipe when you visit my lodge." The Great Father nodded. He scratched a match and puffed a great cloud of smoke that would never find its way to Wakan Tanka through the roof of this lodge.

"Buffalo hides have become quite the fashion here in the east and in Europe. Commercial hunting is big business. Commissioner Parker has a bill we support in the Senate that would protect the herds and your hunting grounds."

Red Cloud glanced at the commissioner. He understood little of the Great Father's words. "What means 'protect the herds'?"

"A law to stop white hunters from killing the buffalo," Parker said.

Red Cloud knit his brows. He cut his eyes to Spotted Tail. The Brule shrugged. He turned to the Great Father. "My people cannot eat white man's law."

"Our treaty includes generous provisions to feed your people on the reservation while they learn to feed themselves by farming."

Red Cloud shook his head. "Lakota hunt. Treaty food does not feed the people. We get too little flour, too many worms, too little meat. When we complain to Agent McSerley, he says he will report it to the commissioner." Red Cloud fixed Parker with an accusing glare.

The Great Father took a sip of his coffee. "What do you know about this, Ely?"

"The agent in charge of the Red Cloud Agency is Avery McSerley. I reviewed his reports for the past year in preparation for this meeting. There is no mention of food shortages. The vouchers he submitted for payment indicate the full measure of our treaty obligations are available to the people living on the agency." Parker held the president's eye. Both knew the likely cause of the discrepancy.

"Friend Bradburn, have you observed the circumstances Chief Red Cloud describes?"

"I haven't done an accounting of the allotments distributed, but I have heard the chief's complaints. I have also heard Agent McSerley say he reported them to Commissioner Parker."

The Great Father turned to Red Cloud. "Thank you for bringing this matter to my attention. It appears we have a problem. Ely, see that Red Cloud's charge is brought to the attention of Secretary Delano and Secretary Boutwell. Secretary

Hoar will order the U.S. Marshals Service to investigate McSerley's stewardship of the reservation. If an audit of the agency finds that we have violated the terms of our treaty, Secretary Hoar and the Justice Department will bring charges and prosecute the case vigorously to the full extent of the law."

Red Cloud sat back. "White man's law protects the white man."

The Great Father shook his head. "The law protects us all, Chief Red Cloud. We shall see to it."

The Great Father stood by his words. The Great Father met his eyes.

"We will correct any injustice done your people in this matter. Longer term we need your help. Your people must take advantage of the land, stock, and equipment provided them to learn farming."

Red Cloud pulled a frown. This the Great Father did not understand. "Lakota hunt."

"There will always be game to hunt, but perhaps not enough to feed your people. Learn to farm. Plant the land. Feed the people. Live as neighbors with the white men among you."

The black preacher nodded.

The Great Father's words reached Red Cloud's ears.

Parker knew the words did not enter his heart.

Chapter Twenty-Seven

Red Cloud Agency
North Platte River
Wyoming Territory
July 1872

Harness jangle and the steady clop, clop of the team announced the heavily loaded freight wagon. "Whoa there!" Tobias hauled lines in front of the agency.

Avery McSerley smiled at the sound of money. He scraped his chair back from his desk. He crossed the wood plank office floor to the shaded porch and the shimmering heat of the day beyond. A dust devil swirled across the parched clay where the wagon parked. "Tobias." McSerley greeted the freighter.

"McSerley." The freighter nodded. "Got a bigger shipment for you this trip."

McSerley noted a tall dusty stranger in a slouch hat riding shotgun in the box. "Who might this be?"

"Name's Corby, I took him on to help with this load."

Corby said nothing.

McSerley turned to the canvas covered wagon bed as Wood stepped down from the box. The freighter pulled the canvas back for McSerley to inspect the load. "We got flour, calico, coffee, sugar, and blankets."

"Could'a used two wagons for this load." McSerley scratched the stubble of beard at his chin.

"With Corby's help, we could have." Wood thumbed his hand

in the direction of the rough-shaven freighter lounging against the wagon box.

McSerley caught the freighter's suggestion. "Two wagonloads and two bills of lading, double the profits. I believe you're right Tobias, I believe you are right. Let me tally this up for the both of you."

Wood smiled and sent a stream of tobacco juice slicing off a wagon wheel. "Let's just don't stand in the hot sun all day."

McSerley hurried through the motions of tallying the wagon contents. "Step into the office while I fill out the paperwork," he said leading the way up the plank step to the porch.

Wood and Corby clumped up the step behind him. Little about the shadowed office provided relief from the heat. McSerley sat heavily in his desk chair, opened a drawer, and drew out two forms. He dipped a pen in the ink pot and began scratching figures on the bills, pausing only to wave at a persistent fly attracted to his unwashed scent. At length he sat back and picked up the two pages. Giving each a cursory glance he handed one to Wood and the other to Corby. "That look about right?"

"Always does." Wood stepped in front of Corby to the front of the desk. He picked up the pen and signed the inflated bill. A pistol cocked behind Wood. He froze.

"Put your hands where I can see 'em real easy."

Wood whirled, menacing a move to the .44 on his hip. He came up short, caught in Corby's cold blue eyes, and the gun bore leveled between his eyes.

"Don't do anything stupid, Wood. You're both under arrest."

McSerley eased back in his chair.

"Keep your hands where I can see them, McSerley, or I'll ventilate the both of you. Strictly in the line of duty you understand."

"Under arrest, by whose authority and on what charge?"

"Permit me to introduce myself properly. The name's Abel Corby, U.S. Marshal. The charge is fraud."

Red Cloud Agency
North Platte River
Wyoming Territory
September 1872

Red Cloud stood beside the black preacher watching them come. They shuffled through the dust, round eyed and sober, facing the uncertainty of this thing the wasichu called school.

The black preacher swept his arm across the scene unfolding before them. "Behold the future of your people, Red Cloud. Here your children will learn to speak English. They will learn to read and write. Words will open their ears and hearts to the message of God's righteous will and salvation."

Red Cloud glanced at the black preacher's fevered eyes. "The Great Father spoke truth. The agent McSerley no longer cheats the people. For this our children come to your school."

"Red Cloud is a man of his word." Bradburn nodded.

"Red Cloud cannot say they will stay. Red Cloud cannot say the children will accept your wasichu god."

"Oh, but they must do both." Bradburn raised a long bony finger to the sky. "Education is the path to knowledge and enlightenment. Enlightenment leads to faith in the true God and His merciful salvation. It is our sacred duty to see to it. Have no fear, Red Cloud. Your people will be saved. Your people will be led to enlightenment by their children."

Red Cloud watched the children climb the schoolhouse steps. One by one they disappeared inside. He remembered his war. The great victory that drove the pony soldiers from their forts on the Bozeman Trail. He won the Paha Sapa. He won the Powder River hunting grounds. The words of the white man's treaty made record of his victory as the people might remember it in song. When the words of the treaty fell hollow, he took the people's complaint to the Great Father. The Great Father stood by the words of his treaty. He made white man's law protect the Lakota. Still the whites came. The hunting grounds grew barren. The people depended on the wasichu to feed them. The Great Father was a warrior. Red Cloud found much he could admire in him. The Great Father did not understand Lakota ways. Young men hunt. They do not farm. What would become of these little ones in this thing the white man calls school? They would be taught to turn away from the old ways. White man's school would smother the old ways in the eyes of their children. He did not have a good feeling about this. He gave his word to feed the people. He kept his word. The children came. Victory grew bitter on his tongue.

CHAPTER TWENTY-EIGHT

White House
Washington, D.C.
November 10, 1872

A steward in a starched white jacket stepped into the ballroom.

"The President and First Lady of the United States."

The guests in the grand salon broke into genteel applause as a blue uniformed Army band ensemble struck up the familiar chords of "Hail to the Chief."

The president made his entrance to the reelection celebration with Julia on his arm. A short, stout pleasant hostess, the First Lady chose a striking purple gown for the occasion. The salon glowed, festooned with braces of candles and softened lamplight. Cabinet officers, congressmen, senators, diplomats, and invited dignitaries created a dark suited canvas to the palate of colorful gowns worn by their wives and escorts. White gloved waiters circulated among the gathered guests serving silver trays of champagne, delicacies, or the guest's preference in libations.

The President and First Lady circled the room greeting their guests and accepting hearty congratulations. One by one the dignitaries came forward: Justice Department Secretary Ebenezer Rockwood Hoar, Treasury Secretary George Boutwell, New York Senator Roscoe Conkling, Secretary of State Hamilton Fish. Each offered his congratulations and good wishes.

"Congratulations, Mr. President," Ely Parker offered a firm handshake. "I am pleased you will be able to continue the important work of your Indian policy. There is much remaining to be done."

"Thank you, Ely. I know there is. I'm confident that with your help, we shall finish all we set out to do," Grant passed on to his political confidant.

Congressman Elihu Washburne spoke below the hum of guest conversation for the president's ears. "Congratulations, Sam."

"Thank you, Eli." Grant took Washburne's hand with a warm smile. "I couldn't have done it without you."

Washburne lowered his eyes, "Thank you, Sam."

A waiter presented a tray of champagne. "I believe I'll have some of that good Kentucky sour mash. Care to join me, Eli?"

"Don't mind if I do, Mr. President, don't mind if I do."

Julia wrinkled her nose. "This conversation suddenly has the aroma of politics about it. Sam, if you'll excuse me, I believe I should see to the rest of our guests."

Grant patted her hand as she slipped it off his arm and drifted into the crowd. A waiter appeared with two crystal glasses of whiskey on a tray. Grant took one and handed the other to Washburne.

"To success in your second term, Mr. President," Washburne raised his glass and took a swallow. "I believe when the full results are tallied, you will have won sixty percent of the popular vote if not more. It is truly a stunning endorsement, Sam."

"The American people have spoken, Eli. I'm gratified by what they had to say."

"The Democrats and their Liberal Republican allies must be beside themselves," Washburne chuckled.

Grant swirled the contents of his glass. "Greeley was a formidable opponent. The backing he got from his own paper was expected. The fact that his fellow editors across the nation anointed him to the office made the race appear more difficult than it proved to be in the end."

"The people voted your record, Sam. Greeley and the Democrats owned the newspapers, but the people weren't taken in by the rhetoric of your political adversaries."

"We can be thankful for that. I hope it translates into support for our second term platform, though regrettably I have my doubts. I suspect the strength of our victory will only serve to harden the voices of our opponents."

"That's politics, Sam."

"Yes, well politics is a bit like war. It's tough enough to hold the high ground in this town against the opposition you know about. One doesn't need the newspapers conjuring up a scandal under every carpet corner and affixing blame on those who had no part in it. Political patronage has been around as long as the Republic. Hell, President Lincoln elevated it to an art form. To read it as Greeley and his cronies across the country print it, you'd think I invented it."

Washburne signaled a passing waiter. "Best have another one of these to fortify us for the next four years."

Department of the Missouri
Office of the Commanding General
Chicago, Illinois
December 1872

Custer admired his reflection in a windowpane, darkened by heavy gray clouds swirling with a fall of new snow. He curled the tips of his mustache and smoothed a lock of hair off the shoulder of his fringed buckskin jacket. He wondered what Phil had on his mind, a new assignment perhaps? He could only hope. It seemed only fair. He'd been restless ever since his victory on the Washita. His reward for that had been garrison duty at Fort Riley and a tedious administrative assignment at that. His campaign record should have counted for more than a desk job. He hated desk soldiering. He had his detractors, of course.

A tight-assed desk commander or two in the War Department envied his record. They'd been bent on ruining his career since that ridiculous dereliction of duty business. Fortunately, he'd had General Sheridan's confidence. He hoped this meeting would return him to command of his beloved Seventh. What other reason could Phil have for summoning him to his headquarters?

"The general will see you now, sir." The pasty faced orderly called him back from reflection.

Custer stalked across the reception in long angular strides. Gleaming knee-high riding boots struck a staccato tattoo at his passing.

Sheridan sat behind a massive polished desk in his spacious office. A portrait of President Grant hung above his credenza, flanked by the stars and stripes in a standard.

Custer came to attention in front of Sheridan, offering a casual salute, "Colonel Custer reporting for duty, sir."

"George," Sheridan looked up from the file he'd been reading. "Have a seat." Sheridan directed him to a pair of visitor chairs drawn up in front of his desk.

Custer took his seat. "When I heard you'd been given the Department of the Missouri I hoped you'd send for me, sir."

"Cump and I talked it over, George. We agreed you were the right man for the job I have in mind for you."

"Why thank you, sir." He preened at the compliment. "You know I'll do my best, whatever the job. Even better if you give me the chance to fight."

Sheridan closed the file, turning his attention to his guest. "The job is confining the hostiles to the reservations and keeping them there."

"Judging by what I read of the president's peace policy in the papers, I'd say any Indian in his right mind would run to the nearest reservation for the handout they're being given." He stretched his legs, crossing his boots at the ankle. The only thing regulation about the boots was the shine.

"General Sherman and I think it might take a bit more, shall we say, persuasion than that. The wild ones cling to the old ways. As long as they can feed themselves they'll follow the herds. Fortunately, the buffalo hunters are thinning the herds at a pretty good clip. That makes agency beef an important part of feeding the tribes. Trouble is the agency system is so corrupt the reservation Indians can't count on being properly fed. They stray off the reservation to hunt or steel beef from nearby ranchers. That's where you'll have to step in and bring them to heel."

"I'm sure you'll find the Seventh up to the task, sir."

Sheridan furrowed his brow at the comment. Custer's self-assurance could be maddening. It could also be counted a useful tool. He couldn't resist the temptation to goad his protégé to a predictable squirm. "Did I mention the Seventh?"

"Oh, ah, well, no sir. I guess I just assumed."

Sheridan chuckled. "Of course it's the Seventh, George. I just didn't want to let you get ahead of yourself again."

"What are my orders then, sir?" The old self-assurance recovered.

"You are to proceed to Fort Abraham Lincoln and report to General Terry. There you will assume command of the Seventh. You will assist General Terry in maintaining peace and order over the reservations in the area using such measures as may be reasonable."

A small smile creased a fine line beneath the whorls of Custer's mustache as he turned Sheridan's order over in his mind. *Such measures as may be reasonable.* It seemed too good to be true.

"You can count on me, sir." He stood, his salute crisper this time.

"I know I can, George. I know I can."

CHAPTER TWENTY-NINE

Fort Abraham Lincoln
Dakota Territory
February 1873

"Colonel Custer to see you, sir."

General Alfred Howe Terry looked up from the Quartermaster's report. "Give me a minute, Miles. I'll come and get him."

"Very well, sir."

The orderly closed the door quietly as Terry pushed back from the rough-hewn camp desk that served his small sparsely furnished office. He needed a moment to think. A swirl of fresh snow skipped across the sunny windswept parade ground outside the office window. He appreciated Custer's assignment to his command about as much as a toothache. At least you could have an aching tooth pulled. The hawks in the War Department favored an aggressive policy in dealing with the tribes. General Sheridan stood prominent among their number. He'd long been a Custer supporter. He was clearly responsible for the appointment. You couldn't justify appointing a man with Custer's record and reputation to a sensitive command if your purpose was to maintain the peace.

In Terry's estimation, the president's peace policy represented a reasonable attempt to right the wrongs done the plains tribes and preserve a lasting peace. Unfortunately, the president's policy routinely fell victim to corruption in the Bureau of Indian Affairs. War Department hawks disagreed with Grant's policy and passively resisted it. They overlooked abuses in the reservation system that served to destabilize the situation on the frontier. Hungry people do desperate things. Provocations gave the hawks cause for actions they were predisposed to take against the tribes. By some accounts, Custer's attack on Black Kettle's village was just such an action. Black Kettle was widely known to be a peace chief. Custer attacked his winter camp well within reservation lands. He reported the village hostile, owing to an allegation involving stolen cattle. Rumors arose not long after the newspapers' glowing initial accounts. Significant numbers of women and children were among those killed. The character of the rancher whose cattle were the subject of the complaint was called into question. Still more questions arose, following the murder of the Washita reservation agent. He died at the hand of a tomahawk wielding hostile. A subsequent audit of the agency confirmed criminal irregularities in the agent's administration. Custer had command of the post that housed the agency. He was never proven complicit, but you couldn't dismiss the suspicion. On a small post, he had to know. All of this called to question justification for the firebrand colonel's actions.

Sheridan was among the most outspoken of the War Department hawks. He had Sherman's ear and was the strongest voice in the general staff in support of Custer. The hawks might not want to openly defy the president's policy, but they had a perfect instrument for doing so in Custer.

Terry didn't appreciate having Custer sent back to the field on his watch. Given the slightest opportunity, Custer would overstep his orders and there would be hell to pay. Terry knew it and so did Sheridan. The fact that he'd been posted to Abe Lincoln was no bureaucratic coincidence. They'd tossed a calculated appointment with a lighted fuse in his lap. He'd need to be very clear about his orders to the volatile commandant of the Seventh. He rose with a sigh, very clear indeed.

He found Custer waiting in the tiny outer office.

"Colonel Custer?"

"General Terry, George Custer at your service, sir." The salute was crisp though somehow out of keeping with his nonregulation fringed buckskins. The uniform suited Custer's reputation for flamboyance.

"Miles, ask Major Brystol to join us." He wanted a witness for this meeting.

"Yes, sir." The orderly hurried out.

"Right this way, Colonel," Terry said showing Custer the door to his office. "May I offer you a cup of coffee?"

"Thank you, sir."

"Cream or sugar?"

"Black is fine."

Terry poured two cups and handed one to Custer. "How was your journey?"

"Uneventful, sir."

"Not easy traveling the Dakotas this time of year."

"Train travel takes you only so far it's true. The last legs of the journey are certainly demanding, but then we are soldiers, General. We are given to do things other men might shirk."

"Yes, yes, I suppose we are." Terry appraised the man, confident, no, cocky, utterly self-assured. The hair, the tunic, the boots, gave every bit the look of a self-absorbed, strutting peacock.

"You sent for me, sir?" Mitchell Brystol, West Point class of '63, was a bright young officer. He'd made his mark in the latter stages of the war and was posted to the Department of the Missouri with the cessation of hostilities. He moved up rapidly courtesy of the same postwar reduction in command structure that caused Custer the loss of his general's star.

"Yes, Mitch. Colonel Custer, meet my Adjutant Major Brystol. Mitch, Colonel Custer has just arrived to take command of the Seventh."

"Major Brystol, my pleasure." Custer's deference to the junior officer had the glossy veneer of form about it.

"It is a pleasure to meet you, sir. I've long admired your record."

Custer preened.

Brystol knew how to lay it on, Terry thought. "So, Phil's reunited you with the Seventh," Terry made the observation sound congratulatory.

"Yes, sir and may I say it will be an honor to fight under both of you."

Custer knows how to lay it on too. "Well, George, we hope we don't have to fight. The reservations are mostly peaceful now. The president's policy seems to be working. Our job is to keep it that way."

"I understand, sir. General Sheridan briefed me on the situation when he gave me my orders."

"I'm sure he did, Colonel, but for the record let me make myself clear. The reservations are peaceful. Your job is to keep it that way."

"Thank you, sir. Like I said, General Sheridan made my instructions perfectly clear."

"Good then. We understand one another."

"We do, sir," Custer said with a nod.

Terry doubted they did. Any understanding the colonel had would last as long as it took him to clear the gates on patrol. He'd made his position clear, with the benefit of a witness.

"Has Mrs. Custer accompanied you?"

"She plans to follow in spring, once the weather improves."

"Splendid, I think she will be most comfortable here. The officers' wives are good company."

Grasshoppers in Summer

Capitol East Portico
Washington, D.C.
March 4, 1873

Ely Parker stamped his feet, fighting for circulation against numbing cold stone steps. Icy wind added to the discomfort of the modest crowd hardy enough to attend. A gray curtain of steam rose from the muffled heads of the dignitaries seated in rows behind the rostrum. Below the capitol portico, a sharp north wind turned the steaming breath of the onlookers to thin wisps that disappeared in chill gusts.

Chief Justice Salmon Chase managed to preserve some semblance of decorum summoned by the Oath of Office in spite of the wind whipping his black robes and beard. Julia Grant shivered noticeably as she held the Bible on which the president placed his left hand. He raised his right.

"I, Ulysses Simpson Grant," Chase projected as much voice as he could muster against the wind.

"I, Ulysses Simpson Grant . . ."

"Do solemnly swear . . ."

Parker lost the familiar words of the oath in the bitter howl. In spite of his discomfort, he took personal satisfaction from this historic occasion. This president and his enlightened policies represented the Indian's best chance for peaceful coexistence with the nation's westward expansion. Much had been accomplished in the past four years. Much remained to be done.

The president's political adversaries mounted a vicious campaign to block his reelection. The eastern intellectual elite rallied behind the newspaper man Horace Greeley. They attacked the president for patronage practices that had become institutionalized by decades of political appointments. They ignored Grant's reform policies, endeavoring instead to make him responsible for corrupt practices of the past. Thankfully, those accusations did not sway the American people. People voted the president's record, sweeping their hero back into office with nearly sixty percent of the popular vote.

His swearing-in complete, the president took his place at the speaker's rostrum to deliver his second inaugural address.

"Fellow Citizens,"

The crowd stood motionless as though frozen, were it not for flapping cloaks, billowing bonnets, and streamers of breath.

"Under Providence I have been called a second time to act as Executive over this great nation."

Parker strained to hear. The president's words cut the icy wind punctuated by wisps of steam. Many of the themes were familiar: the continuing challenges of reconstruction, assuring the rights of freedmen in the south, and, more recently, assuring stability of the currency. It would gall the papers who opposed him to report his remarks, though faithfully report them they would. The First Amendment right of a free press bore a responsibility to honor the difference between reporting the news and editorial opinion. The nation could rely on its newspapers to report the truth. That confidence accounted the respect with which people held their journalists. That respect helped frame public opinion, though it had failed to harden political opposition to the president.

He waited to hear the continuing outlines of the president's Indian policy. Here as much as anywhere, more work was needed to secure just treatment of the tribes. The bureau and the reservation system remained an intransigent and vexing problem. They'd made grudging progress in rooting out pockets of corruption. The president's religious friends could be credited with mixed results. They claimed success by white measures such as education and religious conversion, though in some cases their coercive measures struck him as high-handed and harsh. Efforts to protect the buffalo herds bogged down, mired in political stalemate and frustration. Much indeed was left unfinished.

"Our superiority of strength and advantages of civilization should make us lenient toward the Indian."

Parker picked up his attention.

"The wrong inflicted upon him should be taken into account and the balance placed in his credit. The moral view of the question should be considered and the question asked, 'Cannot the Indian be made a useful and productive member of society by proper teaching and treatment?' If the effort is made in good faith, we will stand better before the civilized nations of the earth and in our own consciences for having made it."

The president stood fast by his commitment. The challenge, Parker knew, would come in defining the meaning of words like *useful, productive,* and *society.* The president framed these concepts in white terms. Indian culture does not see these things as white men see them. His job would be to help the president and others to see things as the Indian saw them. To him would fall responsibility to shape the president's policy in ways respectful of Indian culture. It would not be easy. Nonetheless the responsibility was vital, a mantle he must shoulder. Reconciling cultural differences was all that stood between peace and bloodshed. It presented a solemn duty he would not shirk.

White House
Washington, D.C.
September 1873

Grant laid the report on his desk and picked up the cigar gone cold in the ashtray. He fumbled in his vest pocket for a match. The report raised disturbing questions. The match flared in the gathering afternoon shadows. He puffed a great cloud of blue smoke. The Bureau of Indian Affairs and the reservation system stubbornly resisted their efforts at reform. Corruption had deeply entrenched itself in the bureau. You could smell it. As Red Cloud recounted the grievances against his people, corruption became real human tragedy. They'd made comparatively little meaningful progress in spite of the declared goals of his policy. The agencies resisted every step of the way. *Bad for business,* he thought, grinding the cigar in his teeth.

The report's allegations of corruption included the Washita River Agency. It also called to question official accounts of the provocation used to justify the attack on Black Kettle's Village in '68. He recalled questioning it himself at the time. Those questions seemed well placed. The stolen cattle used to justify the action were in dispute. Black Kettle reported his agency beef had been stolen. He identified the rancher who reported the stolen cattle as the culprit. He asked the Army to return them. Custer took no action. Indian survivors of the Washita fight admitted warriors from the village took the cattle. The report concluded the cattle taken by warriors from Black Kettle's village, in fact belonged to the Indians. The Indians engaged in recovering their own stolen livestock, or recovering it in kind, because the Army took no action. Much of the rest of the account was hearsay and accusation. Some evidence suggested that the Washita agent conspired with the rancher to steal the agency cattle and sell them back to the government as replacements. That had never been proven. It seemed the issue came down to a matter of the white rancher's word against Black Kettle's. In the end the white man's word was enough for a lot of people to die.

The action on the Washita helped Custer resurrect his career. He knew the stolen cattle were in dispute based on Black Kettle's complaint. Could his failure to act on the chief's complaint have been deliberate? Did he know the Washita agent might be corrupt? It would be hard to keep such a thing secret on a small post. The evidence might be circumstantial, but where there was so much smoke you could bet something was burning somewhere.

"Horace," Grant called.

The appointments secretary stuck his head in the doorway, "Sir?"

"Get me a meeting with Senator Carswell, I have a matter I'd like his Select Committee on Indian Affairs to look into."

Odd bedfellows. Horace thought, a Southern Democrat and a Republican president.

Chapter Thirty

War Department
Office of the General in Chief
Washington, D.C.
February 1874

"General Sherman will see you, General." The orderly stepped aside, holding the office door.

Sheridan acknowledged the orderly with a nod as he passed.

Sherman rose to greet his friend. "Phil, good to see you." He extended his hand, dispensing with the formality of a salute.

"Good to see you too, Cump." Sheridan smiled.

"Have a seat," Sherman gestured to a pair of wing chairs and a settee upholstered in regulation Army blue at the side of the office. "Care for a cup of coffee?"

"Yes, thank you."

The orderly disappeared to pour coffee.

"What's on your mind, Phil?" Sherman wasted little time on social amenities. Sheridan asked to see him for a reason.

"I've got an idea, Cump, one that might give us final resolution of the Indian problem."

"Good, let's hear it."

The orderly returned with two steaming cups of coffee. He served them on the low table in front of the settee and withdrew.

Sherman took a sip of his coffee and fixed his attention on Sheridan.

"As you know the Indian problem is a work in progress. Red

Cloud and the peace chiefs have taken their people to the reservations, but we still have to contend with Sitting Bull, Crazy Horse, and the other bands who resist complying with their treaty obligations. They hang onto the old ways, following what's left of the buffalo herd and other wild game. We both know it will take force to drive the hostiles onto the reservations. For the moment, that is in direct conflict with Sam's infernal peace policy."

Sherman nodded. "Sam refuses to see that you simply can't negotiate with the likes of Sitting Bull and Crazy Horse. They remain hostile and Sam's got our hands tied."

"I think I may have a way to untie them."

Sherman eyes creased at the corners, his interest piqued. "I'm listening."

"For the past year we've been hearing rumors of a gold discovery in the Black Hills. Trouble is, it's only rumor. Miners prefer to keep their discoveries to themselves for obvious reasons. Still the rumors are rampant and persistent."

"So, you believe them to be true?"

"Most likely, though I'm not even sure that matters."

Sherman scratched his chin. "If there is gold in the Black Hills, those hills aren't the worthless throwaway we wrote into the Laramie Treaty."

"Exactly. I propose we mount an expedition to verify the rumors."

"The Black Hills are off limits, Phil, you know that. They belong to the Sioux. Sam and the secretary will never sit still for us violating that treaty."

"We won't violate it."

"I don't understand, Phil. Where the hell are you going with this?"

"The rumors attract prospectors to the area in violation of the treaty. I propose we send a survey party into the Black Hills to site a new fort. The mission of the fort will be to protect the reservation from the growing problem of white trespassers. If the survey party happens to confirm the discovery of gold what's to be done about it?"

"If word gets out, and it surely will, we'll have a gold rush on our hands."

"We couldn't keep the miners out of reservation lands with a hundred thousand troops. The Sioux think those hills are sacred. The hostiles will fight to protect them. The miners will be U.S. citizens. Sooner or later, the Army will be sent in to protect them. The public will demand it. The treaty will be broken and our hands will be untied."

Sherman sat back. The plan was bold yet simple, brilliant really. It surely could work. "Phil, I think you're on to something here. If we do this, it needs to stay between us and whoever leads the survey party. That will be a sensitive assignment. We need somebody we can trust. Have you got anyone in mind?"

Sheridan clasped his hands across his belly. "Custer."

Sherman pursed his lips thoughtfully and nodded. "I'll have to convince the secretary and likely the president that a new fort is needed. Under the circumstances that shouldn't be too difficult as long as we make sure the tribes know the survey party comes in peace. That'll be up to Al Terry."

"Abe Lincoln is due for a post inspection. I'll do it myself. I'll give Terry his orders and then have a private conversation with George."

Sherman nodded again. "All right, Phil, get to it."

Fort Abraham Lincoln
Dakota Territory
April 1874

Terry stood on the rough-cut plank porch fronting his office. He squinted into the afternoon sun. A chill spring breeze ruffled

Grasshoppers in Summer

the graying whiskers at his chin. He clasped his hands behind his back in his habitual parade-ground rest position. The inspection party accompanied by a small escort rode through the gates. Fort Abraham Lincoln was the most important post on the northern plains with a standing garrison of some twelve hundred men. The stockade surrounded a large parade ground, corrals, stable, barracks, commissary, and offices for the post commander and provost marshal, along with a handful of neat whitewashed clapboard homes to quarter the officers.

Terry considered the post inspection a formality really. He ran a tight ship. Abe Lincoln would rate a top fitness report. Curious that General Sheridan would come all the way out here to do the inspection himself. He could easily have assigned another field grade officer to make the trip. Terry couldn't help wondering if the general had something more on his mind.

Once inside the gates, Sheridan signaled a halt. He gave instructions to the lieutenant in command of his escort. The lieutenant ordered his men to dismount. They led their horses to the paddock while Sheridan and his aide trotted across the parade ground toward Terry. One of the Army's most senior officers, he was still a cavalry man at heart, Terry observed. He might ride a desk most of the time but he still sat a horse like he could lead a column. Sheridan drew rein in front of the office.

"Welcome to Fort Abraham Lincoln, sir." Terry saluted.

Sheridan returned the salute with a nod and stepped down. He brushed trail dust off his blouse and britches as Terry's orderly stepped forward to take his horse. He clumped up the steps to join Terry. The two men shook hands. "Good to see you, Alfred," Sheridan smiled.

"It's good to see you too, Phil."

"May I present my aide, Major Cartwright."

"Major," Terry nodded. "Miles, show the major to the officers' quarters and have someone see to their horses. Come on in, Phil, care for a cup of coffee?"

"It's been a long ride up from Cheyenne, Alfred. If you've got any whiskey, I believe I'd have a drink."

"I think that can be arranged." Terry showed Sheridan into his sparsely appointed office.

Sheridan drew a camp chair up beside Terry's desk and lowered himself heavily with a sigh. "A couple days in the saddle is enough to remind a man why the Army has him sitting behind a desk at this stage in his career."

Terry produced a whiskey bottle from the cabinet behind his desk and poured two generous glasses. He handed one to Sheridan and dropped into a chair across from him. They lifted their glasses and took a swallow. "So, what brings you all the way out here, Phil? It can't be a post inspection."

"No, not entirely." Sheridan set his glass on the desk. "Cump and I have been concerned for some time now about the rumors of a gold discovery in the Black Hills. The presence of even a few miners is a clear treaty violation. If the rumors prove true, we could have a gold rush on our hands. If that happens, the non-treaty hostiles will fight."

"It is a legitimate concern."

"The president agrees. We need to take steps to protect the tribe's treaty rights and head off the prospect of a gold rush before the situation gets out of control. If we don't there will be no way to turn back the tide. We've got a job for Custer and the Seventh. Major Cartwright has the orders. Basically, we want George to site a new fort in the Black Hills. We need you to tell Red Cloud and the other reservation chiefs we are doing it to protect their land."

Terry nodded thoughtfully. It made sense. He knew how important the Black Hills were to the Sioux from his experience at the Fort Laramie negotiating table. If gold prospectors rushed the Black Hills the wild bands under Sitting Bull and Crazy Horse would surely fight. Terry supported the president's Indian policy. He understood the importance of protecting Indian treaty rights. The Black Hills were a cornerstone of the Fort Laramie Treaty. That treaty had held for six years now, and while a few remaining wild bands refused to go to the reservation, they weren't on the warpath either.

"That makes sense, Phil. I've been worried about those rumors myself. Getting the message to Red Cloud and the other reservation chiefs is easy. The tougher question is what do we do about Sitting Bull, Crazy Horse, and the other non-reservation bands? They're the ones most likely to take offense at the presence of a new fort."

"I told Cump you'd have an answer to that problem." Sheridan smiled, taking a swallow of his drink.

"You flatter me, Phil. Getting word to those bands is like tracking smoke in the wind. The only thing tougher than finding them is getting them to believe what you've got to say."

"So what do you suggest?"

"We can ask Red Cloud to help. I don't know if that will work, but it's got a better chance than anything else I can think of."

"All we can ask is that you try, Alfred."

Terry nodded. "How long will you be staying with us?"

"Just long enough to do the post inspection. The way you run your station, Alfred, I shouldn't think it would take more than a few days." Sheridan drained his glass. "Now, if you don't mind, I'd like to get cleaned up before evening mess."

"Let me show you to the general officers' quarters, Phil. It's just down the street."

"Thank you, Alfred." Sheridan rose from his seat. "Is Custer on post?"

"He is, or soon will be. He took four companies out on maneuvers this morning. I expect them back anytime now."

Walking back to his office from the general officers' quarters, Terry turned Sheridan's presence over in his mind. On its face, the concern about the Black Hills made sense. What didn't was the fact that the concern was being expressed by known hawks like Sherman and Sheridan. The president, he could understand. Another thing troubled him. Why had Sheridan seen fit to come all the way out here to deliver his orders personally? He could have done that with a telegram. It also raised the question as to why Sherman and Sheridan selected Custer to lead the expedition. Assignment responsibility would typically have been his as post commander. He might as easily have chosen him, but why take the decision out of his hands? Custer was a Sheridan favorite. Phil promoted his career going back to the war. At some level it made sense, though there wasn't much career glitter in leading a survey party. *Still,* Terry scratched his head. *Why come all this way to deliver the orders in person?*

A knock at the door announced his visitor. Sheridan looked up from the post supply inventory report spread on the small desk in the general officers' quarters. "Come in."

"Colonel Custer reporting as ordered, sir."

Sheridan absently returned Custer's salute, noting his buckskin jacket and boots with a sidelong glance. He extended his hand. "George, it's good to see you. How have you been?"

"I'm as well as can be expected for a warrior assigned to a peaceful post. I was pleased and a little surprised when I heard you were coming out to do the post inspection. Is anything wrong?"

"No, no just some things I needed to do personally. Sit down, George."

Custer took a chair across from the desk.

Sheridan set aside the report he'd been reading. "It's been a while, George. How's that lovely wife of yours?"

"Libbie's just fine, Phil. Thank you for asking. I'm sure she will want to have you over for supper while you are here. She is always pleased to see you."

"I'll look forward to that. She's a wonderful woman. You're a very fortunate man, George. I'm surprised she puts up with you." They chuckled. The general sat back and folded his hands across his paunch. "George, I wanted to talk to you privately about an assignment we have for you. General Terry has orders for you to organize a survey party for the purpose of locating a new fort in the Black Hills."

"I thought the Black Hills were off limits."

"They are, but you can't tell that to gold prospectors."

"I've heard the rumors." He smoothed his mustache between thumb and forefinger.

"Cump convinced the president we need a fort out there to protect the territory from illegal prospecting. The orders General Terry has for you direct you to lead that effort."

"You can count on me, Phil."

"Not so fast, George, there's more." Sheridan shifted in his chair, changing his demeanor from routine assignment to something more. "George, we both know it's going to take force of arms to move the hostiles onto the reservation and keep them there. Sam's fool Indian policy stands in the way of the final resolution we both know is necessary. He's got our hands tied."

Custer nodded. "I agree, but there doesn't seem to be much we can do about that."

"Actually, there is something we can do. That's the second part of your mission George, the part only you, Cump, and me are to know about."

Custer liked the sound of this already. They were making him an insider on an action at the highest levels of command. Whatever they had in mind might yet win him his general's star. "I'm listening, Phil."

"You're going to site a fort all right, but in the bargain you are going to confirm the discovery of gold. Take some of your newspaper friends with you. Prospectors don't announce what they find. All you get is rumor. Newspaper people will trumpet it from the mountaintops. It's sure to trigger a gold rush. The hostiles will fight to protect the Black Hills. In the end, the Army will be called in to protect the miners."

"And that will be the end of the president's peace policy." Custer's mustache lifted in a knowing smile. There'd be a fight for sure and he and the Seventh would be right in the middle of it. He could almost see the general's star on his epaulet.

"You can count on me, General."

"We know, George. We know."

Chapter Thirty-One

Red Cloud Agency
North Platte River
Wyoming Territory
May 1874

The black preacher Bradburn and an unknown pony soldier stepped out of the darkness into the circle of firelight. Red Cloud and the elders sat in council.

"Red Cloud, may I present Major Mitchell Brystol."

Red Cloud nodded to the pony soldier. The two white men sat across the fire from Red Cloud. The deep etched features of the Oglala chief became a mask of light and shadow in flickering firelight. He regarded the officious black preacher with suspicion. His words were filled with the will of the wasichu god. This god did not speak to the heart of the people. The black preacher did not hear Wakan Tanka. The people found little to believe in his words. What god would entrust his words to such a man?

Bradburn flicked his eyes around the circle of elders, giving him the appearance of a wary serpent. "Major Brystol is from Fort Abraham Lincoln. He has a message for Red Cloud and his people from General Terry."

Red Cloud turned to the pony soldier. He had light hair in the white way, touched by red in his drooping mustache. He sat with his boots crossed in front of him, his blue coat dusted from the trail.

"I bring Red Cloud and the Oglala people greetings from General Terry."

Red Cloud nodded. Terry was known to him for his part in making the Fort Laramie Treaty. He had proven to be a man of his word. He would choose a messenger to speak his words wisely. Red Cloud would listen to the young man with open ears.

"General Terry and President Grant are concerned that white men have entered the Black Hills illegally in search of gold. This violates our treaty with the Lakota."

Red Cloud nodded. "We have heard of these white men. Our brothers who live the old ways have fought with some of them. If more come, there will be more fighting."

"The president has asked General Terry to stop these men. General Terry wishes to send Army surveyors to the Black Hills this summer. They will come in peace to find a place for a new fort to protect Lakota lands."

Red Cloud scowled. "Bluecoats made forts in the Powder River country to protect whites crossing the Bozeman Trail."

Brystol understood the point. Red Cloud led his people to war against those forts. "That was before the Fort Laramie Treaty." Brystol held the chief's eyes. "The treaty put an end to fighting between our people. It is better for the Army to stop our people from violating the treaty than for the Lakota to fight them."

Red Cloud considered Brystol's words. He did not like the idea of a fort in the sacred lands of the Paha Sapa. He also knew what happened when white men found yellow stones. They came in great numbers and that would bring war. If the wasichu built a fort to keep their people from searching for yellow stones, it might prevent a new war. "If my people agree to this, where will you build this fort?"

"That is what the survey party will be sent to find out."

Red Cloud sat in silence for a long moment. The snap and crackle of the fire sent showers of sparks to the night sky. He offered them to Wakan Tanka as a prayer for wisdom. "The Paha Sapa are sacred to the Lakota. If my people allow this survey, we must agree to the building of this fort."

Brystol smoothed his mustache and rubbed his chin. Red Cloud was asking for the right to approve the site. This was not something he'd been authorized to offer. Then again, he needed something more from Red Cloud. Granting Red Cloud's request might exceed his authority, but he knew his boss. All things considered, General Terry would always agree to talk. "We will speak with the Lakota about the location of the fort, if Red Cloud will help with the survey."

Red Cloud tilted his chin, puzzled at what he might do to help such a thing.

"We ask Red Cloud to send word of this survey to Sitting Bull and Crazy Horse. Tell them the survey party comes in peace."

Red Cloud pursed his lips. "This I can do. I cannot say my brothers will hear these words in their hearts."

"We only ask that you try."

Red Cloud nodded.

Brystol stood. Bradburn led the way as they disappeared into the night beyond the circle of firelight.

"Mahpiya-luta," Thunder Man spoke at Red Cloud's side. "I do not trust the wasichu."

Red Cloud raised an eye to his brother. "General Terry has spoken true words before. We hear him now." Thunder Man was not the one to take word to Sitting Bull and Crazy Horse. He turned to Iron Crane.

"Mazahzahgeh, find the camps of Tatanka Iyotanka and Tashunca-uitco. Tell them the wasichu survey comes in peace. Tell them they come to keep the wasichu who search for yellow stones away from the Paha Sapa."

Iron Crane nodded.

Red Cloud could do no more.

Fort Abraham Lincoln
Dakota Territory

It took two months to assemble the survey party. A thousand troops mustered under Custer's command to escort two hundred scientists, surveyors, and engineers. Consistent with Sheridan's private instructions and Custer's personal habit, three newspaper reporters joined the civilian party. Sixty Arikara scouts led the expedition. The survey party departed Fort Abraham Lincoln in early June to the rousing bars of the Seventh's regimental song, "Garry Owen."

Custer rode at the head of the column with Major Marcus Reno, his second in command, and his Adjutant Lieutenant W.W. Cooke. With over one hundred wagons the column of twos stretched nearly two miles. The reporters trailed behind Custer in position to record every move made by the nation's most celebrated Indian fighter.

Day by day the column wound its way through vast dun-green grasslands and rolling hills. Jagged buttes and spires of red, black, and brown rock stood sentinel over the sun-soaked prairie. Here and there clumps of gray-green sage, pale blue chicory, and patches of yellow mustard dotted the waving grasses. Spiny rock ridges fringed lush valleys, their ancient sand-colored faces layered by the centuries, cut by the wind and punctuated in rockfalls. A sea of grassy waves flowed over the valley floors, spilling into creek beds splashed green and silver by pine, scrub oak, and Russian olive trees lining their banks. Deep gullies, ravines, and dry washes gashed and veined hills rising to pine blanketed peaks. Each day the scouts rode out from the column, probing the ragged line of black hills growing along the south and western horizon.

Spotted Hawk lay in the shadows of a high rocky butte watching the long bluecoat line with their white covered wagons invade the Paha Sapa. He watched with grim expectation. The eagle feathers in his braids twisted in the breeze. The bluecoats and their wagons stretched as far as the eye could see. Red Cloud said they came in peace. Why were so many pony soldiers needed for peace? White men never brought peace to his people. They came to take Indian lands and drive his people to ever smaller reservations. These sacred lands were given the people by the last white man's treaty. Why did pony soldiers come to the Paha Sapa? The spirits of the land cried out in warning. Spotted Hawk heard them. His heart filled with anger and fear for his people. No good would come of this.

The long knife Custer led them. Spotted Hawk's blood boiled with hatred for the man who murdered his people and took his wife. He remembered the loss he suffered that bloody day on the Washita. He nearly lost his life. Part of his heart died with the loss of Autumn Snow. She never spoke of the long knife, or the evil he did her. She need not. Spotted Hawk knew it in his heart. One day he would kill the pony soldier chief. One day when these pony soldiers who came in peace came to steal the Paha Sapa.

Custer made base camp in a sheltered valley in the heart of the Black Hills. The confluence of two small streams provided ample water for the large party. Campfires dotted the valley floor as evening settled. Troopers pitched Custer's tent in the center of the camp. Six places were set at two camp tables for the colonel to entertain guests at a dinner prepared by his personal cook.

They gathered around the lantern-lit table in the early

evening gloom. Custer sat at the head of the table, holding court for his guests: three journalists, the chief surveyor, and Major Reno. The cook served steaming plates of roast beef, biscuits, and beans. Custer passed a bottle of whiskey around the table to flavor steaming cups of coffee.

The senior journalist, a balding heavyset man from Omaha named Bixby, cocked his head toward Custer, a forkful of roast beef halfway to his mouth. His smudged spectacles made him appear a blind owl in the reflected lantern light.

"Tell me, Colonel, you've heard the rumors of a gold discovery in the Black Hills. Do you think they could be true?"

Custer stroked the patch of whiskers at his chin, considering his answer. Never at a loss to assert self-importance, he seized the opportunity posed by the question.

"For the present, rumors of gold in these hills are just rumors. It is the Army's duty to protect these lands and honor our treaty commitments to the best of our ability. A fort will give us a sustainable base of operations and the best opportunity to carry out that mission. My orders come from Generals Sherman and Sheridan with the concurrence of the president. In that, our purpose here is of the highest national import." Custer turned to the senior surveyor, a man named Billings.

"Mr. Billings, a man in your position must have some basis to judge. What do you think about the prospect for gold in these hills?"

"I'm afraid I have no special insight into that, Colonel. If I did, I'd be out there in a stream somewhere with a pan instead of taking instrument sightings on these interminable rocks."

"I've no gift for such things myself," Custer admitted around a mouthful of roast beef. "But I do know one thing." He stabbed the air with his fork for emphasis. "The rumors have gone on for some time now. If there is nothing to them, why do they not simply die out? I think, gentlemen, where there is that much smoke, somewhere there is a fire."

"But, Colonel, you must understand the Black Hills are the centerpiece of the Fort Laramie Treaty." Bixby pressed his spectacles to the bridge of his shiny nose. "If the rumors of a gold discovery prove true, does the Army seriously believe the presence of a new fort will hold back a gold rush?"

"A perceptive observation, Mr. Bixby." Flattery curried favor. "If gold were discovered here, the way of progress might no longer indulge us in the luxury of our treaty commitment. Ultimately, history will judge the right of that. For now, I think it fair to say, you may see history made by this expedition."

All three journalists scratched at notepads beside their plates.

Dinner finished with more coffee, whiskey, and cigars. "Well, gentlemen," Custer said. "Tomorrow we ride southwest to inspect a site the scouts have been telling me about. I expect you'll all want to get a good night's sleep."

They rose from the tables amid a mumble of thank-yous and good evenings. Custer stalked off to his tent as the others drifted off to the dim shadows of the darkened camp.

Early the following morning Curly led Custer, the survey team, and a company of sixty men deeper into the hills southwest of base camp. The column wound its way through a rugged maze of gorges and buttes. Early summer sun beat on the rocky terrain radiating intensity to the heat. At midday the Crow scout drew rein near the mouth of a narrow canyon. A fast running creek wound its way down the canyon floor.

"Hidden Wood Creek," Curly said pointing to the glittering stream.

Custer nodded and stood in his stirrups to have a look around. He squinted through bright sunlight at the dead trees lining the canyon walls overhead.

"Hidden creek, looks more like deadwood."

Captain Benteen, commander of the escort company, grunted agreement laced with contempt. *The man loved nothing better than the sound of his own opinion.* Custer settled back in his saddle. Sullen and belligerent most of the time, Benteen owed his sour disposition in part to habitual hangover. Privately he was among those in Custer's command who regarded the colonel a reckless, pompous ass. The colonel drove his men hard in a constant quest for personal glory. *What military unit took newspaper reporters into the field? Custer's Lord a'mighty Seventh,* Benteen finished his own thought. Newspaper accounts of his deeds fed his ego and his reputation.

"We'll take our midday meal here and have a look around, Captain."

Benteen offered a half-hearted wave at a salute, then wheeled his horse and rode off to see to his men.

"Sergeant Major Kane, have someone brew us a pot of coffee if you would," Custer said as he dismounted. He led the way to a shady spot under a rocky outcropping. Lieutenant Cooke, the surveyor Billings, and the newspaper man Bixby followed along. Custer dropped into the shade and took off his hat. He wiped sweat from his forehead where his hatband plastered his hair.

Billings appraised the rugged landscape with a dubious shake of his head.

"Are you sure about this area, Colonel? We haven't seen enough flat land in one place for a fort all morning."

"Don't need a fort here." Custer replaced his hat. "We need one nearby."

Billings looked a trifle annoyed. "If we're not lookin' to site a fort here, then why'd we ride all the way up here in this infernal heat?"

Custer's eyes narrowed under the shadow of his hat brim, unaccustomed to being questioned. He arched a brow as if to enlighten the dull-witted.

"This is where our scouts tell us they've seen prospectors."

"Coffee, sir?" Sergeant Major Kane approached with a fresh brewed pot and a stack of tin cups.

"Yes, thank you, Sergeant." Custer took a cup for Kane to pour.

Billings stood, properly chastened. "In that case, I believe I'll wander down to the creek and have a look around."

He ambled off in the rising shimmers of glaring heat. The rocky canyon floor tumbled down to the creek. The stream ran clear and cool, gurgling over the rocky bed. He climbed upstream along the bank, his boots crunching loose stones. Sunlight played over the rippled surface of running water. He fixed his gaze on the bottom, intent on the bed beyond the glare. Here and there a large stone raised a swirl in the shallow flow, the echo of a white-water rapid left from the spring runoff. Something caught sunlight in a small eddy. Billings bent to his knee and picked at the creek bottom in the shallows. The water felt cool against the heat. He turned over a bright stone lodged among the gravel at the creek bottom. He picked the stone free and turned it over in the palm of his hand. Sunlight caught a wet gleam beneath the sandy silt. A shiver of excitement ran up his spine. He looked deeper into the eddy. There were more, two, three, no four. He picked them one by one, rinsing away sand and mud in the current. His eyes bulged as the realization deepened.

"Gold! Gold!"

He ran up the bank from the stream. He held his fist in the air clutching the yellow stones. The main body of the survey party and soldiers roused themselves from their lunch break and gathered to meet the surveyor. He held out his find in triumph. Bixby jumped up and waddled off toward a knot of men gathered around the discovery as fast as his stubby legs would carry his girth. Other men only needed to hear the word.

They rushed down the hill to the stream.

Custer let the import of the discovery sink in. Now they would come to these hills. There would be no holding back the flood of fortune seekers. The foolish Fort Laramie Treaty could not hold them back. Nothing would keep them away. These Black Hills would be taken for gold. Hills the Lakota held sacred. For this they would fight. Custer looked off to the northwest toward the horizon where the non-reservation tribes roamed the Powder River country. A slow smile creased his eyes at the corners.

"It's true, Colonel, the rumors are true after all." The portly journalist wiped perspiration from his bald pate as he huffed back to where Custer stood. "There's gold in these hills. They've found gold!"

"Indeed, Mr. Bixby. Soon these hills shall become freedom's trail. You may quote me on that."

Freedom's trial, you may quote me. Benteen shook his head. Colonel Iron Butt's road to personal glory would be closer to the truth. *You may quote me on that.*

Chapter Thirty-Two

*Office of the Commanding General
Department of the Missouri
Chicago, Illinois
July 1874*

Gold in the Black Hills!

Headlines screamed the news from New York to San Francisco at the speed of the telegraph wire. They proclaimed it *"American El Dorado."* Sheridan put down the paper. He rose from his desk, clasped his hands behind his back, and strode to the window. He stared out at a dull gray sky. Rain spattered the cobbles in the street below. Fat droplets traced brown streaks in the dusty film on the other side of the glass. *The die is cast.* Sam's Indian policy may be well intentioned, fit for some misplaced piece of moral high ground. It no longer mattered. Nothing could reverse the forces now set in motion. Gold brought wealth. Greed drove men to seek it wherever it was found. No Indian treaty ever stopped gold seekers before. This one would be no exception. The miners would come. Their numbers would grow. Nothing could stand against the tide. The hostiles would take to the warpath. Some of the reservation tribes might join them. America would demand protection for her citizens. The Army would be called to final resolution of the

Indian problem. It could end no other way. It was no more now than a matter of time.

White House
Washington, D.C.
"Commissioner Parker to see you, Mr. President."

Grant glanced up from the newspaper. Horace Porter waited patiently beyond a curtain of cigar smoke. Yes, of course, Ely would ask to see him. He clenched his jaw, uncertain what to say. Then again, Parker had a way of finding practical answers to thorny problems. His Buffalo Bill came to mind. They'd lost that battle to partisan politics. Damn shame really, it offered a common-sense approach to a vexing problem. Well they had another vexing problem on their hands for sure. It was vexing all right, along with a healthy dose of guilt. He'd been talked into a bad move with the Custer Expedition. He should have seen this coming. Custer, the man had a penchant for bad ends. Porter cleared his throat.

"Ah yes, send him in, Horace."

The aide stepped aside. Parker burst past him, a newspaper clenched in his fist. He crossed the office on long fluid strides.

"I assume you've seen the news, sir."

Grant nodded. "Have a seat, Ely."

He sat heavily in an upholstered side chair. "I was afraid of something like this. The whole idea of sending the Army on such an errand never sat right with me. I can't think of a worse result."

"On the merits, Cump made a sound argument. The intent was to protect the tribes' rights. I must say, I didn't expect this."

"I should have seen it. I should have raised a stronger objection."

The president relit his cigar. "It's not your fault, Ely. I made the decision. I'd likely have overruled you if you had objected more strenuously. The question now is, what's to be done about it?"

Parker closed his eyes and shook his head. "I wish I knew. We can remind the public the Black Hills are protected Indian land. You can order General Sherman to deploy troops to protect the reservation."

"We can do those things and we will. Still, gold fever is a powerful thing. It's big country out there. I can put myself back in Cump's chair and appreciate the difficulty of protecting it from here."

"We've made so much progress, Sam. Not enough by some measures, but a good deal by others. For all its faults, the Fort Laramie Treaty has kept the peace. We must find a way to preserve the peace."

"I don't have the answer, Ely. Give it some thought. You have a knack for tough problems."

"I appreciate your confidence, Mr. President. I wish I felt up to it."

Dakota Territory
October 1874

"They come from the four winds." The Oglala war chief Tashunca-uitco spoke. His words rose in steam on the chill night air. Crazy Horse spat into the crackling fire, sending a sizzling shower of sparks into the blanket of stars in the black autumn sky.

Tatanka Iyotanka, the Hunkpapa Chief Sitting Bull, nodded angrily. "Yellow stones make the Paha Sapa a thieves' road."

"The yellow hair long knife is chief of thieves." Crazy Horse's eyes blazed with anger.

Spotted Hawk sat with the young warriors beyond the circle of firelight, listening to the chiefs at council. A courageous war chief, Crazy Horse inspired the young warriors. They saw him for a leader committed to preserving the old ways. His farseeing black eyes radiated deep kinship with his people.

Sitting Bull counted his first coup at fourteen summers. A courageous warrior, he became leader of the Strong Heart warrior society. Now as a medicine man, the people revered him for his wisdom and spiritual leadership. Short and stocky he had a round face, a broad nose, and a resolute set to his jaw. His wide-set eyes burned with determination. A fire of rage smoldered in his heart at the treatment of his people. An endless succession of broken promises and wasichu lies cheated his people of their land and life.

"We must drive the white devils from our sacred land," Crazy Horse said.

Spotted Hawk's heart burned with his words. He and the rest of the young warriors believed these two would lead them to victory over the whites.

Sitting Bull passed the pipe to Crazy Horse. "Come, my brother, let us take our people to the Powder River country for the winter. There our medicine will grow strong. When we return in the spring, we will kill our enemies."

A shrill chorus of war cries rose in a great cloud of moonlit steam from the young warriors in the darkness beyond firelight.

CHAPTER THIRTY-THREE

Capitol Offices
Washington, D.C.
November 1874

A soft knock at the door roused Carswell from his reading.

"Come in," he glanced up as the door opened. "Ah, Mason, come in, come in. Have a seat." Carswell gestured to wing chairs drawn up beside the desk in his spacious office. He closed the folder he'd been reading and turned his attention to his guest.

Mason Pierce served as general counsel to the Senate Select Committee for Indian Affairs. A bright young attorney from a fine old Georgia family, he had an intense work ethic. He headed the committee's investigation of the Bureau of Indian Affairs. Recently he'd been working on the circumstances surrounding the Washita River Agency.

"So, how's the investigation progressing, Mason?"

"The evidence appears to confirm many of our suspicions. As you may recall the action taken against Black Kettle's village was initiated to recover cattle allegedly stolen from one Luther Hatch. Indian survivors of the battle maintain that the cattle were actually agency beef reported stolen by Black Kettle. They say the warriors took only what belonged to the tribe when the Army took no action to recover the cattle. Unsubstantiated allegations charge that Hatch conspired with the Washita agent," Pierce paused to check his notes. "One Roscoe Denton; they planned to sell the cattle back to the agency as replacements for the cattle Black Kettle reported stolen."

"Yes, yes, Mason, I'm well acquainted with all of that." Carswell drummed his fingers on the desk impatiently. "What's the point?"

"I think you'll find Mr. Denton an interesting character, Senator. It seems he specialized in getting what he wanted at other people's expense. Prior to his service as the Washita agent he held, shall we say, lucrative administrative positions provided for under the Reconstruction Acts."

"Damn Yankee carpetbagger lining his pockets at our expense you mean." Carswell had seen his fill of the type.

"Of course, some of his policies were none too popular with the locals. When things got uncomfortable in Biloxi he moved on to Mobile. He stayed there until a hooded delegation of city fathers threatened to stretch his neck at the end of a rope. When government administration opportunities ran out in Alabama along with his tax collecting authority, Denton found a new position in the Bureau of Indian Affairs."

Pierce paused to flip through several pages of notes. "He found opportunity in the terms of the treaties intended to provide for the needs of the tribes under his supervision. It was a simple matter for a man of his, shall we say, talents to turn a handsome income at the expense of his charges. He had complete control as long as the Indians didn't take matters into their own hands.

"He understood the value of security from his experiences in Alabama. He made a point of cultivating his relationship with the Army who afforded his agency the accommodation of a modest office on post at Fort Larned. The post commandant, Colonel George A. Custer, then of the Seventh Cavalry, made a perfect foil for Denton. Custer was reportedly desperate for an opportunity to resurrect his military career. In the west, the most likely cause of noteworthy action would be some sort of

Indian uprising. He may have been complicit in Denton's activities, or at the very least turned a blind eye to them. If the tribes were aggrieved by administration of the agency, he might have seen it more as a matter of opportunity than injustice or criminal wrongdoing."

"That is a rather strong allegation, Mason. Have you any proof?"

"Not yet. There is a strong pattern to the circumstances, but we have more work to do. There is one other interesting item in regard to Mr. Denton's appointment." Pierce slid a sheet of paper across the desk.

Carswell scanned the sheet. A slow smile creased the corners of his mouth. "Yes, this is good, Mason. This is very good, far more interesting in fact than Colonel Custer's role in all this. I suggest you concentrate your inquiry on this aspect of the case."

"I thought you might see it that way, sir."

Fort Abraham Lincoln
Dakota Territory
February 1875

Custer read the War Department dispatch again. It informed him that he'd been subpoenaed to testify before the Senate Select Committee on Indian Affairs. The committee would hold hearings concerning the performance of the Bureau of Indian Affairs including administration of the Washita River Agency. The subpoena ordered Custer to appear before the committee in that regard.

Custer laid the dispatch on the small desk in his cramped office. He twisted his mustache, weighing the substance of the testimony he'd be asked to give.

He'd known the Washita River Agent Roscoe Denton was corrupt. Denton looted much of what Congress appropriated for support of the reservation. He'd chosen to overlook it.

Desperate people did desperate things. It had only been a matter of time until he had the provocation he needed to take action against the tribes. The stolen cattle incident had a certain inevitability about it. The fact that the rancher who made the allegation was a man of low character had no bearing on the facts as they were reported. Hatch was white. Little more need be said. Rumor held that Hatch and Denton conspired to steel the cattle from the reservation. They planned to resell the herd to the agency to replace the stolen herd. The rumor had never been proven. With Denton dead, the truth of the allegation likely died with him.

Custer rose from his desk, clasped his hands behind his back, and paced in thought. He paused at the small office window, considering the possibilities. Clearly, he'd acted within his authority when he attacked Black Kettle's village. The recovery of stolen cattle was not in dispute. He scraped a patch of frost off the window glass with his thumbnail, revealing the snow-swept parade ground somehow soiled in gray afternoon light. His conduct could not be called to question. The committee may have evidence of Denton's malfeasance. They'd found an inflated bill of sale after Denton's death that seemed to confirm the rumor of his complicity with Hatch. His testimony would need to corroborate that, but that all came to light after the fact. There was nothing to suggest he had any foreknowledge of agency corruption. Satisfied he could give plausible testimony, he set the matter of the subpoena aside.

A trip to Washington offered attractive prospects for putting his career to rights. Washington would give him the opportunity to call on Sherman, reminding him of his glorious victory on the Washita. The newspapers had been full of heroic accounts of his actions. He'd seen to that. His presence would remind Sherman he was the warrior to resolve the Indian problem once and for all. Privately, he expected he'd receive the general's approval for the success of his survey mission.

His testimony would give him visibility on Capitol Hill. Political influence never hurt a military man. In fact, he'd call on Sherman after his testimony. That way the general would be reminded of his political notoriety along with his success on the battlefield. Yes, that would be perfect. All of it should help rebuild his fortunes.

He'd take Libbie with him. No need for her to sit here on the frontier when he could show her off to the Washington social scene. His presence was sure to be in demand at the most important social functions once word spread that he was back in town. His friends in the Washington press would see to that too. Those functions would afford yet another opportunity to rub shoulders with the rich and powerful, more good reason to take advantage of his notoriety. Thoughts of a lovely early spring in the District warmed him to the idea.

Chapter Thirty-Four

White House
Washington, D.C.
February 1875

Grant tossed the War Department brief on his desk. "Significant white incursion on reservation land in and about the Black Hills," the report said. *Significant incursion my ass,* he clenched his jaw. *If I've learned anything about bureaucratic dissembling since taking this job, the damn reservation is overrun with gold miners.* He picked up his cigar gone cold in the ashtray. He relit it and blew a cloud of smoke at the window. Cold rain splattered wet cobblestones in the drive beyond. Dark heavy storm clouds matched his mood. *It's happening again. We're breaking another treaty, one I pledged to uphold.* They'd given public notice as Ely suggested. He'd ordered Cump and Phil to use whatever measures they might deem necessary to protect the reservation. *It's not working. We've got to do a better job of controlling this situation.*

"Horace," Grant barked.

His secretary appeared at the door to the office, "Sir?"

"Get word to Secretary Belknap. I want to see him, General Sherman, and General Sheridan as soon as Phil can get here from Chicago. The subject is the situation in the Black Hills."

"Yes, sir." Horace closed the office door quietly.

White House
One week later

"The president will see you now." Horace Porter summoned Secretary of War William Worth Belknap, General Sherman, and a travel-weary General Sheridan into the presidential office.

The president rose from his desk to greet them. "William, Cump," Grant gestured to the settee at the side of the office. Both men acknowledged the greeting with a nod. Grant clapped Sheridan on shoulder, "Thank you for coming such a long way on short notice, Phil."

Sheridan took the wing chair Grant offered. "I understand the urgency, sir."

"Coffee, gentlemen?" Grant asked. Heads nodded all around. "Horace, if you please." Grant settled into the wing chair across from Sheridan. "Gentlemen, let's get right to the point." Grant charged ahead without waiting for the coffee to be served. "The situation in the Black Hills is intolerable. Gold or no gold, it is a clear violation of our obligations under the Fort Laramie Treaty. If there is gold in the Black Hills, by right it belongs to the tribes."

"The Indians have no interest in gold, Mr. President," Belknap said.

Grant cut him off. "Then that is their right. I'm not interested in gold at the moment either. I am interested in seeing that we uphold our treaty obligations for once. Phil, you're closest to the situation out there. What is to be done about it?"

Sheridan shrugged his shoulders and shook his head. "We're talking gold fever, Mr. President. It's like trying to stop a river from flooding its banks in the spring. I'm not sure we could effectively control that area with a hundred thousand troops. I've got precious few more than ten thousand in the whole of the department."

Grant glowered. He didn't like the answer, but he understood

Sheridan's command of the situation's tactical practicalities. Like so many things that came to this office, his job was to make the best of a bad lot.

"Maybe we could come to some accommodation with the tribes."

"Accommodation?" Belknap said.

"Yes, trade the Black Hills for something or buy them outright."

Sherman shook his head. "I don't know, sir, the Indians consider those hills sacred. I learned that much sweating my ass off all summer at Fort Laramie. I'm hard pressed to believe they'd sell them."

"You may be right, Cump, but damn it, man, we have to do something. Leave that to me. Now what is the situation with regard to the safety of those miners?"

"That is the other side of the coin, sir." Sheridan took up the question. "Red Cloud and the other peace chiefs don't like the situation, but they haven't shown any sign of a hostile response. They seem to be waiting to see what we do about it. It's the wild bands under Sitting Bull and Crazy Horse, I worry about. They're always a hair trigger away from the warpath. If they decide to take defense of the Black Hills into their own hands, the Army will have a hard time protecting our people. We don't have a presence in the region. Our nearest fort is Abe Lincoln."

Grant pondered the problem. The Army's presence in the area might well be taken for just the sort of hostile act to trigger another Indian war. Still, treaty violators or not, Grant felt an obligation to provide for the safety of American citizens. It smelled like another one of those odious compromises that so often seemed destined for this office.

"All right, gentlemen, let me see what can be done to defuse the situation with diplomacy. The odds may be against us, but we must at least try. If we can come to an accommodation with the tribes, the issue may yet be settled peaceably. In the meantime, Phil, do the best you can to stop the flow of miners into the Black Hills. I appreciate the difficulty of the assignment, but treaty violations are against the law. If diplomacy fails, we may have to take further action, but I don't want an offensive show of force out there. Are we clear on that point?"

"Very clear, Mr. President." Sherman and Belknap agreed. Sherman and Sheridan exchanged a knowing glance. *Very clear indeed, it's only a matter of time.*

White House
Washington, D.C.
March 1875

"Senator Allison, thank you for coming." Grant rose to take the senator's hand.

"A pleasure as always, Mr. President." Senator William B. Allison took the offered hand.

"Please sit down." Grant gestured to the settee.

Allison took his seat. "What can I do for you, Mr. President?" Allison, like Grant, wasted little time on amenities.

"I'll get to that. Care for a drink?"

"Why, thank you, I believe I shall. It's been a rather long day on the hill."

Grant went to the sideboard in the gray light of early evening. He selected two cut crystal glasses and opened the matching decanter. The whiskey would be stiff, relaxing, and purposeful. He returned to the settee and handed Allison his glass. He took his seat in the facing wing chair. They lifted their glasses and savored swallows. Good Kentucky bourbon still merited an appreciation brought on by the memory of war shortages.

"Oh, that's good, Mr. President. That's very good."

"We're here to do some business, Bill. Please, call me Sam."

"So, what can I do for you, Sam?"

"I've got a bill coming out of the House. It authorizes us to offer up to six million dollars to purchase the Black Hills from the tribes who own them under terms of the Fort Laramie Treaty. I need your help to shepherd it through the Senate. I intend to appoint a presidential commission to negotiate the purchase. I'd like you to chair that commission."

"That's flattering, Sam. Thank you." Allison paused, considering the practicalities of the problem. "The first challenge will be getting it through the Senate. After the last congessional election, we'll need some help from the other side of the aisle to get it done."

Grant's gut tightened. He knew where this was headed, and he didn't like it one bit. "You mean the Senate Select Committee on Indian Affairs."

"I do, sir."

"That means that son of a bitch Carswell. You know Senator Carswell and I have a history. He's responsible for killing Ely Parker's Buffalo Bill the last time I had anything come before that committee of his."

Allison sipped his drink and nodded.

"So, what makes you think the aforementioned SOB will help us with this?"

Allison thought for a moment, "Because you'll appoint him to the commission."

"Eat crow, you mean." He opened the humidor on the table and held it out to Allison. "Cigar?"

"No, but thanks anyway, Sam."

Grant bit the tip off a cigar and spit the end on the carpet. He fished in his vest for a match, struck it, and puffed, turning the cigar between his thumb and forefinger. "What the hell good will it do to appoint Carswell to the commission? Other than embarrass me."

"You're not going to eat crow, Sam. You're going to give him the visibility of an opposition appointment to a high-profile presidential commission. Not just any commission either. This one is charged with negotiating peaceful resolution of a crisis much in the national interest. No politician alive could resist such a heady elixir."

"Damn it. If that doesn't amount to eating crow, I don't know what does."

"Sam, you've already seen what he can do to your policy if he puts his mind to it. Invite him into the tent. Make him part of solving the problem instead of letting him oppose you on principle."

"You make a good point, Bill. In fact, you're probably right. That doesn't mean I have to like it. Here, let me refill that for you." He took Allison's glass and went to the sideboard.

It still amounts to eating crow. The son of a bitch ends up holding high cards at every turn.

Chapter Thirty-Five

Senate Chambers
Washington, D.C.
March 1875

Libbie Custer sat in the second-row guest chairs in the spacious Senate hearing room. Early spring sunshine poured through the chamber's floor to ceiling windows. Polished wood guest chairs, witness table, and committee bench bathed the room a tawny glow. Her handsome husband stood beside the witness table preparing to testify before the Senate Select Committee on Indian Affairs. He cut a dashing figure, she thought dreamily. He always did in his dress blue uniform. He'd swept her off her feet from the moment they first met. The uniform had surely been part of it. He was a national hero and could do no wrong in her eyes. Oh, she heard the mean-spirited things some people said. Some said he was arrogant and self-serving. Others said he was reckless. She dismissed it all as petty jealousy. She knew him for a caring husband and one of the bravest officers the Army had.

Pretty and well educated, Libbie had charm and ambition to match her husband's. Her delicate dark beauty masked a strong-minded woman and a fierce supporter of the husband she adored. She watched the committee members file into the chamber to take their places on a raised platform behind a long polished wooden bar that might have seated a panel of judges. They made a distinguished group of older men dressed in dark suits that, along with the room, exuded a palpable feeling of power. She could picture George among them someday. A political career when he finished military service seemed a good possibility. He already enjoyed a national reputation for his war service and his exploits in the Indian campaigns. In fact, he might one day ride that reputation all the way to the White House. *President George Armstrong Custer.* She turned the possibility over in her mind. It had a nice ring to it. *First Lady Elizabeth Bacon Custer,* she smiled. George definitely belonged in the seat of Washington power.

Committee members began to take their seats with the arrival of the Committee Chairman, South Carolina Senator Thurman Carswell. *A military man,* Libbie thought. Surely George would win his admiration even if the distinguished senator fought for the Confederacy.

Senator Carswell glanced around the hearing room. The members were in their places. He nodded to the witness and rapped his gavel.

"The committee will come to order. The Senate Select Committee on Indian Affairs is now in session for the purpose of hearing testimony from Lieutenant Colonel George A. Custer, U.S. Army Department of the Missouri. The Parliamentarian will swear in the witness."

A small bespectacled bald man in a brown frock coat stepped to the witness table. Custer stood at attention. He placed his hand on the Bible the man offered. "Raise your right hand. State your name."

"Colonel George Armstrong Custer." Self-promotion never acknowledged the more junior lieutenant grade.

"Do you swear to tell the truth, the whole truth, and nothing but the truth so help you God?"

"I do."

"Then be seated, Colonel Custer, and thank you for coming." Carswell's drawl melted like butter over hot cornbread as the Parliamentarian withdrew. The witness chair scraped the hard wood floor. Custer took his seat at the table facing the committee.

Carswell paused, letting the room quiet down. "I have a few opening remarks before we hear the colonel's testimony." As a Dixie Democrat and political opponent of the administration, Carswell saw these hearings as an opportunity to expose the dirty underside of Grant's highly touted Indian policy. Corruption ran rampant in the Bureau of Indian Affairs. For all the president's avowed purpose to clean it up, little progress had been made. Now in his second term, political adversaries felt privileged to lay blame at the president's feet. Carswell believed corruption caused all manner of problems including the so-called uprising on the Washita River Reservation Custer put down with his attack on Black Kettle's village.

"Let the record show that Colonel Custer appears before this committee as a decorated war hero who has distinguished himself by his service in numerous Indian campaigns including his glorious victory in the Washita River battle."

Custer smoothed his mustache, preening in the glow of the senator's recognition. His achievements would now be a matter of congressional record. He had center stage before sixteen U.S. Senators, sixteen of the most powerful men in America. Any one of these men could advance his career with little more than an offhand word in the right ear.

"This committee is well aware of the administration's peace policy toward the plains tribes. The Senate regularly approves House appropriation bills authorizing funds for the maintenance of Indians inhabiting reservations. These sums amount to millions of taxpayer dollars. Yet there is a considerable weight of evidence to suggest the benefits of these expenditures do not reach those for whom they are intended. A recent Treasury

Department report estimates that as little as twenty-five cents of each dollar appropriated actually reaches the tribes. The rest disappears in the administration of the reservation system. This committee has seen example after example of graft, corruption, and fraud in the administration of these programs, which brings us to the substance of today's hearing.

"Colonel Custer, the records before this committee indicate that you were in command of the Seventh Cavalry posted at Fort Larned during the summer and fall of 1868. Is that correct?"

"It is, Senator." Custer projected his answer with a commander's crisp confident clip.

"On November 27th of that year you mounted an offensive against the Black Kettle band in the vicinity of the Washita River. Is that correct?"

"It is, sir."

"The news accounts and your own report describe the glorious victory you achieved in that battle. You and the Seventh are to be congratulated in that."

Custer smoothed his mustache under his thumb and forefinger, masking a self-satisfied smirk. He nodded acknowledgment.

"Is it true, Colonel, that Black Kettle and his people moved to the Washita Reservation as required by treaty and lived there in peace?"

"Yes, sir, up until they took to raiding for cattle."

"Describe for this committee the circumstances that gave rise to the action you took that day."

"In late October, we received a report from a rancher in the area complaining that a war party from Black Kettle's village stole a herd of cattle. I sent out a patrol to confirm the allegation. I reported the incident to General Sheridan and requested authority to recover the cattle in question." Those were the facts. The rumors had never been proven.

"And did General Sheridan authorize the action you took?"

"He did, sir."

"Did you recover the cattle, Colonel?"

"We did, Senator, at least most of them. Some scattered when the fighting broke out."

Carswell studied his witness. Custer was relaxed and confident in his testimony. It was time to get to the meat of the matter. "Colonel, how well did you know the Washita River agent?" Carswell paused referring to his notes. "One Roscoe Denton, I believe."

"I knew him. I can't say that I knew him well, Senator, but I knew him. The agency office was on post. Fort Larned isn't all that large. Everyone knew each other."

"Were you aware the U.S. Marshals Service suspected him of defrauding his agency?"

"I do recall hearing something about a bill of sale they found after Denton's death. The bill appeared to have been inflated."

"You say you recall hearing something."

"Yes, Senator, I was recalled to Fort Riley shortly before Denton was murdered."

"Did you have any reason to suspect Denton might be corrupt?"

Custer considered his reply, aware that the room was becoming uncomfortably warm. He didn't like the direction of these questions. He'd known Denton was corrupt. Denton's little cattle business gave him the provocation he needed to move against the Cheyenne. The rumors about Hatch were just that, rumors. "None that I recall, Senator."

"How would you describe Denton's relationship with the tribes under his care?"

He could feel a hard edge in the senator's question and the intense gaze that accompanied it.

"I'm not sure what you mean, Senator."

"Did he exhibit concern for his charges? Did they have a cordial relationship?"

Custer calmed himself under the softer tone of these questions. "From my observation, I would describe the relationship as professional." *Where in hell was he going with this?*

"Denton was murdered in the spring of 1869. Can you describe the circumstance of his murder for the committee?"

"As I've said, Senator, the Seventh had been reassigned to Fort Riley by that time. I do recall seeing reports of the incident."

Carswell hunched forward, closing on the point of his questioning. "What do you recall of those reports, Colonel?"

"He was ambushed on the road east of the fort."

"And the nature of his death?"

"He was killed by a blow to the head. The official report suggested a tomahawk."

"So, there may have been some among the tribes in his charge who harbored animosity toward Mr. Denton, enough animosity to murder him."

"It would seem so, Senator."

"Now one final question, Colonel. Did Mr. Denton ever speak about how he came to be appointed to his position at the Washita River Agency?"

"Not specifically, Senator. He was fond of making it clear he had powerful political connections in Washington when it suited his purpose."

"So, it wouldn't surprise you, Colonel, to learn that Roscoe Denton's appointment to the Bureau of Indian Affairs came at the recommendation of Orville Grant, the president's brother?"

The hearing room broke into a surprised hum at the revelation. Custer sat dumbstruck. He hadn't seen any of that coming. His best hope of escape was that the senator had made his point and would end the hearing.

"Must I repeat myself, Colonel? Would you or would you not be surprised to learn that Roscoe Denton's appointment came on the recommendation of the president's brother?"

Custer sat silent, trapped. He felt all eyes in the hearing room bore into him. How do you answer that question? Yes? He'd already said Denton flaunted his political connections. No? The question had him boxed.

"Colonel," Carswell demanded.

Custer shrank from his usual bravado. "No, sir, I don't expect so." His testimony would not be well received at the White House.

Carswell sat back. It was weak confirmation, but it was confirmation. "No further questions."

CHAPTER THIRTY-SIX

White House
Washington, D.C.
Next Day

Grant threw the morning edition of the *New National Era* onto his desk in disgust. He bit the end off a cigar and spit it on the carpet. The headline glared back at him through the match flame as he lit his smoke.

President's Brother Implicated in
Indian Agency Corruption
Senate Investigation Continues

He clasped his hands behind his back, hunched his shoulders forward, and paced the office, trailing a cloud of blue smoke. He looked like a storm cloud wreathed in fury. Lightning flashed in red faced anger. His neatly trimmed beard now flecked in gray did nothing to soften the twisted scowl clamped around his cigar.

He'd come to expect this type of political bullshit from the likes of Carswell. That's what Democrats did. The newspapers pounced on the story. They never missed an opportunity to attack his administration. This time they'd found more than even Carswell had. They'd uncovered evidence of Denton's scallywag reconstruction crimes in Biloxi and Mobile. Denton could have been the mold for a carpetbagger. How in hell did Orville get himself mixed up with such a disreputable miscreant?

Then you had that idiot Custer. The man was a loose cannon and he'd never served a day in the artillery. He had to have known that Denton was corrupt. You couldn't keep that sort of thing secret on a post as small as Fort Larned. Grant stopped to stare at the headline again through a cloud of smoke. He couldn't do anything about Carswell or his cutthroat accomplices over at the *National Era*. Orville was his brother and no help for that. But Custer, he could do something about that son of a bitch.

"Horace," Grant barked for his administrative secretary.

Porter appeared at the office door, "Sir?"

"I have a message for you to deliver to Secretary Belknap over at the War Department."

War Department
Appointments Office
May 1875

"Colonel George Armstrong Custer reporting as ordered, sir." It galled him to report to a pen and ink commander with a brigadier's star.

Brigadier General Meriweather Dawes looked up from the piles of paper and file folders that covered the top of his desk, credenza, and the small conference table in the corner of his crowded office.

"Ah, yes, Lieutenant Colonel, thank you for coming." He made a point of correcting Custer's self promoting reference to his rank. Custer's legendary arrogance wouldn't make this any easier. Shit rolled downhill in the War Department, Dawes reminded himself. Well, that's what they paid him for.

"I have new orders for you, Lieutenant Colonel," he said, extracting Custer's folder from the stack on his desk.

"New orders?"

The man hadn't expected this. Given the circumstances Dawes couldn't imagine he hadn't considered the possibility. Then again, he'd finished last in his class at West Point for a reason. Intellect apparently wasn't his strong suit. That probably accounted for his fighting record and the casualty counts.

Custer opened the file and scanned the page. He skipped over the administrative bullshit recounting name, rank, serial number, current assignment, and the rest of it. The first line of the orders leaped from the page.

Relieved of command effective immediately and assigned to administrative leave.

Custer exploded red faced. "And just what the hell is this supposed to mean?"

"It seems rather straightforward to me." Dawes ignored the outburst, turning to the open file on his desk.

"Does Cump know about this?"

Dawes looked up from his file, clearly annoyed. "General Sherman approved the assignment."

Custer straightened himself to command bearing. "We'll see about that. I need to see the general, now."

"General Sherman said to express his regrets. He's busy."

This is a general, Custer thought in disgust. He's nothing more than a secretary. He turned on his heel and strode out of the office.

CHAPTER THIRTY-SEVEN

Fort Abraham Lincoln
Dakota Territory
June 1875

They gathered for the parley outside the main gates of the fort. The commissioners sat at a row of camp tables beneath a canvas tent top, deflecting the worst of the hot summer sun. The canvas smelled clean and starchy as it gently flapped in the breeze. Senator Allison sat at the center table flanked by Senator Carswell and General Terry. Terry was an experienced negotiator, having been the primary draftsman of the Fort Laramie Treaty. The commission's purpose intended to amend terms of that treaty.

The Lakota delegation headed by Red Cloud sat on blankets across from the commissioners seemingly unbothered by the beating sun and buzzing flies. Red Cloud laid down his arms and moved his people to the reservation seven years before after signing on to the treaty that ended his personal war for control of the Powder River hunting grounds. He'd taken his grievances to the Great Father and heard his words in the white man's great house. The Great Father kept his word. He had the evil agent McSerley arrested. More of the treaty promises made their way to his people, despite the children suffering the black preacher's school. The Great Father did right by his word. Now he would listen to new words the Great Father sent him.

Senator Allen addressed the assembly. "Great Father Grant

and all the people of the United States welcome the chiefs of the great Sioux Nation to these talks. We wish to discuss an equitable arrangement to obtain mineral rights to the gold in the Black Hills. The United States government is prepared to pay for the right to remove this gold from your treaty lands. The Lakota have no interest in these yellow stones. The Great Father will pay you to let us have them."

Red Cloud and the others listened. They did not understand much of what the white man said. It was always so with the whites. They spoke only of their ways. They did not understand the ways of the Lakota. They did not understand the importance of the Paha Sapa. These yellow stones they spoke of were nothing to the spirits of their ancestors.

Red Cloud exchanged a few words with the chiefs on his left and then on his right. They all nodded. "We will talk among ourselves. We will speak again under the next sun." Red Cloud and the Sioux chiefs rose and returned to the cluster of tipi set off from the walls of the fort.

Terry looked down the commissioner's table. The politicians were eager to begin negotiations and confident they could bring them to successful conclusion. Terry had his doubts. As important as Red Cloud was, he did not speak for all the tribes. The chiefs who came with him were reservation chiefs. The non-reservation tribes would be the likeliest source of trouble and they were not represented. Sitting Bull refused to attend outright. Crazy Horse made no response. For all they might do here, this delegation could bring no substantive resolution to the issue. They might give the commission the appearance of a resolution. It might satisfy the newspapers covering negotiations and maybe the president's desire for justice in the matter. But in the end, Terry's gut told him the miners would stay and the hostiles would fight.

★ ★ ★ ★ ★

They met again the following day and the day after that. The chiefs had many questions. The more they talked among themselves the more questions they found for the white men to answer. They did not understand mineral rights. They did not understand land ownership. In the Lakota tradition, people belonged to the land. Land did not belong to the people. Only the white man's paper words said the Paha Sapa belonged to the Lakota. The land was not the white man's to give with his words. The Lakota belonged to the Paha Sapa.

August 1875

Curly squatted on his heels at the back of the tent top waiting for the parley to begin. He would translate if the Sioux spoke Lakota. Red Cloud spoke English. Most often he spoke for his people. Curly would be called only if needed. He knew the hearts of the Sioux. For all the words the sides spoke to one another that summer, very little understanding passed between them. He listened to the white men talk.

"It's like pushing rope uphill," Carswell grumbled. "Three months of talking and all the talk goes in circles. I thought Washington could be frustrating." Carswell mopped his brow as he stood to pace in front of the camp tables. The canvas tent top provided scant shelter from the blistering heat.

Allison fanned himself with the pages of the final offer they would make today. "Everything has its price, Thurman. It's only a matter of time."

"Time be damned. We've been sitting under this stinking canvas, eating dust all summer. We make offers. They go off and parley. They come back, make long speeches, and stare at us. We make another offer and the shit starts all over again. They're making us look foolish, Bill. Even the newspaper stories are beginning to question whether they'll ever agree to anything."

"I know it looks bad, Thurman, but this offer is the best we've got. Once Red Cloud understands this is 'take it or leave it,' he'll come around and bring the rest of them with him."

"I hope you're right, Bill. I came on this commission as a bipartisan gesture to the president. I'll not be played for a fool by a bunch of savages."

Bipartisan gesture, my ass, Allison thought. Carswell accepted the appointment because Grant had to come crawling to his committee to get what he needed. "Take a seat, Thurman, the chiefs are coming."

Carswell returned to his seat. Dark figures crossed the dusty plain between the cluster of tipi and the fort. Shimmering waves of heat made a ghostly apparition of the procession. *Ghostly about summed it up,* Carswell thought. These people are governed by phantoms, spirits they call them. Ghosts they said haunted the Black Hills. For that they would hold the wealth of the nation hostage. Rubbish! This nonsense must stop. He cut a sidelong glance at Allison. "Final offer, Bill." Allison nodded imperceptibly.

Three months and they still don't understand. Terry dismissed the politician's rant. "Final offer" had no meaning for these people, even less to the non-reservation bands. The Army understood. The Army understood that everything depended on Sitting Bull, Crazy Horse, and those who followed them. None of the words, or mules, or blankets, or corn exchanged here would count for anything with the non-reservation bands. They would do what they would do. Terry feared they would fight.

Red Cloud led the procession of chiefs and elders. He stopped across from Allison and took his seat. The others fanned out on either side of him. Red Cloud folded his arms across his chest and tilted his chin toward Allison. He said nothing, waiting expectantly.

Allison cleared his throat. "We have talked many days now. The Great Father has given generous promises. You have asked for mules, blankets, and corn. All these have been granted you. Still we do not have an agreement for removing the yellow stones from the Black Hills. The Great Father has offered much, Red Cloud. You have offered us nothing."

Red Cloud sensed the white man's anger. Still he knew his brothers' hearts. He bowed his head searching for words to make the white man understand. "Red Cloud and his brothers cannot offer what is not ours to give."

Allison could feel tension chill the heat. Carswell clenched his fists on the table before him, his knuckles white.

"Now see here, Red Cloud." Allison's frustration boiled over. "Must I remind you that rights to the Black Hills were ceded to the Lakota by the Fort Laramie Treaty? If you and your brothers had the right to accept the land, clearly you have the right to make this agreement." Allison paused to mop his brow.

Red Cloud and the others made no reply. The silence grew awkward.

A fly buzzed about Allison as if to mock him. He waved it away nearly striking Carswell with the gesture. Like pushing a rope uphill, Carswell had said. Three months and it seemed they were no closer to a resolution than when they'd started in June. The savages must be made to understand.

"The time has come for you to make a bargain. The Great Father is running out of patience, waiting for the Lakota to meet us fairly in this. We are prepared to offer six million dollars to purchase the Black Hills. It is a handsome sum. It is our final offer. Do you understand? When we next meet you must accept this offer or these talks are over."

The words hung in the heat between them filling another awkward silence. The white man had said all he had to say. Red Cloud turned to his brothers on the left. One or two heads nodded. He turned to those on his right. Three or four more heads nodded. He turned back to Allison.

"We go to council." He got to his feet. They filed off toward their village, their footsteps raising dust to the breeze as they walked away.

"What do you think?" Carswell hissed out of hearing.

"Some of them seem to understand," Allison offered hopefully. "We shall see if they can persuade the rest."

Terry watched heat waves swallow the dark figures shimmering against the distant tipi. At least they'd reached the last scene in this Act. For all the drama, nothing had changed.

They came from council the following morning. Dark silhouettes against the blazing sun crossed the plain to the white tent top flapping in the breeze. The commission waited. Senator Allison sat in the center flanked by Carswell and Terry. Allison remained hopeful reason would prevail at the last.

Privately, Carswell had become a skeptic.

Terry kept his cynicism to himself.

Curly watched from behind the commission table. He held his bearing without expression. He knew.

A small crowd had come down to the gates to watch. The fort was abuzz with expectation. The long negotiations would at last come to an end. To what end? The question hung over commissioners and onlookers alike. The peace chiefs would speak at last. The unasked question was, speak for whom? A few among those assembled knew for whom they would speak. Most did not.

The chiefs took their seats around Red Cloud, who sat across from Senator Allison. They sat in silence. The rustle of canvas and buzzing flies were all that could be heard. Allison had no patience for this.

"Has your council reached a decision to accept the Great

Father's generous offer?"

Still silence.

Allison could not abide the void. "You do understand this is our final offer."

Red Cloud rose majestic as the red rock sentinels standing watch over the Black Hills.

"Paha Sapa," he intoned, his voice resonant.

Allison raised a hand to stop him, recognizing that the chief would render their decision in Lakota. He waived Curly forward to translate, and gestured to Red Cloud to continue.

"Paha Sapa Kin Wiyopeya Unkiyapi kte sni yelo." He folded his arms across his chest. His brother chiefs grunted agreement. The council spoke with one voice.

Allison and Carswell turned to Curly. Terry did not.

"Red Cloud say, 'Lakota will not sell Black Hills.' "

Another silence fell. The chiefs rose one by one to stand with Red Cloud. Red Cloud turned and led them on the dusty trek back to the land of their ancestors.

The commissioners sat stone faced. The handful of reporters, observing the scene, scrambled off in search of a telegraph key.

Chapter Thirty-Eight

"Played us for fools all summer," Allison fumed, tossing back his drink. He refilled his glass and topped up Carswell's. They sat in the parlor of the small officers' quarters where they'd spent the summer. A scarred wooden table and chairs provided what passed for amenities. A kerosene lamp gave the shadowy surroundings a dim yellow glow.

"I could have told you that would happen, Bill." The deeper the two men got into the whiskey bottle, the less partisan their differences became.

"So, what do we do now?" Allison stared bleary eyed at his whiskey. "Tuck our tails between our legs and sneak back into Washington empty handed."

"Not exactly, Bill. You've got to report to the president." Carswell did enjoy the prospect of his Republican colleague having to deliver a message of failure to his president.

Allison took another swallow. "What am I supposed to say beyond the obvious?"

"Ah, and that's where statesmanship comes in."

"What the hell are you talking about, Thurman, or is the whiskey talking?"

"Some of both, I expect. Hear me out. We both have the same problem you know. Neither one of us want to take the blame for this, shall we say, impasse."

"Impasse, stalemate, call it whatever the hell you want. We

failed. Now we get to go back to Washington and admit it to the president."

"Correction, William, you get to admit it to the president. The more interesting question is, what is to be done about it?"

"That I expect will be up to the president."

"William, William, William, a statesman doesn't leave his president to twist in such a wind."

"A statesman, is it? And I suppose you have something better to offer."

"As a matter of fact I do. We tell the president and the press that despite our best efforts to bargain in good faith, the Sioux rejected the path to peace. Tell the president to issue an administrative order requiring the non-reservation tribes to report to the reservations or be considered hostile and in violation of the Fort Laramie Treaty. When the hostiles fail to report to the reservation, which is a certainty to hear General Terry tell it, congress can repudiate the treaty."

Allison pressed his fingertips together. "Hmm, sounds like a sensible course of action."

"It is sensible; and probably our only alternative." Carswell poured another drink. "Once the treaty is set aside, the miner's presence will be legal. They're U.S. citizens. There'll be a public outcry to protect them. The president will have no choice. He'll send in the Army to defend the miners and force the hostiles onto the reservation."

Allison warmed to the idea. "Everybody gets political cover, including the president."

"And we get credit for taking back the Black Hills, treaty or no treaty."

Allison lifted his glass. "You are a clever bastard, Thurman. No wonder you're so damn difficult when you're on the other side of the aisle."

White House
September 1875

They gathered in the large conference room awaiting the arrival of the president. French doors opened to lawns toasted green gold by late summer sun. A gentle breeze ruffled the dark blue draperies cooling the stuffy room. Senator Allison sat at the end of the table closest to the head chair that awaited the president. He wasn't looking forward to this meeting. You could polish it up like Carswell's shiny red apple, but when you took a bite the worm was still in there. They'd failed to win agreement to modify the treaty, plain and simple. Carswell for all his brilliant advice sat at the other end of the conference table as far away from blame as he could get. Others in attendance included Secretary of War William Belknap, General Sherman, Secretary of the Interior Columbus Delano, and Wesley Swinton, Under Secretary for the Bureau of Indian Affairs. All rose as the president entered the room.

"Gentlemen, please be seated." Grant drew back his chair and sat down. He turned to the chairman. "I've read the newspaper accounts of the negotiations, Senator Allison. Would you be kind enough to give the official commission report and recommendations for the record?"

"Certainly, sir. As you know the commission negotiated with the tribes in good faith for three months. We met every reasonable demand with fair and generous terms. Despite our best efforts the tribes simply refused to agree to terms. We can only assess their intentions in the most dire terms."

"Do you have any policy recommendations for this administration to consider?"

"We discussed a number of possibilities. The most sensible appear to be these. We should order the non-reservation bands to report to the reservation by a stated date. If they do not report as ordered, they shall be deemed in violation of the Fort

Laramie Treaty and therefore hostile. In General Terry's estimate, it is near certain Sitting Bull, Crazy Horse, and those that follow them will refuse to comply."

Grant turned to Sherman. "Is that how you see it, Cump?"

"It is, sir."

"Very well then, continue, Senator."

"With the tribes in clear violation of their obligations, introduce legislation to repudiate the treaty. Once the treaty is abrogated, the miners' presence is no longer illegal. In sum the tribe's refusal to bargain will seal their fate."

Grant shook his head. Another broken treaty, the very wrong he'd resolved his administration to right. Oh, it gave the appearance of blame to the tribes, but they only sought to preserve that which had been given them. He could hear Ely Parker's objections in the reservations voiced by his own conscience. He'd made a deliberate decision to leave his Commissioner of Indian Affairs out of this meeting and the deliberations that would attend to it. He felt guilty about it, but that wouldn't solve the problem. Who could have foreseen the discovery of gold? The miners were there. Nothing could be done about that. Right or wrong, they were U.S. citizens. This was the part of the job he hated, doing what was necessary even when it didn't seem right.

"Secretary Delano, issue the order to report to the reservation."

"Yes, sir."

"Secretary Belknap, you'll end up enforcing this. Have you anything to add?"

Belknap deferred to Sherman with a nod

"Give them until January to comply, Mr. President. That will give us time to mount whatever action may be warranted."

"Very well then." Grant turned to Allison. "Senator, let me offer my thanks to the commission for your efforts. I understand the difficulty of the task you undertook."

Sherman folded his hands. The die was cast. It had taken longer than they'd expected. They hadn't foreseen the attempt to buy the Black Hills. In the end, Red Cloud sealed the fate of his people. It struck him as ironic. The great war chief had sown the seeds of defeat with his greatest victory.

Chapter Thirty-Nine

Winter Camp
Powder River Country
October 1875

The lodge fire crackled, sending sparks to the smoke hole and the chill night sky beyond. Sitting Bull and the Hunkpapa elders listened to the words of the Oglala, Swift Pony. He spoke of the treaty talk with the white eyes sent by the Great Father.

"Each day Red Cloud and the chiefs heard the words of the Great Father. At first the one called Allison spoke of buying the yellow stones in the Paha Sapa. Red Cloud and the chiefs spoke among themselves in council. They asked the Great Father for mules, coffee, corn, and blankets. The Great Father offered them all these things. They could not agree among themselves how much of these things would be enough. They asked how many whites would come to take the yellow stones. The wasichu did not know. They asked how long the wasichu would stay in the Paha Sapa. The Great Father's men did not know."

The Hunkpapa chief curled his lip in a sour frown. "They should have asked Sitting Bull. Sitting Bull could tell them. They will come, as many as grasshoppers in summer. They will scar our sacred land with their stinking forts and villages. They will come and they will never leave.

"This talk continued many days. Then the one called Allison spoke of buying the Paha Sapa. The chiefs spoke much about the meaning of this at council. Red Cloud said it meant more than taking only the yellow stones. He said the wasichu would take the Paha Sapa and never leave."

Sitting Bull nodded. "It is good. Red Cloud's wisdom has not blown away with the smoke of his reservation lodge fire."

"The wasichu Allison spoke of the generosity of the Great Father and the great sum he would pay for the Paha Sapa. In council that day no one could count the value of his words. Our brothers knew only that the whites would never leave our sacred land. The next day Red Cloud spoke for the people."

"Paha Sapa Kin Wiyopeya Unkiyapi kte sni yelo!"

"It is good." The words passed around the circle of firelight like the sacred pipe.

"What will the wasichu do now?" The words of Sitting Bull's younger brother, Pizi, known as Gall, hung heavy in the fire smoke.

"They will not leave the Paha Sapa," Sitting Bull rumbled. "They will do what they have always done. They will break their treaty and take our land."

"The white chief Terry says all tribes must go to the reservation this winter," the messenger said. "If we do not, they say the treaty will be broken. Then the pony soldiers will come to force us onto the reservations."

Sitting Bull shook his head. "Who would move women and children in winter? This is foolishness. White men have no respect for the dangers of snow."

"Then we must fight!" A young warrior shouted from the back of the lodge. All heard his words.

Sitting Bull searched the hearts of his brothers in the circle of elders. He gathered his thoughts. "We must summon our brothers." Sitting Bull held his voice soft and low, though none could mistake his defiance. "Gather the great Sioux Nation, our Cheyenne brothers, and the Arapaho. Tell them we meet on the Greasy Grass in the Moon of Making Fat."

Gall spoke. "Send our brothers the war pipe!"

Sitting Bull closed his eyes. He prayed. "I cannot say send the war pipe. It may come to be so. Wakan Tanka will guide us in this. We must wait for this wisdom. Tell our brothers we gather to dance and to pray."

Department of the Missouri
Chicago, Illinois
November 1875

Storeman sat at a small desk outside General Sheridan's office. Colonel Custer paced the sparsely furnished reception area like a caged animal. Storeman did his best to ignore him. The eccentricities of the flamboyant cavalry commander were legendary. He'd come to Chicago all the way from Washington, presented himself unannounced, and demanded to see the general. Sheridan didn't usually have much patience with that sort of behavior, but for some reason he allowed it with Custer. The colonel served under him during the war. He'd proven a ferocious fighter though he had a reputation for recklessly aggressive tactics. He'd drive his troops to the point of exhaustion and take risks that resulted in high casualties. Neither set well with the troops under his command.

"Storeman," the general's muffled voice could be heard through the closed office door. The aide went to the door and opened it.

"Sir?"

"Send Colonel Custer in."

"Very good, sir," he turned to the expectant Custer. "The general will see you now."

Custer squared his shoulders and strode purposefully across the outer office. He came to attention in front of Sheridan's desk and saluted. Sheridan made a casual wave at returning it. The credenza at his back was piled high with paper below the president's portrait. The pictured image stared at him as though the president meant to overhear the conversation. It served only to harden his resolve. He wasn't about to take this insult lying down.

"At ease, George, have a seat." Sheridan gestured to the two leather covered wing chairs at his desk. Custer took his seat. "Now what's on your mind, George?" The question was perfunctory. The general knew perfectly well what was on Custer's mind. The hard part was the fact he doubted much could be done about it.

Custer's gaunt frame hunched forward, making an awkward contrast to the comfortable line of the chair. His eyes glittered with the wolf-like intensity of a wounded predator. "May I speak freely, sir?"

"Of course, George. When has protocol ever stopped you from that?" Sheridan rocked back in his chair and made a thoughtful steeple of his fingers at the point of his chin. He expected a broadside.

"It's bullshit, Phil! I've been relieved of my command in some political reprisal over that damn Senate hearing. Carswell intended to embarrass the president all along. I just happened to be sitting in the witness chair when he did."

"I understand, George. I'm not happy about it either. Cump tells me the order came from the War Department."

"The damn paper-pushers over there have no business meddling in appointments to field command." Angry spittle foamed at the corners of his mouth and mustache.

"Well, there's truth enough to that. I've little doubt the order came from the White House. The press had a field day with the story. Sam's got enough problems with that bunch. Most of them are still pissed off over the election results. They beat him mercilessly at every opportunity. You can't expect the president to overlook what happened at that hearing. Maybe Carswell did trap you. Sam can't do anything about him. His brother did what he did. You ended up in the wrong place at the wrong time. Shit spills downhill, George. You've been in the Army long enough to understand that."

Custer slapped his bunched gauntlets against the palm of his hand and ground his teeth. "What am I supposed to do, Phil, stand here and take it? We've got a job to do out there. The hostiles made a mockery of the damn Allison Commission and Sam's peace policy. We need to bring them to heel. The Seventh needs to be part of it. I need to be with the Seventh."

Sheridan understood. Custer could be a pain in the ass, but he was a warrior. Warriors deserved better than political bullshit. "I'm going to Washington next month to talk to Cump about a summer campaign. Maybe the two of us can reason with Sam. I can't promise anything, George, but I'll try."

Custer nodded. It wasn't much, but at least he had hope. "Thank you, Phil."

War Department
Office of the Commanding General
Washington, D.C.
January 1876

Congress Reclaims Black Hills!
Hostile Violations Blamed for Treaty Abrogation

Sherman folded the paper and set it on his desk. He took the last swallow of coffee gone cold in the cup. It had taken a couple of years but things turned out pretty much the way Phil predicted. They hadn't foreseen Sam's attempt to negotiate with the tribes. In the end though, gold gave them what they needed. The Allison Commission recommendations put icing on the cake. Now Congress had cleared away the last obstacle. The summer of seventy-six would bring final resolution to the

Indian problem. After that, Phil could have this chair. Sherman resolved to go off to a well-deserved retirement, knowing he'd accomplished his mission.

Bureau of Indian Affairs
Washington, D.C.
January 1876
Ely Parker gazed out the window of his small office lost in thought. He fixed on the White House, across a snow-swept Pennsylvania Avenue beyond the black iron fence. Gray skies and a swirl of new snow matched his mood. He draped bitter disappointment in stoic Seneca bearing. Seven years, seven long years it had worked. It took months to fashion that treaty and negotiate terms equitable to both sides. He'd taken personal satisfaction in that. They'd endured the long summer, winning approval of the tribes. Then there'd been the rough and tumble backroom struggles to win ratification in the Senate. Western interests opposed it on principle, but they'd managed to overcome the opposition and it worked. The opposition was deep seated and staunch. Be that as it may, for seven years it worked. It worked, only to have victory undone by the very man who'd set him to the task.

He'd seen the storm clouds gather with the discovery of gold in '74. Custer had to have been the instrument of higher command. Sheridan's sympathies were widely known, but that expedition had to have the support of Sherman and yes, even the president. Trusted advisors persuaded him. The logic at the time seemed plausible enough. Plausible hell, one word of the gold strike was all it took. Once word got out, there'd been no way to stem the inevitable. The president had been duped. There could be no other explanation. In the end, he'd failed. The Great Spirit knew he tried. His voice had been that of one crying in a powerful wind. He should have been part of the Allison

Commission. Had he been, he might yet have averted disaster. That he'd not had a seat at the table spoke to the powerful forces drawn up against him. He should have seen it coming.

The president's political opponents killed the Buffalo Bill. He should have foreseen that as a harbinger of the future. It was only later he learned they did it at the bidding of railroad interests. Little meaningful progress had been made on reforming the reservation system. Corruption ran deep, often with powerful political patrons to protect the perpetrators. The religious groups the president enlisted proved more interested in evangelizing the Indian and stamping out his culture than preserving a way of life in harmony with their white neighbors. In the end, destiny some considered manifest, had proven too powerful to resist. The final chapters remained to be written, yet the outlines, the end of a saga, already emerged into sight.

For all the well-meant intention, he could not shake the conclusion, the president let him down. He'd lost the courage of his convictions. He'd succumbed to political pressures and the influence of his old comrades in arms. Parker felt he'd failed his people. Not that the plains tribes were Iroquois, but they were Indian. He'd let them down. He'd let himself down. He should have found the words or the wisdom to carry the force of his argument to the president.

He shook his head sadly and left his vision to cold stark winter. He turned to his desk, took up his pen, and wrote.

Dear Mr. President,
It is with deep regret that I tender my resignation as Commissioner of Indian Affairs . . .

Chapter Forty

War Department
Office of the Commanding General
February 1876

"Damn it, Cump, I want Custer!"

Sheridan came straight to the point, with the same dogged determination he took to the field in a fight. Sherman recognized the style he respected in battle. Now he found himself on the receiving end. It didn't make for a comfortable conversation.

"Cigar, Phil?" Sherman opened the box at his elbow.

"I'd prefer Custer."

"Damn it, Phil, you know he's poison. He shit in his mess kit once too often. Belknap will never sit still for reassigning him." Sherman bit the end off his cigar and spit it in the general direction of his waste can. He scratched a match on the wooden frame of his desk chair and let his words sink in through a cloud of blue smoke.

Sheridan anticipated the objection. "I'm not suggesting we leave it up to the secretary, Cump. You know as well as I do the order to relieve George came from the White House. It's up to us to convince Sam that he overreacted. George didn't get Sam's brother in trouble. Orville did that all by himself. Carswell would have embarrassed Sam with or without George."

Sherman rubbed his temples. At times like these it seemed the only useful purpose of his job was to get the politicians out of the Army's way. In this case that meant reminding Sam that he was a soldier. He'd had time to cool off. Maybe he'd listen to reason, presuming a reasoned case could be made.

"There's a fight brewin' out there, Cump. You and I both know it. I need a warrior. You and Grant can call the son of a bitch whatever you like, but you promised me Custer when I took this job. Now it's time to deliver. When do we talk to Sam?"

Sheridan was in no mood for a reasoned conversation with the commander in chief. "We don't, Phil. That's my job. I'll talk to Sam. Sometimes you just have to remind him where he came from."

White House
Washington, D.C.
March 1876

"I don't like it, Cump! I don't like it one damn bit!" Grant hunched his shoulders, resting his arms on the desk as he fixed his General in Chief with fire in his eye. "The son of a bitch is nothing but trouble. The more I hear about his actions down on the Washita the more convinced I am that a lot of innocent people died down there owing to yet another one of his vainglorious gambits. How many more people need die before you and Phil have seen enough?"

This wasn't going to be easy. Sherman leaned back in the wing chair. He'd guessed it wouldn't be. Now confronted by the president's anger, he knew he had his work cut out for him. He'd thought through his line of reason. Now he wondered if it would prove reason enough. No help for that. He'd have to make do with what he had.

"We all know George has his faults, but he's a warrior. Give him a job and he'll get it done. Phil's sitting on a powder keg out there, Sam. The hostile bands are out of our control. They never signed on to the Fort Laramie Treaty. Repealing it has no meaning for them. They think the Black Hills are sacred. The number of miners out there grows by the day. Right or wrong they are U.S. citizens, Sam." Sherman dropped into a familiar tone he hoped took them back to a camp table in a command tent where they drank whiskey, smoked cigars, and planned strategies to whip Johnny Reb. "The wild ones will attack if we don't subdue them first. Our commander in the field is telling us he needs to strike and he needs warriors to do it."

"I see that, Cump. But what has that got to do with Custer? Are you telling me we don't have another competent cavalry commander in the whole of the United States Army?"

"Phil thinks George is the man for the job. They've been together a long time, Sam. Phil's the man to keep George under control."

Grant scowled. He stood up, clasped his hands behind his back, and hunched his shoulders in his habitual way and began to pace the office.

At least I've got him thinking, Sherman thought. "May I speak freely, sir?"

"When have the trappings of this office or any other dissuaded you from doing that, Cump?"

"George didn't get your brother in trouble. Orville did it all by himself. Carswell used him to embarrass you. It was a political stunt. George just happened to be the foil at hand. If it hadn't been George it would have been someone else. You've got a commander in the field who wants his man for a tough job. You know the right thing to do as well as I." Sherman sat back, letting his words and the chain of command do their work.

Grant bit the end off a cigar and flicked a match to light on his thumbnail. His eyes met Sherman's through a veil of smoke.

"Phil's the man to keep Custer under control, is he? Well if he does, it will be a first." He studied the tip of his cigar.

"He's the commander in the field." Those words had weight

with a military man. In truth that distinction fell to Al Terry, but Phil was close enough for this purpose. Silence settled over the president's pacing.

"All right, Cump, give Phil his man. You be damn sure they both understand if Custer so much as steps in a horse apple out there, there'll be bloody hell to pay. I'll have his sorry ass busted to buck private before I throw it out of the Army for good."

Sherman nodded. "Thanks Sam." *Bloody hell* about sums it up.

Department of the Missouri
Office of the Commanding General
Chicago, Illinois
March 1876

Sheridan and Terry huddled over the map table in the corner of Sheridan's spacious office. "The non-reservation bands gather in this general area," Terry said tracing an oval north and west of the Bighorn Mountains with his finger. "They'll camp for several weeks to celebrate their summer dances."

Sheridan scratched his chin. "That's where we hit them. There's no point to chasing them all over the Dakota and Montana Territories. We hit the biggest bunch we can find with enough force to drive them onto the reservations or destroy them. After that we mop up any bands that may be left or those that get away."

Terry nodded. He'd seen this coming all the long hot days of last summer while the commission hoped in vain for a better outcome. Now the inevitable hour approached.

"General Crook will lead a column northwest out of Fetterman." Sheridan traced a line on the map.

Fetterman, the symmetry touched Terry. The fort named in memory of the man who set these events in motion nearly a decade ago.

Sheridan shifted his reference point west. "We'll bring Colonel Gibbon east out of Ellis. Alfred, you'll lead your Abe Lincoln command west. If the three of you coordinate your strike, the hostiles should be forced to capitulate or die. Do you agree?"

"I do, sir. The tribe's religious rituals deliver them to the anvil where our hammer blows shall ring true."

"A carefully coordinated three-pronged strike can't help but prove decisive. I'll leave the care and coordination in your capable hands, Alfred."

"Thank you, sir, I'll see to it." Terry straightened preparing to take his leave.

"Oh, one more thing, Al."

"Sir?"

"Sam and Cump have come to an agreement. I'll be reassigning Colonel Custer to your command for this operation."

Terry paused, taken aback. "I must say, I'm surprised. I rather thought Colonel Custer's career might be finished this time."

"It may have seemed so to some, but there are those in the chain of command who value the part a warrior like George might play in the conflict before us."

"I see. He certainly has the reputation for a warrior. We shall have to make our orders for this campaign very clear. Careful coordination doesn't allow for his brand of self-appointed authority."

"I'm sure George can be made to understand his part, Alfred. I shall make sure he understands his responsibility and leave the rest in your capable hands."

"I shall rely on you for that, sir. Thank you." Terry turned on his heel. A coordinated campaign with Custer in the battle plan, it felt like another toothache. He shook his head as he closed the office door, *probably too late for a transfer.*

★ ★ ★ ★ ★

Custer sat on the edge of his chair. Sheridan's demeanor gave no indication of whether the news from Washington was good or bad.

"Cump got it done. You're reassigned to the Seventh."

Custer let go a breath he hadn't realized he'd been holding. "Thank you, Phil."

"He had to spend some personal capital to get Sam to agree. Cump says I'm to hold you to a short tether. Sam insists he'll personally drum your ass out of the Army for good if you so much as get horseshit on those shiny boots of yours. General Terry has command of the summer campaign. It's to be a coordinated campaign involving three columns. You'll lead the Seventh as part of General Terry's column. He'll fill you in on the operational details when you get to Abe Lincoln. I expect you to play the part you are given, George. You're not to go off on some road to glory of your own invention. Do you understand?"

"I do, sir."

"Mess up this chance and no one will be able to save you."

"I won't, sir."

"See that you don't."

Custer rose and presented his salute. *Washington is a long way from the action.*

Chapter Forty-One

Fort Abraham Lincoln
Dakota Territory
April 1876

"Old Hard Ass is back." Captain Frederick Benteen entered the small whitewashed clapboard bachelor officers' quarters. He rummaged in the trunk at the foot of his bunk looking for his bottle. "The son of a bitch has more lives than a cat."

Lieutenant W.W. "Cookey" Cooke looked up from his boot polishing. He glanced at the clock on the table between the bunks. Three o'clock, early to start drinking even by Benteen's liberal standards.

Benteen fished a half empty bottle up from the bottom of the trunk. He pulled the cork with his teeth, spat it on his rumpled bunk, and took a pull. He sat heavily. The cot groaned. "I thought we were done with the son of a bitch this last time. No Army officer alive should walk away from embarrassing the damn President of the United States. Somehow Old Iron Butt does."

"You'd best mind your mouth, Frederick." Cooke spit in his boot black. "Like it or not the colonel's in command of the Seventh."

"Much to the detriment of those condemned to serve under the popinjay peacock. Anybody with a brain sees it for a death sentence. The only men happy about this are the likes of his brothers and them few as kiss his scrawny old hard ass."

Cooke let the slur slide. Benteen had rank and no sense when drunk, which was most of the time.

"Got himself back here just in time for the action he did, just in time to cover himself in glory with the blood of his command. How many times he done it, Cookey?" Benteen slurred around the neck of the bottle. "How many men is dead or maimed on account of that bastard? Some day the Lord Almighty's gonna tally them up for him. I just hope I ain't on the list by then."

Benteen stood unsteadily. He fitted the cork in the empty bottle and slapped it with the palm of his hand. "I need some air. A walk over to the officers' mess should do me some good." He lurched toward the door.

Cooke watched him go. *Fresh air hell, a fresh bottle is what he meant.* Benteen's rant was more than the sentiment of one belligerent drunk. The men of the Seventh who served under Custer were of two minds in regard to his return. Those who had yet to form an opinion soon would. The colonel had his admirers, as Benteen had so colorfully described them. They were caught up in the promise of glory he proclaimed. Others knew his war record and feared it. Vainglory came at a price. The captain's raving over casualty counts stated it clearly. The new men would soon encamp on one side or the other.

Fort Abraham Lincoln
Dakota Territory
May 17, 1876

General Alfred Terry led his column out of Fort Abraham Lincoln to the pomp of the regimental band. Civilians, wives, and the small post garrison turned out to see them off. Custer and the five hundred ninety-seven officers and men of the Seventh Cavalry headed the column followed by their Arikara and Crow scouts, three companies of infantry, a battery of Gatling guns, a supply train, and a herd of cattle.

Custer sat his horse at the head of the column, turned out in buckskins, polish, and brass. The regimental band struck up the rousing strains of "Garry Owen" as the Seventh passed in review. The air fairly crackled in anticipation of what was to come. Libbie watched from the porch of the small whitewashed house they shared on post, fair near bursting with pride at the sight of her Autie. Sunlight gleamed in his hair and flashed on his saber. He cast a long shadow over the taciturn commanding general, riding beside him. Fortune would soon change all that. Her Autie would find his rightful place in the general staff and a fitting cap to his military career. From that she envisioned a powerful political career, perhaps rising to the most powerful office in the land. She felt destiny in her bones.

Custer sent out scouts as soon as the column left the routinely patrolled perimeter around the fort. Each day they probed the line of march searching for sign of hostile movement. For the next three weeks he set an aggressive pace, pushing ever west over the sun-soaked rolling grasslands. The march pace wore on men and animals alike.

Late one afternoon he drove the column west as the sun sank toward distant peaks. Terry estimated they'd covered nearly thirty miles that day. The men were tired. He could feel his own fatigue. At last Custer halted the column of fours. A lone rider galloped toward them from the west. The Crow scout Curly returned with a report. He drew rein beside Custer.

"River not far there." The scout pointed west.

"We've struck the Little Missouri," he proclaimed for the benefit of those within hearing. "We'll camp there and cross in the morning."

The last rays of sunset settled into darkness as the men finished pitching their tents. Cookfires came to light up and down the riverbank. Troopers and officers alike would eat a quick supper and fall into exhausted sleep. Custer seemed unaffected by the rigors of the march.

Terry had never seen him so energized. Even now he stalked off to the riverbank, a solitary silhouette against the shimmer of moonlight on the rippled surface of the water. The promise of battle excited the man. He had a voracious appetite for glory. The coming conflict reeked with the scent of it. He pushed the column hard, twenty-five to thirty miles a day, seemingly unconcerned for the strain on troop morale and energy.

The firebrand divided sympathies among his officer cadre. His second, Major Marcus Reno, concealed his misgivings better than most. A handsome, competent officer, he was an experienced professional soldier who'd taken command of the Seventh during Custer's absence. Still Terry observed the occasional shadow of doubt or unspoken question in the man. Captain Benteen, on the other hand, wore his disdain for the Seventh's flamboyant commander on his sleeve, likely emboldened by his fondness for the bottle. Benteen best be cautious lest his whiskey hazed judgment turn disapproval to insubordination. Custer's junior adjutant, Lieutenant Cooke, plainly idolized the man. Cooke's adulation along with Custer's brother, Tom, and a few like-minded veterans polished the colonel's ego to a luster sufficient to blot out the undercurrents of darker sentiment. Either that or Custer simply chose to overlook anything that disagreed with his own self-estimation.

They'd had little conversation at supper, most too tired for talk. The officers took to their tents as Custer trudged up the banks from the river. Only Terry, Cooke, and the ever-present reporter Kellogg remained at the camp table when Custer eased his gaunt frame into a camp chair.

"General Terry, would you care for a drink, sir?"

Terry nodded.

"Cookey, would you do the honors, please?"

Cooke scurried off to Custer's tent. He returned moments later with a bottle and four tin cups. He poured a measure in each, serving his superiors before taking his seat.

"If we hold to this pace, General, we should link up with Colonel Gibbon's column on the banks of the Yellowstone. I should think we will have some sign of the hostiles by then." Custer lifted his cup. "To a great victory then, I can see it. I can feel it." Custer tossed off his drink.

Terry raised his cup in turn. "Let's hope so." He took a swallow.

Cooke refilled Custer's cup. "Hope has nothing to do with it, sir. The Seventh will ride to glorious victory! Make no mistake about it."

"Need I remind you the Seventh isn't acting alone, George. There are three elements to this campaign. We are but one. Our charge is a coordinated strategy."

Custer pursed his lips. "Likely as not it will come to the Seventh, General. Crook is the weak link. He's likely to turn tail and run at the first sight of war paint. Of course, you mustn't print that, Mr. Kellogg."

Kellogg nodded and passed his cup to Cooke for a refill.

"General Crook is a fine officer," Terry said. "He will serve with distinction."

Custer raised a finger as if to rebut the point, but thought better of it. "Mark my words, General, in time it will be up to the Seventh to prevail and prevail we shall."

"I hope you're right, George. Under the circumstances, I expect we will encounter a rather determined enemy perhaps in significant numbers."

Custer swept the notion aside with a wave of his gauntlet. "The Seventh whipped Black Kettle at the Washita. We shall whip Sitting Bull in similarly fine fashion wherever we find him." He took a pull on his cup. "My greatest concern is that the hostiles will run rather than risk a fight."

Custer troubled Terry. The man was spoiling for a fight plain enough. With him it was more about personal glory than accomplishing the mission. The Washita was a peaceful village asleep in winter camp. Sitting Bull and Crazy Horse would be neither. The trouble with Custer was his arrogance. He turned a blind eye to the possibility that Sitting Bull and Crazy Horse might present a formidable fighting force. Keeping the man in check would not be easy. He'd known that from the start. The flamboyant commander had General Sheridan's full support and that made matters more difficult as his commanding officer. The fact that General Sherman himself had gone to the president to win the man's reinstatement spoke volumes. It fed his already considerable ego. He'd made his orders clear. This was to be a coordinated campaign. Still he could not shake a sense of apprehension at what Custer might do when they encountered the enemy. With luck, Crook would find them first. With luck, Custer's Seventh would play a supporting role in the ensuing action. *With luck.*

Chapter Forty-Two

Rosebud Creek
Dakota Territory
June 6, 1876

Sitting Bull sat alone in the dim steamy lodge. His naked body ran with sweat. It poured off his brow, burning his eyes. The burden he carried weighed heavy on his heart. The presence of wasichu desecrated the Paha Sapa. The people looked to him for wisdom. He had no answer to give them. For this he would offer himself to the Great Spirit, Wakan Tanka, in the Sun Dance. He would dance for his people. He prayed Wakan Tanka would give him wisdom and strength to lead his people. His prayer must find favor with the Great Spirit. Much depended on it.

Outside the sweat lodge a pole, symbolizing the sun, stood in the center of the village. Three thousand Lakota and Cheyenne gathered for the summer dances. Their lodges sprawled along the banks of Rosebud Creek. Soon the sun would call the dancers to its sacred center. Other dancers would join Sitting Bull. They would come to pray for other needs.

The setting sun lit the top of the sun pole, summoning the dancers. Sitting Bull belted his breechclout. He would wear a prayer shirt of blood for this dance. The warm evening air felt chill on his skin as he crawled from the sweat lodge. He felt strong in his prayers after punishing his body with the rigors of fasting and sweat.

He stood before the sun pole. The people came from all directions, shuffling through lengthening shadows. They gathered in quiet reverence, forming a circle around the sun pole to watch and pray. The dancers came forward taking their places. Sitting Bull offered his knife to the sun shining atop the pole. His voice rang loud and clear.

"Wakan Tanka, give me wisdom. Wakan Tanka, give me strength." He pressed the blade to his shoulder.

"Wakan Tanka, give me wisdom." A thin line of bright blood appeared in the cut.

"Wakan Tanka, give me strength." Sun glittered on the blade. Another cut ran red.

"Wakan Tanka, give me wisdom."

"Wakan Tanka, give me strength."

"Wakan Tanka, give me wisdom."

"Wakan Tanka, give me strength."

Fifty cuts on his right arm, fifty cuts on his left, Sitting Bull raised his arms to the sun pole, bathing his body in a prayer shirt of blood. The people stood silent, watching the holy medicine man seek wisdom to lead them. He stepped to the sun pole and chose a bone barb hanging at the end of a long rawhide tether.

"Wakan Tanka, give me wisdom. Wakan Tanka, give me strength." He pierced his breast with the bone, his prayers bound to the sun. Blood covered his belly and thighs, falling to earth mother at his feet.

One by one, other dancers came to the pole, Spotted Hawk among them. One by one they pierced their breasts on the sharpened bones, joining their prayers to the sun. Drums signaled the start of the dance, calling softly as the sun faded behind the distant hills firing the clouds purple and orange.

"Wakan Tanka give me wisdom. Wakan Tanka give me strength."

The people chanted prayers for the dancers as they circled

the pole. Darkness enfolded the village. Gentle drumbeat floated on the night breeze with the songs of the people. Dark shadows flickered in torchlight, circling the sun pole to the rhythms of the dancers' steps. The dancers prayed in sacrifice, blood, pain, cold, sweat, and thirst.

Sitting Bull took his strength from the circle of the people. His steps became the beat of the drum. The songs of the people carried his prayer.

"*Wakan Tanka give me wisdom. Wakan Tanka give me strength.*"

Three days Sitting Bull danced to exhaustion. On the third day Wakan Tanka honored his prayer with a vision. He sank to his knees before the sun pole, his body covered in crusted brown blood. He had no more to give. Earth mother cradled him in her bosom. The sun burned blood red. A vision took shape out of bright white light, shimmering before his eyes. Pony soldiers came. They fell from the sky upside down. Their hats fell to the ground. Their ponies' hooves pawed the air as they fell into the Lakota camp. Warriors attacked them in great numbers. The bluecoats could do nothing. They disappeared, lost in the power of the people. The vision foretold great victory.

Spotted Hawk fell beside Sitting Bull. He too was blinded by the sun. A familiar dark shape formed before his burning eyes. He saw a dark notch, a rifle sight. It rested on the shadow of a man. The sun glinted on his long knife. Yellow light touched his hair. Wakan Tanka would grant his prayer. He would fulfill his vow. He would avenge Autumn Snow.

The Lakota chiefs gathered at council in the circle of lodge fire. Crazy Horse sat beside Sitting Bull, listening over the crackle of the fire as he described his vision of the pony soldiers falling from the sky. When he finished the council sat silent and thoughtful.

Crazy Horse considered the meaning of Sitting Bull's vision.

It spoke of a Lakota victory in some coming fight with the pony soldiers. They were coming. His wolves told him this. *The Chief of Thieves would lead them.* Now he knew they would win. He felt his medicine grow strong.

"Wakan Tanka has granted Tatanka Iyotanka a powerful vision. It speaks of a great Lakota victory. The Lakota with our Cheyenne and Arapaho brothers will drive the wasichu from the Paha Sapa. It is the will of Wakan Tanka."

Spotted Hawk listened to the chiefs at council with other young warriors. His blood ran hot. *The yellow hair comes with his long knife.* He lifted his eyes to the night sky. His Sun Dance vision filled his mind's eye. The evil one who hurt his Autumn Snow appeared on his rifle sight. He let out his breath. He felt the trigger, a gentle squeeze. The vision lifted his spirit. He joined his medicine with Crazy Horse. They would taste victory. Wakan Tanka spoke his will through Sitting Bull's vision.

Sitting Bull steeled himself against his private doubts. He believed his vision. It spoke of victory. What victory? Did it speak of a great battle or foreshadow a great war? Did it foretell return of the Paha Sapa? He did not know. He could do no more than tell his vision to the people. They would make of it a meaning of their own. He saw victory gleam in the eyes of Tashunca-uitco. He saw it pass to the young warriors and war chiefs. What victory did his vision promise? Only Wakan Tanka knew.

"It is time to move camp to the Greasy Grass. It is time to join our brothers the Arapaho and Cheyenne. There we shall see the meaning of this vision.

"Tashunca-uitco will not wait for the pony soldiers. My wolves have seen them moving up the Rosebud. Tashunca-uitco and his warriors will go to meet them. Tashunca-uitco will come to the Greasy Grass when the bluecoats have seen our war shirts. We will dance when the bluecoats have tasted our medicine."

The next day Crazy Horse led a band of five hundred Lakota and Cheyenne warriors down the Rosebud in search of the bluecoats. He would meet them. His warriors would defeat them as the vision foretold.

Sitting Bull turned north from the Rosebud. The Lakota would join their Cheyenne and Arapaho brothers on the Greasy Grass. The warriors rode in groups spread among the people. Women rode horse-drawn travois fashioned of lodge poles. The travois were laden with utensils bundled in lodge coverings. Children rode with their mothers or walked with the dogs. The band stretched over two miles, making their way to summer camp.

They reached the grass flats the people called Greasy Grass along the banks of the Little Bighorn River. They made summer camp there, in preparation to celebrate the summer dances. Their lodges stretched more than a mile along the west bank of the river. Day after day brother Lakota, Arapaho, and Cheyenne poured into the camp adding their lodges to the village sprawling to the north. Soon they would number ten thousand, nearly four thousand warriors. Smoke from the lodge fires cast a great cloud over the orange and purple lights of the setting sun. At night cookfires gave the riverbank a warm glow as though the people would speak to the moon and the stars by their lights.

Word of Sitting Bull's vision spread through the camp. Everywhere it was greeted with excitement and wonder. What did it mean? Would the pony soldiers come? When? No one could remember so large a gathering of the people from the summers of their grandmothers' grandmothers. With so many warriors surely the people must defeat any soldiers that might come. Sitting Bull's vision had seen Wakan Tanka. The people felt strong medicine in this sign. With it they could drive the white men from the lands of the people.

These expectations made a heavy burden on Sitting Bull's heart. Wakan Tanka answered his prayers with a vision of victory. What victory he could not say. It could be one battle. It could be a great war. He rode alone in the evenings to the bluffs across the river, overlooking the village. There he prayed alone. He prayed for the people. He prayed for greater wisdom. None came.

"*Wakan Tanka protect us.*"

So it began. The warriors took the vision. Sitting Bull said his prayers.

Rosebud Creek
June 17, 1876

General George Crook led a column, thirteen hundred strong, northwest out of Fort Fetterman. The third element of Sheridan's three-pronged strategy, Crook's mission was to drive the hostiles north into the combined forces of Terry and Gibbon. Late on the morning of the 17th, Crook called a halt on the banks of Rosebud Creek. Early summer heat beat down on the column through the morning march. A light breeze fanned the grassy plain on the creek bank making for an inviting rest stop.

"Major Ainsley, have the men stand down. We'll take hardtack and coffee with our midday rest."

Ainsley saluted the taciturn Crook. At times the general affected a bearing better suited to a schoolmaster than a military commander. He wheeled his mount and picked up a trot to the rear, relaying the general's order to the company commanders. As he rode, he questioned the choice of this rest stop. The grassy plain afforded scant cover. Hilly high ground scored in coulees and washes to the north and east afforded would-be attackers both tactical advantage and cover. They'd come far enough north to be wary of hostile contact. Their Crow and Shoshone scouts reported no sign of the enemy, but Ainsley took cold comfort in that. Hostile territory was hostile territory. Those who respected the fact might live to tell about it.

Up and down the column troopers settled down to rest. Small fires were lit to brew coffee. Their smoke sign drifted into the cobalt blue sky on the breeze. A wagon came forward from the supply train with a camp table and chairs. General Crook and members of his officer staff sat down to a friendly game of whist with fresh brewed coffee.

Ainsley shook his head. Under the circumstances he had little interest in the amusement of a card game and the frivolous chatter that went with it. Crook hadn't even bothered to deploy a proper guard to secure their exposed perimeter. Seen with hostile intent, the column made a fat sleepy target. He couldn't shake the feeling that things were entirely too quiet. It made him restless.

He glanced across the valley floor to the east. Their Crow and Shoshone scouts gathered in the lea of a coulee to rest. Nearly one hundred in number, the scouts would be first to know if trouble presented itself. Gray Wolf, the scouts' leader, had shown himself to be a man of judgment. Ainsley valued his opinion. Unable to satisfy his unease, he stepped into his saddle and rode off to join them. He found Gray Wolf seated in the circle of his wolves, munching jerky. He rose as Ainsley drew rein and stepped down. He said nothing, waiting for Ainsley to speak.

"It is very quiet, Gray Wolf. It doesn't feel right. Are you sure your scouts have seen no sign of hostiles?"

"We see no sign there," he pointed to the north and west.

Ainsley turned to the northeast and the valley wall looming nearby on its climb into the hills. "And there?" he asked.

"My wolves have not yet returned." Gray Wolf squinted at the blue sky touching the rim of the wall. Then he pointed to a faint wisp of dust rising against the sky. "They come now."

They watched as the cloud grew and spread. Three riders crested the valley wall and raced down the face at a gallop. The dust cloud behind them continued to boil up, spreading billows across the ridgeline.

"Somebody's chasin' them and by the look of it more than a few." Ainsley drew his own conclusion. "Put some distance between your scouts and the column, Gray Wolf. We may need a counterattack." Ainsley swung into his saddle and kicked up a gallop back to the column. Behind him he heard war cries rising as a large band of warriors crested the valley wall.

Gray Wolf and his scouts leaped to the backs of their ponies and broke away to the south fleeing down the Rosebud away from the war party.

"Attack! Attack!" Ainsley screamed as he raced back to the column. Company commanders sprang into action ordering their troops into skirmish lines. Crook and his officer staff abandoned their card game and set about the task of closing ranks to meet the assault. The air split with war cries and muffled sounds of rifle reports. The war party stormed over the crest of the valley wall, plunging to the grassy valley floor below. The valley floor shook under the pounding of hundreds of horses' hooves, bearing down on a column in disarray.

Ainsley wheeled his mount southwest, angling down the column to the supply train. His mount slid to a stop at the head of the wagon column. "Wagons ho!" He waved, signaling the drivers to move up behind the skirmish line. Drivers slapped lines and called to their teams, amid the jangle of tack, braying mules, and the crunch of wheels churning on the creek bed. They pulled out along the column. They would provide some cover, though not nearly enough. Ainsley's mount pranced and circled, as he waited for the wagons to pass.

"On me! Double time!" The last three infantry companies fell in column and jogged behind the wagon train. He deployed them along the banks of the creek to secure the column's rear.

Crook stationed himself in the center of his command, waiting to meet the charge. "Hold your fire. Let them come." He raised his saber as the war party closed. There were hundreds of them. The largest Indian band he'd ever faced. At one hundred yards the air sang with bullets. Here and there a soldier fell. At seventy-five yards arrows rained silently out of the blue sky. Most fell harmlessly. A trooper kneeling on Crook's right dropped his rifle. He turned to his commanding officer, his face a twisted mask. He clutched the bloody shaft of arrow driven through his throat. Crook held his attention to the charge. At fifty yards his saber flashed forward in the sun. "Fire!"

Sharps carbines erupted in a deadly volley all along the skirmish lines. Ponies and warriors fell as the attack broke in a sweeping turn to the south. The attackers thundered past the blue line, raining rifle fire and arrows into the clouds of powder smoke and the troopers below.

The war party circled east and north, preparing a second assault. Crook watched them come around to their line of attack. "Reload. Hold your fire." He readied the line for what would become bloody attrition. He swallowed the sour ball gathering in his gut against his will.

As the war party swung back on line to charge the column, war whoops and shooting broke out on the attackers' flank. Gray Wolf and his Crow and Shoshone scouts swooped down out of the hills on their sworn Sioux enemy. They rode through the war party blunting the force of the attack in confusion. Still the main body closed on Crook's position. He raised his saber, silently counting down the range to fifty yards. "Fire!"

The volley spit death into the charge. Ponies and riders fell as the attackers swept past the column, raking the reloading defenders with rifle fire. They circled east and north again preparing another strike. They completed their run north and turned south to their charge.

Gray Wolf and his scouts struck again, this time from the north behind the Sioux. The attack broke down in a confused melee, turning inward on the Crow and Shoshone slashing through their numbers.

Ainsley galloped down the supply train to the back of the column. "Deploy that Gatling gun on the right flank!" The caisson wheeled toward the creek, bringing the big gun on the line of attack. He turned to the driver of the second caisson. "Follow me!" He spurred his mount toward the head of the column. The driver wheeled his caisson out of line and drove forward, one wheel of the gun carriage splashing in the creek bed. Ainsley led the second gun into line on the column's left flank.

The diversion by Gray Wolf and his scouts gave Ainsley time to deploy the Gatling guns with crossing fields of fire. The attackers shook off the scout's harassment and charged the withering blue line. Ainsley let them charge to a distance of one hundred yards. "Fire!" The gunner on the left flank ground the rotating barrels rattling round after round into the charge. The line of assault veered away from the left flank only to have the gun on the right break out a second stream of deadly chatter. Caught in a deadly storm of enfilade fire, the war party turned back to the valley wall. Gray Wolf and his scouts pursued the retreating attackers, hounding them with rifle fire from behind. The war party climbed the valley wall and wheeled on the pursuing scouts from above. Faced with superior force and a hail of bullets, Gray Wolf broke off the attack and returned to the column.

The shooting fell silent. Smoke hung over the column, slowly drifting off on the breeze. Dust settled. Crook studied the war party silhouetted against the skyline at the crest of the valley wall. It looked like they'd taken the fight out of them, at least for the moment. He looked up the column to the left and then the right. Up and down the line men tended the wounded. The dead lay where they'd fallen.

"Major Ainsley!" Crook barked at his left flank.

Ainsley left his post at the Gatling gun, mounted his horse, and galloped to the center of the line. He drew rein at Crook's side, "Sir?"

"Have the company commanders organize burial details. I don't know if we've taken the fight out of the hostiles as yet, but I want to be ready to move out if they do."

"Very good, sir." Ainsley saluted. He wheeled his horse and headed for the rear of the column.

Midday wore into afternoon. The sun rode high and hot. A gentle breeze provided little relief from the heat. The troopers held their line watching and waiting. Crook inspected the line of his adversaries through his glass. The circle of his lens came to rest on a chief riding a horse painted in spots. He wore a spotted war shirt. *Crazy Horse.* He studied his adversary. *It has to be. What is he doing this far south with a war party? Where the hell are Terry and Gibbon?*

Crook snapped his glass closed. Suddenly he felt very much alone. At best, Gibbon and Terry were miles to the northwest. He'd already taken significant losses. How the devil was he supposed to drive Crazy Horse into them? The hostiles appeared to be four or five hundred warriors in strength, at least that's what he'd seen. Could there be more in the area? The only way to know would be to send out his scouts. Under the circumstances that would split his command. If it hadn't been for the scouts' counterattack, they might have been cut to ribbons. He counted the risk of sending out the scouts unacceptable. As he mulled these thoughts, Ainsley rode up.

He stepped down and saluted. "Casualty report sir, thirteen dead, eighteen wounded. The burial details are nearly finished with their work."

"Thank you, Major." Crook set his jaw. *Thirteen dead and they'd expended a good deal of ammunition too.* "What do you make of their intentions, Major?" Crook lifted his chin to the riders silhouetted on the rim of the valley wall.

"Hard to say, sir. If we'd whipped 'em, I expect they'd be running north. Most likely they're bidin' time 'til the medicine's right for another run at us."

Crook pursed his lips, "Or they're waiting for reinforcements. We handled 'em pretty well, but we've taken our share of losses and used ammunition we'll need for a prolonged campaign in the north."

Crook spoke absently as if talking to himself. Ainsley could almost hear the thoughts behind his eyes. Logistics mattered for the whole of the campaign. At the moment, the tactical situation dictated other priorities. Their mission was to drive the hostiles north. They had this band outnumbered. Ainsley thought the situation clear. He'd attack. Mount a two-pronged assault. Direct a force against the valley wall below the hostiles' position. Deploy the Gatling guns at the base of the ridge and saturate the Indians' position. Send a second element up the valley wall to the south. Use this enveloping maneuver to attack the hostiles' flank from the south. That should easily get them running north. From there it became a matter of pressure and pursuit until Terry and Gibbon came to bear.

Crook bowed his head and scratched his beard. At length he drew himself up. "Major, notify the company commanders. We are breaking off the engagement. We are returning to Fetterman to see to our wounded and resupply."

Standing behind Crook, Ainsley's jaw dropped. He rolled his

eyes at the order. *What in hell is he thinking? Gibbon and Terry could be hung out to dry.*

Crazy Horse watched the bluecoats march south. He considered attacking the retreating column as his warriors raised cries of victory. He recalled Sitting Bull's vision of pony soldiers falling from the sky. He did not see Sitting Bull's vision in this fight. Here he and his warriors held the sky. Here too they won as the vision foretold. Sitting Bull's medicine must be very strong. More pony soldiers would come to fulfill Sitting Bull's vision. His warriors had tasted victory. They must take these stories to the Greasy Grass. Victory would encourage their brothers for the fight to come. Better they tell their stories to their brothers than face the rattling guns again. These bluecoats were defeated. He must join his warriors to their brothers.

Spotted Hawk sat his Appaloosa pony flanking Crazy Horse. He did not recognize this long knife chief. He did not see the yellow hair of his vision. His vision must wait for another day. He would take his lead from Crazy Horse.

The war leader wheeled his pony northwest with a victory whoop and led his warriors to join their brothers at Greasy Grass.

CHAPTER FORTY-THREE

Missouri River
Dakota Territory
June 18, 1876

Custer halted the column as the Crow scouts rode in. Curly drew his pony up beside Terry and Custer.

"Plenty big sign come down river." He pointed west.

Terry nodded. "Hold the column here, George. Let's have a look."

"Major Reno, hold the column."

Curly wheeled west to the river. Terry and Custer spurred their horses along behind. The trail of a large band stretched far and wide along the riverbank.

Custer stood in his stirrups to take it in. "Look at this. Ponies, dogs, travois, looks like we've made contact with a good-sized village." Custer could scarcely contain his excitement. He turned to Curly. "How old do you make the sign?"

The scout slipped from his pony to inspect the hoofprints. He toed a pile of dung with a moccasin, "Three, maybe four days."

"With the general's permission, sir, the Seventh can catch them in half that time."

"Permission denied. This column will link up with Colonel Gibbon as planned."

"But, sir, with all due respect our mission is to defeat the enemy and drive them to the reservations. General Sheridan's order gives autonomy to the commanders in the field."

"General Sheridan also charged me as senior officer to assure that our actions in the field are coordinated. Coordination begins when we rendezvous with Colonel Gibbon."

"But, sir, the enemy may escape us by then."

"No buts George, we are doing this my way. Is that understood?"

Custer braced in his saddle and ground his teeth. A blue vein throbbed at his temple. Venom clenched in his teeth. "Yes, sir."

Terry scarcely noted the reply. He wheeled his horse and squeezed up a lope back to the column.

Greasy Grass
Montana Territory
June 20, 1876

A billowing dust cloud at the south end of the valley announced the arrival of Crazy Horse and his Oglala and Cheyenne warriors. They galloped up the east bank of the river filling the air with a chorus of triumphant war cries. The ground shook with pounding pony hooves.

Autumn Snow watched as they galloped toward the village, anxious for Spotted Hawk's return. The war party wheeled into the river and splashed across to Sitting Bull's lodge joining the Oglala and Hunkpapa camps. They churned the river to a froth of white foam with sparkles of water catching the sun. From the manner of their return, Snow knew they must have victory songs to sing and stories to tell. Even at a distance, she picked out the warrior riding the painted pony with the spotted war shirt.

The war party's arrival charged the air in the camps along the river. Dust clouds rose to the north and south as people hurried toward the Hunkpapa camp. They gathered around Sitting Bull's lodge.

Crazy Horse climbed the west bank of the river and drew

rein. His warriors splashed ashore behind him, whooping and shaking their rifles and tomahawks in the air. Sitting Bull waited to greet him. Crazy Horse leaped down from his pony. His voice rang loud and clear.

"My Oglala and Cheyenne warriors have won a great victory."

The assembled villagers took up the cry to a deafening roar.

Sitting Bull raised his arms to quiet the people. "Let us hear Tashunca-uitco tell us of his victory."

The crowd grew as more villagers crowded into the Hunkpapa camp. Most stood quietly, straining their ears to hear Tashunca-uitco's words. Others spoke quietly, passing the account of a great victory to those too far away to hear.

"Bluecoats come from the south. My warriors and our Cheyenne brothers found them on the Rosebud. We attacked them at their campfires. We charged three times before the pony soldiers could bring their rattling guns to defend them. My warriors fought bravely. Many bluecoats died in these attacks. The pony soldiers sent their Crow and Shoshone dogs to fight for them. Bluecoats cannot stand before us. They go back the way they came. Sitting Bull's vision gives our warriors strong medicine." His words were greeted with a chorus of victory cries.

Crazy Horse raised his arms. "This night let all the people sing and dance to our victory!"

The war party took up the cry with the voice of the nation assembled on the Greasy Grass.

Sitting Bull listened. His heart filled as Tashunca-uitco spoke. His vision protected the warriors. They won a great victory. No pony soldiers had fallen from the sky. His vision spoke of more. More bluecoats would come. His warriors would meet them. Once more, victory would be theirs. This much he knew. It eased the burden he bore in his heart. He looked to the sky. Where his vision might lead, he still could not say.

Yellowstone River
Montana Territory
June 21, 1876

Custer crested the ridgeline at the head of the column. Golden prairie grasses turned green in the lush river bottom below. Cottonwood and scrub oak gathered in thickets along the riverbank, dappled in afternoon sunlight and shadow. Further to the south the river forked, the Yellowstone taking a more westerly course while the Bighorn turned south. Custer took little note as he pushed the descent to the river bottom where level ground would hold a faster pace. As he and the first elements of the Seventh reached the east bank, two riders broke the tree line across the river to the west. Military issue hats and loose flowing black hair identified them as scouts. They splashed into the water and crossed the chest-deep shallows in powerful plunges, pushing white foam. Custer drew the column to a halt.

"They're not ours," he said, turning to Terry, who rode beside Cooke. The two newspaper reporters followed closely, never straying far from Custer's side.

"Looks like we've made contact with Gibbon," Terry said. "We'll take a rest stop here and let Gibbon join up." Terry let Custer set the pace, but he was as tired as the rest of the men.

"But, sir, we've got five, maybe six hours of daylight left. Surely Colonel Gibbon can catch up if we tell the scouts we're moving forward."

"We've pushed the men and stock pretty hard, George. Everyone could use a little rest, including me." Terry dismounted, closing the subject.

Custer clenched his jaw. All this coordination and caution bullshit bordered on cowardice. If the hostiles discovered their presence before the scouts found them, they'd disappear like so much smoke in the wind.

Colonel Gibbon's column rode out of the late afternoon sun. They forded the river north of Terry's encamped force and began making their own camp. Gibbon and his second rode south along the riverbank to report to Terry. They found him in front of his tent seated at a camp table with Custer. Terry rose to greet them as Gibbon stepped down.

"General Terry, it's good to see you, sir. May I present my second, Major Danforth."

"Welcome John, Major, make yourselves at home." Terry motioned the orderly to bring up two more camp chairs. "It isn't much, but we've a comfort or two."

Gibbon and Danforth removed their hats and took the offered chairs. A light evening breeze came up across the river as the sun drifted toward the horizon.

"George and I were about to have some supper." Terry motioned to the orderly. "Will you join us?"

"That would be very nice, sir," Gibbon nodded. "It's been a long day." Gibbon turned to Custer. "George, it's good to see you too."

"Indeed," Custer nodded. He sulked moodily over Terry's decision to cut short the day's march.

Terry turned the conversation to the business at hand. "Have you seen any sign of the hostiles, John?"

Gibbon nodded. "We've seen signs of several bands moving south and east, but we've made no contact. I'm guessing there is a summer camp somewhere south of here. How about you, sir?"

"We crossed one trail headed south at the Missouri. That one was a large party. It does seem the tribes are moving toward a summer camp somewhere south of here. From what you say it sounds as though they may be gathering in significant numbers."

"Exactly what we hoped for," Custer said. "Let's give them no quarter from which to escape."

At that a mess detail arrived with steaming plates of beans, biscuits, bacon, and coffee.

"Not exactly Christmas dinner," Terry said, tearing a biscuit.

"Never is in the field," Gibbon said around a forkful of beans. "Even simple fare tastes pretty good when a man's hungry enough."

As the last rays of sunset disappeared into purple shadow, a second scouting party returned from the south. The Crow scout Curly reported to Terry's tent. The general and his commanders sat drinking coffee after finishing their meal. An orderly brought a lamp to the table as the officers turned to the scout expectantly.

"Did you find the enemy?" Custer blurted the question, unable to contain the anxiety of a caged animal.

Curly nodded, "Much sign. Many ponies and lodges move south to Greasy Grass."

"Little Bighorn river valley," Custer said, interpreting for Terry and Gibbon. "We need to move fast, General, before they get away."

Terry wouldn't allow Custer's impatience to run away with the tactical situation. "How far are they, Curly?"

The scout shrugged. "Three days. Maybe two, hard ride." He added this last with a glance at Custer.

Terry hesitated in thought.

Custer blustered into the void. "Sir, send the Seventh south. We'll cross the trail we saw at the Missouri. It'll lead us to their summer camp. We'll come around and strike them from the east before they get away."

Terry took a deep breath. He groped for the word. "I appreciate your, aggressiveness, George, but this is a job for more than the Seventh."

Damn it, Custer fumed privately. *Terry's infernal caution risks the opportunity for decisive victory.*

"Sergeant Major Kane, get my map case." Terry pushed the dishes to the side of the table as Kane returned with the map. Terry spread it on the table and anchored it against the ruffle of the night breeze with the lamp. He located the Little Bighorn river valley with one index finger, then estimated their current position to the north with the other. Gibbon bent over the map beside Terry, his mustache shadowed in lamplight. A disinterested Custer slouched in his camp chair, his boots stretched before him crossed at the ankle. He knew the tactical situation without the aid of a map.

"Very well then," Terry straightened up and stroked his beard. "Colonel Gibbon and I will march down the Yellowstone to the mouth of the Bighorn. We shall take positions there, blocking escape to the north. The Seventh will provide the coordination element for the campaign. George, you take the Seventh southeastward until you locate General Crook. If you cut the trail we crossed back at the Missouri, you will pass east of the camp on your way south. Send word back to us when you join General Crook. Crook can lead your combined force north. You and Crook shall strike a hammer blow against our anvil. Sitting Bull and his people will be caught between us."

Tediously dull tactic, Custer thought. Still he'd been given orders that would put him in proximity to the enemy. General Sheridan's orders gave discretion to field commanders. Discretion was all he needed. Once he had enemy contact, who could say what the circumstances on the ground might dictate? The hint of a smile tugged at the shadow of his mustache.

"It's settled then, we march at sunrise. Goodnight, gentlemen." Terry turned on his heel and went to his tent.

They broke camp in the gray light of predawn. Dark figures

scurried about routine chores, disturbing the early morning quiet with the movement of equipment and stock. Word of the scouts' report circulated through the ranks the night before. The prospect of a large village had become even larger by the retelling. New recruits or men facing their first encounter with Indians wondered what it all meant. Unknown added to the unease soldiers feel preparing for battle. Veterans knew they were in for a fight. Indian opposition would often avoid an organized fighting force. This would be no mere skirmish. The mission was to drive the tribes to the reservation. Sitting Bull, Crazy Horse, and the other non-reservation bands stubbornly resisted every attempt to confine them. There was no reason to expect any different now. A few understood the white presence in the Black Hills might make the tribes' will to fight something none of them had seen before.

The column assembled in the pale light of predawn. Terry, Gibbon and the infantry would march south along the Yellowstone to the Bighorn. Custer and the Seventh would ride south by southeast, in search of Crook's column. Custer rode up to Terry and Gibbon as they prepared to depart.

"Sir," Custer saluted. "The Seventh is ready to move out."

Terry looked up. Custer sat astride his horse, his features draped in shadow. "You understand your orders, George. The Seventh is the coordinating element in this campaign. Your mission is to find General Crook and lead him to the Indian camp."

He nodded.

Privately Terry worried over the man's legendary capacity to exceed his authority. He fixed the gleam in Custer's eye in his. "Now, Custer, don't be greedy. You wait for us."

"I won't." He wheeled his horse and returned to the head of his column, leaving his purposely ambiguous reply behind. He drew rein beside Lieutenant Cooke. "Terry has cut us loose,

Cookey. The Seventh is on its own! Major Reno, column of fours."

Reno cringed. He couldn't imagine the general "turning Custer loose."

"Column of fours!"

The command echoed crisp and clear to the column.

"Left wheel, ho!"

The column picked up a trot.

As the first rays of sunrise broke over the horizon, Custer bathed his face in golden light on the trail to glory. He could see it before him. He could feel it in his breast. No longer fettered to the apron strings of Terry's caution, at last he would have his time in the sun.

For the next two days he set a grueling forty-five mile a day pace worthy of his hard ass sobriquet. The enemy would not escape. The Seventh would have its fight and he would have his victory come hell or high water.

Chapter Forty-Four

Greasy Grass
Montana Territory
June 24, 1876

Sitting Bull rode out of the village at sunset as he often did. He splashed across burning river currents fired in the slanting rays of last light. He picked up an easy lope east across the valley floor, alone with his thoughts. His pony attacked the valley wall at a gallop, easing his climb to the rim. He pulled the pony to a halt at the crest of the ridge. A broad grassy plain stretched before him sloping gently to the top of the bluffs. The pony soldier presence felt strong here. He slid from his pony and dropped his rein to the ground. The pony would crop quietly while he prayed.

He sat, face to the west. The village sprawled along the far riverbank as far as he could see in the dusky light. Cookfires dotted the darkness illuminating nearby lodges, a patchwork of dancing light and shadow. In other places, firelight flared on the black rippled surface of the river. The glow reached to the night sky, spreading his prayers on a blanket of wood smoke over the people below. The burden of his vision weighed heavy on his heart. Many people had come in answer to his call.

Pony soldiers too were coming. When, he could not say. He only knew they would come. He could feel their presence. Would his vision shield the people? He believed it would. Still he fought doubt. The vision had not yet been fulfilled. Above all he must believe. He took his pipe and held it toward the village in prayer.

"Wakan Tanka, pity me. I offer you this pipe for all the people. Wherever we find the sun, the moon, the earth, the four points of wind there you are always. Father save the people, I beg you. We want to live. Guard us against all misfortune. Pity me."

The night breeze freshened from the north stirring his thoughts. *Pony soldiers come. Sand Creek, Washita,* the names whispered death. Death haunted the people. The death of the people haunted him. He prayed again.

"Wakan Tanka protect us, Wakan Tanka protect the people."

He took comfort and strength from the fires. Never in anyone's remembering had so many come to celebrate the old ways. The old ways grew strong in their numbers. The medicine in his vision found strength there too. The pony soldiers would see their strength. Would they go back to their forts like those that met Tashunca-uitco? Sitting Bull saw his vision again. No, they would fall from the sky. They would fall before the mighty Lakota. After that, only Wakan Tanka could know.

Montana Territory
June 24, 1876

They crossed the trail, coming down from the Missouri as expected. It cut southwest toward the Little Bighorn just as the scouts had said. They were close. Custer felt it. The thrill of the hunt fired his blood. It coursed through his veins like an intoxicating elixir and gathered in his breast. He drove the Seventh like a man possessed, relentless in the heat. He pushed his scouts harder still. *Find them, he demanded, find them.*

By late afternoon on the 24th, Benteen reflected the black mood of the troops. *The son of a bitch is a merciless madman. Satan don't dare let him in hell for fear he'd take command.*

Curly and his scouts rode in from the west at sunset. He dropped from his lathered pony at the head of the column.

Custer stepped down to hear his scout's report.

"Major Reno, have the men dismount. We'll rest here. Hardtack and water. No fires."

"Yes, sir."

"Big village on the Greasy Grass." Curly pointed southwest. "See some lodges from the Crow's Nest. Pony herds cover hillsides like ants, big village for so many ponies."

Custer slapped his gauntlets on the palm of his hand. This is it. This is the fight meant for the Seventh. He smiled in the fading light.

"Major Reno, we move out in an hour."

Hardtack and jerky, washed down with a little water. Not much of a supper. An hour's rest. He plans to march all night. A sour ball gathered in Reno's gut. Where was Crook? March all night. March where? Their orders were clear. He feared Custer's intentions. They were also clear.

Crow's Nest
Montana Territory
June 25, 1876

Custer signaled a halt near the base of the notched outlook Curly called the Crow's Nest. He studied the terrain running north. From the vantage point the scout had chosen, he expected they would have a good view of the river valley.

"Captain Benteen, hold the column here. The men may dismount, but hold your formation on the chance we need to mount a swift attack. Major Reno, come along; let's have a look at this village we are about to destroy." He nodded to Curly.

Custer and Reno fell in behind the scout as he wheeled his pony and galloped to the top of the ridge. They dismounted in a notch at the crest. Their exhausted mounts dropped their heads, blowing snorts. The river valley stretched before them hot and sultry, shimmering in a midmorning. The river wound its way through the valley, the banks patched in scrub oak and river willow.

"There," the scout pointed into the distance. The river wound through the hills and bluffs to the northeast, revealing a knot of tipi rambling along the west bank of the river before disappearing from sight.

Custer withdrew his glass from the leather pouch on the cantle of his McClellan saddle. He extended the tarnished brass tube and fitted it to his eye. He swept the hillsides east and west of the village looking for any sign of movement. The village stood quiet. "Doesn't look so big to me." Custer handed the glass to Reno.

Reno took the glass. "The way the river bends it's hard to tell how big it is."

"Pony herd there." Curly pointed to the low rolling hills north and west of the village. "Big herd. Big village. Many warriors."

Reno followed the grassy slopes disappearing in the heat haze rising from the river. The horse herds dappled the hills like a swarm of ants. "It sure enough is a big herd. There might be five hundred head or more and that's just those you can see." He handed Custer the glass.

He took a second look. "I'd say it's big enough to make this the greatest victory in the history of Indian warfare."

Reno winced. He was afraid that's where this was headed. Such arrogant underestimation of the enemy could only portend foolhardy action.

"I'd say we're outnumbered at least two to one and that's without assessing the rest of the village."

Custer laughed. "It doesn't matter, Major, I've seen this before at the Washita. The red devils yonder will scatter before the Seventh like dry leaves in a November wind." He lifted the glass to the valley wall east of the river. "The high ground runs east of the village along the bluffs. We'll take our advance up

Grasshoppers in Summer

that way." He snapped the glass closed and returned it to the saddle pouch. "We'll have to move fast though before they get away."

"Get away, sir?" Reno couldn't follow Custer's point.

"The way I see it, they're breaking camp. They're gettin' ready to run sure as hell."

Reno shook his head. "It looked quiet to me, sir."

"I say they're getting ready to run, Major." Custer laid heavy emphasis on the junior officer's rank. "The Seventh has no choice but to strike now."

The full force of Custer's intent struck Reno like a hammer blow. "I see, sir. What about General Crook?"

"What about Crook? I haven't seen hide nor hair of him, have you?"

"No, sir. The general's column may be still further south. General Terry said . . ."

Custer cut him off with a wave of his gauntlet. "I'm well aware of General Terry's orders. I am also aware of our mission. We are to engage the hostiles and drive them onto the reservation. Crook plainly hasn't arrived in time enough to participate in the engagement. We either strike now or face the prospect of losing contact with the enemy."

"But, sir, the numbers, surely you can see."

"I see a force of undisciplined savages about to be cut down by the finest cavalry in the U.S. Army. Now come along, Major, we'll have this done up before supper I should think." He stepped into his saddle.

Reno stood rooted in disbelief.

Custer wheeled away to return to the column.

Reno shook his head. He can't be serious. He means to attack, outnumbered two to one if not more. Our orders are to link up with General Crook. We're to coordinate the attack. He swung into his saddle preparing to follow old iron butt.

Curly looked again at the pony herd. It spread a dark blanket over the hillsides as far as he could see. Silently he shook his head and turned to his pony.

Custer led the Seventh northeast from the Crow's Nest, approaching the village from the south. He called a halt in the shelter of a draw a mile south of the village. He gathered Reno, Benteen, and Cooke around him at the head of the column and dismounted. He scratched a crude map in the dirt.

"The river runs through the valley here." He drew a soft curved line from north to south. "The village lies here on the west bank. This ridgeline becomes the east wall of the valley rising to a broad plain here." He traced the ridgeline east of the river roughly parallel to it. "We will leave the pack train here with a company to guard it. Captain Benteen, take H, D, and K companies and scout the bluffs west of here toward the river. You will secure our rear and stand ready in reserve. Major Reno and I will advance with the main attack force here." He pointed to the south end of the village. "Questions, gentlemen?" He looked from one man to the next.

No one spoke. No one would. Benteen knew it was pointless. He had a rearguard assignment to be thankful for. Cooke worshiped the ground the man walked on. The lot, if there was one, fell to Reno.

"Sir, begging the colonel's pardon, sir, don't you think it would be wise to scout the village north of the bend in the river? We really can't assess the enemy's strength from here."

Custer scowled. "I see no point to further delay, Major. It only serves the risk the enemy may discover our presence and give them moment to flee. It will be difficult enough to catch them should they scatter at the sound of the charge."

"But, sir, the men are exhausted. We've had two days and a night's forced march. The horses are spent. If we strike at midday, we've little chance of surprise."

"You heard me, Major, we attack. Have I made myself clear?"

Reno glared. "You have, sir."

"Anyone else?" He turned from Cooke to Benteen. The captain offered little more than a sullen shake of his head.

"Very well then, mount up."

Up and down the line troopers swung to their saddles amid jangling tack, creaking leather, and the rattle of sabers. When the troops were mounted Custer turned to Reno.

"Major, column of fours."

"Column of fours, forward, ho!"

The column surged forward at a trot, giving the appearance of a parade. Custer sat his saddle straight and proud at the head of his beloved Seventh. The standard-bearer rode at his right flank; the red and blue unit battle flag snapped in the hot summer breeze. Quiet calm settled over him in supreme confidence. He savored the coming victory without pause to consider he might have misjudged the strength and disposition of his enemy. It mattered not. He led the Seventh. Anything was possible to him.

Reno followed accompanied by the bugler. Privately the village filled the telescope in his mind's eye with a great white expanse. The hillsides to the west darkened by a vast pony herd. How many warriors were camped with Sitting Bull? They didn't know. The realization ate at his gut. Could the Seventh inflict decisive force on such a large encampment? He had grave doubts compounded by the fact Custer had already divided their force. The colonel's bravado wagered everything on the expectation the hostiles would run rather than fight. Even Terry's plan rested on that belief. Sheridan at least had ordered three columns into the field. Where the hell was Crook? Did any of them expect they would encounter such a large concentration of the enemy? No one could have anticipated this. He answered his own question. Custer fancied himself beneficiary of some epic moment engineered by fate for his personal glory. An icy ball of apprehension roiled his stomach.

Custer called a halt at the base of the ridgeline that climbed to the bluffs above the village. "Major Reno, take M, A, and G companies. Cross the river and attack the village from the south. I will take companies C, E, F, I, and L north. If the hostiles return your attack we will counter. If they run, press your attack. We will cut off their retreat."

Reno blinked. Custer was dividing their force yet again. Old Hard Ass had ordered him to attack the largest village anyone had ever seen with three companies, fewer than one hundred forty men.

"But, sir."

Custer raised a gauntleted hand to silence him.

"You have your orders, Major."

Reno fixed Custer's eyes with unspoken challenge. Everything in his better judgment screamed at the foolhardy recklessness posed by this course of action. He wheeled his horse, "M, A, and G companies, left wheel! Ho!"

He led them west to the river at a canter.

Custer watched them go.

"Forward, ho!"

He squeezed a canter up the ridgeline to the north. From there he could assess the enemy's disposition and tactics.

CHAPTER FORTY-FIVE

Oglala Camp
Greasy Grass
June 25, 1876

Pony soldiers rode into the valley south of the village under a thin haze of dust. They turned west and splashed across the river. They spread a line across the west bank of the river and advanced on the village from the south. Villagers, mostly women and children caught at the riverbank, ran from the bluecoat line. The pony soldiers charged, riding down on those fleeing before the attack. Those that did not fall ran screaming and crying for the safety of the village.

Sitting Bull's brother, Pizi, known as Gall, saw the soldiers advance. He watched his wife and child run from the riverbank. He stood helpless as pony soldier bullets cut them down. His vision ran red with their blood, his heart turned black with rage. He ran to his pony and vaulted onto his back. His war cry rallied warriors at the south end of the village. Everywhere warriors ran to their ponies to join him. Soon the war party at the south end of the village swelled to more than four hundred. Gall led them out to meet the pony soldiers. Fierce with courage and rage, he threw himself into the attack, inspiring the warriors who followed him.

The ground shook where Snow stood as warriors stormed out of the village. The air filled with war cries and rifle fire. As the battle engaged, she could see little more than swirling dust.

The clouds drifted south as the pony soldiers pulled back toward a grove of cottonwood trees.

Custer watched Reno fall back from his vantage point on the ridgeline above the valley. "It looks like there's some fight in this bunch, Cookey. Get me a messenger." Custer penciled a note to Benteen.

Come on, big village. Be quick. Bring packs.

He handed the note to a young trooper.

"Hurry, son."

The messenger saluted, wheeled his mount, and galloped to the rear.

Custer snapped his telescope open. He couldn't make out exactly what was happening south of the village for the dust. The situation there seemed to be deteriorating. Elements of Reno's command broke from the cottonwoods; some mounted, others on foot. They ran for the river. Indians pursued them as they splashed across the river. Some were cut down; others made it to the low hills and ravines leading up the ridgeline away from the river.

"Should we counter Major Reno's position?" Cooke's tentative question brought Custer back to his promise of support.

Custer swung his glass to the main body of the village. Dust rose in great dun clouds everywhere. "Look there, Cookey," Custer pointed. "They're breakin' camp gettin' ready to run. Benteen will relieve Reno. We need to cut off the main body's escape."

Cooke's eyes widened in disbelief. For all his lack of experience and respect for the colonel, his gut told him this enemy wasn't running away.

Custer snapped his telescope closed without taking note of Cooke's reaction.

"Forward, ho!"

Suddenly a cloud of dust boiled up below the ridgeline ahead. Custer signaled a halt. He squinted against the shimmering heat waves rising along the dun grassy slope. Dark shadows, horses, and riders crested the ridge from the west as though rising out of the ground to meet them. The party halted some distance off. They appeared some thirty or forty in number. Seeing the Seventh drawn up before them, they wheeled their ponies and galloped back down the ridge returning to the village. Custer smiled. *They ran,* exactly as he knew they would.

"Bugler, sound the charge!"

A bugle call sounded alarm beyond the valley wall to the east. A dust cloud rose behind it, staining the blue sky. Snow watched a war party gallop down the ridge wall to the valley floor. As they reached the river bottom, she saw pony soldiers pour over the ridge wall above in pursuit. The words of Sitting Bull's vision beat in her heart. The war party split the hot dry air with warning cries as they raced across the grassy flats to the river. The bluecoats fought their ponies, slipping and sliding down to the valley, billowing clouds of dust. The warriors splashed across the river to the village. Alarm spread all around her. *Pony soldiers come. It is Sitting Bull's vision.* Warriors ran to their ponies. Women gathered their children.

Sitting Bull saw his vision spill over the valley wall. Pony soldiers fell on the village as if from the sky. All around him warriors took up their weapons and mounted their ponies. This day he would know the truth of his vision.

Spotted Hawk heard the bugle call. He saw the pony soldiers fall from the sky. He looked beyond the dust cloud, staining the sky at the ridgeline. High above where the sky remained blue, a lone hawk circled the plain. Spotted Hawk saw his vision. This day he would find the yellow hair long knife.

"Yie yie yee!" He ran to his pony.

Hunkpapa and Arapaho under Low Dog thundered out of the village to meet the pony soldier attack. Their ponies turned the river white as they galloped across. The pony soldiers no more than reached the valley floor when they saw warriors charge into the river like great dark clouds running before a storm. Sunlight flashed the splashing river water like lightning. Thunder rumbled under the hooves of more than a thousand ponies as the storm broke over the east bank of the river across the grassy plain.

The bluecoats faced the largest fighting force ever assembled by the people. They were trapped against the valley wall. They turned and ran. The warriors sensed victory. They rode with strong medicine. It filled their hearts. Tired pony soldier horses labored to climb the valley wall to the ridgeline. The high ground they charged down now slowed their retreat. The smell of fear followed the retreating bluecoats as the warriors pursued them across the valley.

Sitting Bull lifted his eyes to Wakan Tanka. He held out his arms in prayer over his warriors. "Wakan Tanka protect the people."

Women and children ran to the riverbank to watch the warriors pursue the bluecoats. Snow ran with them. She watched the warriors overrun stragglers who fell behind the main body in retreat. The pony soldiers reached the rim of the valley wall and disappeared. Low Dog and hundreds of Lakota and Arapaho followed. Soon the plain beyond the ridgeline swirled in great clouds of dust building in and spreading under the hooves of more than a thousand attacking ponies. Gunshots and war cries carried faintly on the hot summer breeze. A great battle took place on the plain above the village beyond the seeing of the women and children. Powder smoke colored the dust clouds as the battle raged furious.

Crazy Horse led his Oglala and Cheyenne into the river following Low Dog to battle. Spotted Hawk followed his war leader. River water splashed his face. It made his heart clean and strong. His spirit soared with the great hawk circling the plain above. He splashed up the east bank of the river and put his heels to his pony's flanks, anxious to join the battle, eager to fulfill his vision. He galloped with his brothers. The ground shook beneath the power of their charge as they raced across the valley floor. The washes and draws at the base of the ridge swallowed their numbers. He urged his pony up the coulees and ravines that etched their way to the crest of the ridge. The ponies caught the scent of battle and stretched out in powerful strides.

Spotted Hawk led a small band up a narrow wash climbing gently to the grassy slope above. Halfway up the wash he saw a rider picking his way down the same rocky slope his pony climbed. The rider saw Spotted Hawk's band and tried to climb out of the wash. His pony stumbled. The stony bank would not hold his footing. As they closed, a flicker of recognition tugged at Spotted Hawk. Something about this man spoke to him. He was Crow, one of the yellow hair's scouts, judging by the unbraided flow of his hair. Killing a hated enemy would be victory in a greater victory. He saw the black wave in his top knot. He remembered Autumn Snow's words. One of his brothers fired at the man. Spotted Hawk spun on his pony's back.

"Don't shoot! This one is mine." He checked his pony as the others galloped past up the draw. He walked his pony across the draw to the Crow and slipped to the ground. The scout stepped down from his pony soldier saddle. The two men stood silent, lost in the moment, the sounds of the battle a distant reminder of the conflict.

"You are the one they call, Curly?"

The scout nodded. "How did you know?" His words caught in his throat. Recognition flickered in a distant memory of another battlefield. His eyes widened at the sight of a ghost.

"You," he gasped. "You are dead. Curly counted coup at the Washita."

"You counted coup on the near dead. The Great One Above gave Spotted Hawk new life. Autumn Snow told Spotted Hawk of your kindness to her. You freed her to return to me."

The scout nodded. "It is good she found you. I did not know if she would find her people. There is no honor in white man's slavery."

Spotted Hawk turned to his pony and pulled his blanket off the saddle. He tossed it to the man called Curly. "Here, put this on and ride out of here. No one will trouble a brother Cheyenne."

"You would do this for a Crow?"

"Spotted Hawk does this for the man who showed kindness to his wife. Spotted Hawk does this for the man who set her free. Now, go in peace. Spotted Hawk has a vision to fulfill."

Curly watched Spotted Hawk swing up on his pony with a whoop. He kicked his pony into a gallop up the draw toward the sounds of gunfire above. He counted the Cheyenne a worthy coup as he threw the blanket over the pony soldier saddle. He stepped up and let his pony pick his way down the draw.

Spotted Hawk's pony gathered his hindquarters in a powerful surge that broke the valley wall rim. He checked the pony to a stop at the base of a long sloping rise. Dust boiled up the slope toward a flat at its crest. The land trembled with pounding pony hooves. The air sang with the rattle of gunfire and war cries. Smoke and dust hung like winter mist over the hillside. Bluecoat soldiers huddled in small knots surrounded by Lakota, Cheyenne, and Arapaho warriors. Some of the bluecoats shot their horses and hid behind them. Others knelt or stood to fire into the dust storm circling around them. One fell with an arrow buried in his chest. Another jerked as a bullet struck him. He jerked again and then again as he fell.

Spotted Hawk rode from one fight to the next searching for his vision. These pony soldiers would die to the last man. He and his brothers were too many for them. He searched for the one pony soldier he came to kill. He rode north along the ridgeline. There he saw it. The red and blue flag whipped by the summer wind. He kicked his pony into a gallop. He would find the yellow hair with the little red and blue flag.

He drew his pony to a halt. Crazy Horse led his warriors in a circle of death, trapping the pony soldiers with the little flag inside. Warriors rained bullets and arrows on them. Many bluecoats and horses already lay dead. Others lay wounded still trying to fight.

The yellow hair stood beside the red and blue flag, his pistols in hand. His yellow hair, shorter now than Spotted Hawk remembered, fluttered on the hot summer breeze. He looked whiter now. His eyes knew fear. Spotted Hawk's medicine grew strong at the sight of him.

He slipped down from his pony. He fixed his eyes on the long knife. He walked through the storm of his brothers' flying ponies. Warriors cut their mounts left and right to avoid him. One painted pony skidded to a halt and reared, pawing the air and nearly throwing his rider. Spotted Hawk moved as if in a dream, not seeing his brothers, not hearing the bullets whine through the air like a swarm of angry bees. He paid no attention as he stalked his vision. Dust choked his breath. Gun smoke burned his eyes. His rifle felt smooth and light. He felt rage in his breast and peace in his heart as he followed the vision given him in the sacred Sun Dance. Strong medicine freed him from harm as it shielded other great warriors.

He stalked his enemy, close enough to see into his eyes. Close enough for the hated long knife to see into his. He lifted his rifle, fit the stock to his shoulder, and leveled his aim. His vision danced on the sight, blackened against the bright summer sky. Bullets whistled and whined around him. They struck the ground and kicked up dirt at his feet. Spotted Hawk did not notice. Such things could not touch him.

The bluecoat chief sensed him. He turned. His eyes flickered over the rifle sight. He raised his pistol and took careful aim. Their eyes locked over the sights of their weapons. The long knife squeezed his trigger. No one heard the metal click over the battle roar. The yellow hair felt it. He knew it.

Spotted Hawk's vision filled his rifle sight. He squeezed. The rifle charged. No one heard this report mingled among the war cries and shots filling the air. The bullet struck the long knife chief at the same instant as another. A dark killing hole appeared on the rifle sight. A red flower of life greeted death. His vision fulfilled, he watched the yellow hair fall. He raised his arms wide, shaking his rifle in victory.

He turned his back on his enemy. He turned away from a victory the people would forever remember in song. He walked through the killing circle of his brothers, back to his pony. He swung up on his back as the sounds of gunfire began to die away. A chorus of victory cries rose from more than a thousand throats. Spotted Hawk wheeled his pony and squeezed up a lope back to the village, back to his Autumn Snow. His spirit felt light. His heart soared with the mighty hawk, circling above his brothers, counting coup on the last of their enemies. He sought his vision. He found it. He filled it. The circle of his quest complete.

The scene from the riverbank changed little over the short time before the warriors began returning to the village. Other pony soldiers joined the fighting on the valley wall south of the village. These ran away with those that survived Gall's attack. Great clouds of dust dirtied the blue sky above the battlefield to the north where Low Dog and Crazy Horse fought. Shooting punctuated the shrill wail of war cries in the distance. When the shooting fell silent, the dust clouds slowly drifted off on the late afternoon breeze. The warriors returned victorious. The pony soldiers with their long knives lay dead, they said.

Spotted Hawk was among the first to return. Autumn Snow let out a small sigh when she saw his pony splash across the river toward the village. Relief flooded her heart. He drew rein in front of her and slipped to the ground. He took his wife in his arms.

"The yellow hair is dead," he said softly. "He fell to Spotted Hawk's vision."

Autumn Snow lifted misty eyes to his and rested her head on his breastplate.

The village slowly filled with joyous victory celebration. The singing and dancing would go on through the night. The wind freshened. The carrion on the hill would become the work of wolves and vultures.

Sitting Bull rode out alone again at sunset. He splashed across the river, fired in the slanting rays of last light. He picked up an easy lope across the valley floor to the east. His pony attacked the valley wall, climbing the ridge at a gallop. He pulled him to a halt at the rim. The broad grassy slope stretched before him again. The spirits of the pony soldiers sang their death songs on the night breeze. The smell of death hung in the air. This was the gift Wakan Tanka foretold. Was it the fulfillment of his vision or only the beginning? He slid from his pony and dropped his rein to the ground. The pony dropped his head to crop quietly.

Many soldiers would come after this victory, too many even

for such a great number as this. Wakan Tanka gave the people a great victory, but what had they won? He remembered Red Cloud's war. He won a great victory. He won peace. He won treaty lands. White men broke the treaty. They took the land. They took the Paha Sapa. Now Red Cloud lived captive to the white man's reservation. What would come to his people from this victory? They would sing and dance in celebration. The warriors would tell stories of great deeds and triumphs. How long would they tell these stories? The people would sing songs. How long would they sing these songs in freedom? Wakan Tanka knew the answers to these questions. Wakan Tanka did not speak. Sitting Bull did not know. He knew only the questions weighed heavy on his heart. Tomorrow the people must go to the four winds.

CHAPTER FORTY-SIX

Department of the Missouri
Chicago, Illinois
June 30, 1876

Sheridan set the telegram aside. He rubbed the tension throbbing at his temples. George was a warrior to the last. He'd done the job they knew he would when he and Cump fought for his appointment. He'd never intended the man to die. The eulogy he read in the morning *Tribune* glorified his memory with the courage and valor of his daring successes. There'd been no mention of any of the darker aspects of his career. Likely they could thank the grieving widow for that. Libbie had proven as adept as George in maneuvering the press to her purposes.

So be it then. The man made the supreme sacrifice. Those who knew him might question his prudence and motive in his actions, but that would be little benefit to the country. By this last act, he gave the country the national will to demand nothing short of final resolution to the Indian problem. That was the goal he and Cump set out to achieve. It had taken three years to achieve; but it played out almost as they envisioned, including the part George played. He hadn't intended to send the man to his death. Then again, he knew from the outset he could count on George to seize the decisive moment when he encountered it. For all his faults Sheridan valued Custer as a fighting man. He'd counted on George to be George. This time it ended in tragedy. For that he must bear some responsibility for the man's death and the deaths of his command. That came as a heavy burden, mitigated only by the survivors' reports. Those reports were either highly exaggerated or George blundered into an assault on an enemy force many times his strength. Such an action could be considered reckless beyond even Custer's liberal standards. Nothing could be done for that now. All he could do to honor the death of those men was mount an aggressive campaign to bring the hostiles to heel. They would inevitably win final resolution of the Indian problem, in part, thanks to George Custer. Admiration of his memory seemed small enough tribute for that.

White House
Washington, D.C.
June 30, 1876

Custer Lost!
Seventh Cavalry Command Massacred!

The headlines screamed injustice and outrage. The newspaper accounts mourned the tragic loss of a dashing young hero savagely cut down in the carriage of his duty. Editorials across the nation opined the action on the Little Bighorn proved beyond reproach, that peace with the hostiles would only be found in total military defeat.

Grant folded the paper and tossed it onto the clutter of paper heaped on his desk. Twilight turned the office dusky gray. He scratched a match and lit the desk lamp. He trimmed the wick. Low light suited his dark mood. He went to the sideboard and poured a generous measure of good Kentucky bourbon. He loosened his tie and threw open the glass doors to the gardens. The soft voices of night sound crept in on a gentle breeze. He sipped his whiskey.

History will lionize the son of a bitch. They'll turn him into a hero. *Two hundred ten good men dead and for what? The brass bit of a general's star he thought he deserved.* Grant shook his head and knocked back his drink. He poured another and crossed to the office settee.

He sat heavily, weary at the end of the day. Weary as he neared the end of his presidency. He took a cigar from the box on the coffee table and bit the tip. He spat it on the carpet. The match flared yellow sulfur smoke in the shadows. He let the chemical burn off and drew the flame to the tip. The cigar glowed red. He blew a cloud of smoke into the darkness, the fragrance a familiar comfort.

History would record Custer a hero, his persona a carefully polished looking glass no matter the facts. It was the reflection people wanted. It played to their preconceptions of right and wrong, good and evil. Custer and his command were victims of a savage attack, carried out by the white man's mortal enemy. Custer hadn't lived to savor the glory, but his death would now secure total defeat of the First Americans the president's peace policy had sought to protect. The public would demand no less. No amount of reason could be made to prevail.

He'd failed. What place would history accord him for that? he wondered. He contemplated the twilight of his presidency. How would history record it? He came to office with the intentions of a reformer. What he got for his troubles were scandals, a financial panic, and a legacy of corruption in the Bureau of Indian Affairs. This last hurt worst of all. He'd hoped to do for the Indian all that Lincoln had done for the freedmen of the south. In this he'd failed. Had Custer paid the price for his failed policy? Is that how history would record it? Who could say? Newspapers across the country idolized the man's flamboyance. In life, the man had never been any more than a thorn in the side of his presidency. Now it seemed he would remain so in death.

Hell, maybe Cump and Phil were right all along. It seemed so now. Thanks to the public outcry over Custer they were sure to have their final resolution to the Indian problem. Righting the wrongs of past policies would be left to some other presidency, if such justice were ever to be done.

"Sam, will you be coming up to dinner?" Julia called from the door.

"Yes, dear, I'll be along directly."

He examined the tip of his cigar. We'll both be off to private life soon. Thankfully, he expected, with no questions about what might be recorded of that. It would be a welcome respite from the office at hand. He tossed off his drink, stubbed out his cigar. He hoisted himself off the settee and crossed the office to his desk. He glanced around the office wistfully mindful of all the events that swirled around his presidency these past eight years. He considered the presidencies that preceded him and those that might follow. If these walls could talk, they could record history. Sadly, that task was left to men. Men recorded events as interpreted through the lens of their own viewpoint. That lens would shine brightly on Custer. Dare he hope for an enlightened view of his efforts? He shrugged off the shadow of doubt. He cupped a hand in the glow of the soot-stained chimney and blew out the lamp. He crossed the office gloom, his passage marked by the hollow echo of footfalls. The office door clicked softly closed behind him.

Little Bighorn River
August 1876

Death's stench hung over the grassy bluffs and river bottom like a pall. Weeks had passed since the massacre. Wolves and vultures gorged on carrion. The sight of it sickened Crook. Burial details retched at the remains, gasping for fresh air, which seemed in short supply in the heat. Even at a distance, the air smelled tainted, sweet, and foul. Most of the dead were ruined beyond the decency of identification and proper individual burial. The best that could be done was to avenge the atrocities done them.

The sheer size of the camp sign staggered the imagination. It stretched nearly two miles along the west bank of the river. How many warriors might have inhabited such a village? Two thousand? Three? The advance elements of Custer's Seventh numbered some six hundred men. Surely his scouts must have warned him of so large a village. He could not possibly have blundered into it by surprise. What possessed the man to engage a force so vastly superior? According to reports by Major Reno and Captain Benteen, Custer had not only attacked the village, he'd divided his force in doing so. He was known to be aggressive, some even said reckless, but this? This was beyond reckless. This was foolhardy. He doubted Terry and Gibbon combined could have prevailed in the face of such force. Crook took some solace in that for his own retreat from the Rosebud. A prudent commander respected superior force. Not Custer. His thoughts ever rode to glory.

And what of the village? The greatest concentration of hostiles in the history of plains warfare vanished like so much morning fog. Sheridan vowed to avenge Custer. He dispatched the Army in force to scour the Powder River country and "Bring the hostiles to heel if it takes until spring."

Crook had no illusions about the chances of finding roving bands during the summer hunt. The chances amounted to luck as luck would have it. Hound them, harass them, drive them to ground in their winter camps. That's where decisive blows might be struck. Crook meant to be at the forefront, striking those blows. He needed victory to silence the voices of those who held his withdrawal from the Rosebud responsible for the loss of Custer and the Seventh.

Monroe, Michigan
September 1876

Livid, her anger so strong it tasted bitter on her tongue. Anger overcame sorrow so deep she felt its pain to the core of her being. She may appear delicate, petite, porcelain. The appearance masked a steel spine and iron will. She squared her shoulders and paced, her heels tapping the polished wood floor. Bright autumn sun filtered through lace curtains, pooling before the fashionable formal furnishings of her parents' parlor.

How could he be so spiteful? How could he suggest such a thing of her Autie? He was President of the United States and a soldier for all that. He knew better. He had to. Seemingly he did not. She'd not allow it. She'd never accept it. George could never be responsible for his own death or the deaths of those worthy men serving under him. Those men knew George. They loved him, just as she loved him. She couldn't sit by. She wouldn't sit by.

An awaited knock at the door released her frustration. She glanced in a passing mirror as she made her way to the foyer. She smoothed an errant tendril behind her ear. A tall, thin figure stood in the shadow beyond the curtained window. She twisted the knob, opening the door to the porch. A pinched scarecrow of a man greeted her with sad eyes.

"Mrs. Custer, Frederick Whittaker." He extended a soft bony hand. "Please accept my condolences. I appreciate your willingness to see me at such a trying time." The cultured English accent rolled off his tongue, dripping in sincerity.

"Mr. Whittaker, please come in." She stepped aside, closed the door behind him, and led him to the parlor. "Please, have a seat. Would you care for a cup of tea? I've just made a fresh pot."

"Why, yes, thank you. That would be lovely."

"I'll only be a moment." She went to the kitchen and returned with a china tea service on a silver tray. She set it on a low table before the settee and poured two delicate cups. She handed one saucer to her caller, picked up the other, and took a seat in a wing chair drawn up beside the settee. The chair might have swallowed her petite frame had it not been for a certain determination in her bearing.

"Now, Mr. Whittaker, as I understand it, you wish to write a book concerning my husband's life."

He nodded. "I have long been an admirer of your husband, Mrs. Custer. I believe the public should know him better. I can't think of a better way to do that than a biography of his life and accomplishments."

She lowered heavy lashes in silence for a time. She lifted their veil. "Yes, I'm prepared to agree with your premise. There are those, including the president, who blame my Autie for what happened." She paused, gathering herself, "Out there."

He nodded.

"It's not true." She squared her shoulders. Her eyes flashed defiant. "George was the bravest man ever. He served his country with valor and distinction in the war. He served her so again in the Indian campaigns. He made the ultimate sacrifice for his country. That is the George people should know. Is that the story you wish to tell, Mr. Whittaker?"

"It is, Mrs. Custer. I wish to write a true and complete life of Colonel George A. Custer."

She met his eyes, "General George A. Custer, a complete life of General George A. Custer."

"Yes, of course, I'm sorry, General George A. Custer."

She held his eyes, measuring the man. "You will tell the true story? You will not be misled by those who wrongly blame George for what happened? He is a hero. Your book will testify to the truth of that?"

"It will, Mrs. Custer. With your help, we shall have a true and complete testament to the life and accomplishments of General George Custer."

She sat silent a moment more. "I believe you, Mr. Whittaker. We shall have just such a testament."

CHAPTER FORTY-SEVEN

Powder River
Hunting Grounds
The spirits of life and death followed close after Greasy Grass. More pony soldiers came that summer and into the whispers of autumn. They pursued the people living the old ways without rest. In her heart, Snow knew they would know no peace until they moved to the reservation. Tashunca-uitco must know it too, though he gave no sign of it. He led the people on the path of following the old ways. The path grew hard. Hunting was poor. Much time was lost to breaking camp and running from the bluecoats. Winter would protect them if they found enough food. Winter moons would give rest until spring. Then it would begin again. How long could they go on?

Spotted Hawk rejoiced in the victories they won. His heart sang the songs of the Rosebud and Greasy Grass. His medicine grew strong in fulfilling his vision and telling his story. She carried the seed of that strength in her belly. Spotted Hawk believed his son would grow to be a great warrior in the old ways. She could feel his power. Still she feared for her son. The old ways may not be there for him to grow into.

She remembered the Washita and the hardships of the white man's reservation. She remembered the dark husk of a worm in the white man's flour. The old ways died there. The white man's reservation came hard to a warrior of the old ways. She had seen it in Spotted Hawk. Spotted Hawk and the other young men struggled to find manhood in the ways of the white man. It would grieve her to see such a thing in their son. Crazy Horse would not accept this. Spotted Hawk would follow wherever he led.

She too had a vision. She saw a fork in the trail. The white man's reservation followed one path. Crazy Horse led them down the other, the path of the old ways. This is the path Spotted Hawk chose. Snow feared this path led only to death. The old ways led to a warrior's death. Spotted Hawk would choose the warrior's death. She saw the death of the old ways on the path to the white man's reservation. The vision troubled her heart. The path of death struggled with the life in her belly. What path would they choose for their son? He would know only the ways of the life he lived. They would be his ways. He would choose to die for the old ways only if he lived them.

Powder River
Montana Territory
October 1876

Wind whipped the feather in his hair with a cutting edge. Icy fingers knotted in his belly. Spotted Hawk watched the long blue column wind its way up the valley from the Greasy Grass. Surely, they had seen their fallen brothers. They knew the Lakota victory. They came as he knew they would, many more this time. Up and down the long line the little wagons with the rattling guns and guns that spoke thunder rode among the pony soldiers. They came to fight the people. This time they made a blue forest of long knives with walls of bullets. He saw the rattling guns at the Rosebud. He had not seen the guns that spoke thunder before. He knew the stories. The white men protected their forts with them. Now they brought them out against the people. The bluecoats would fight behind the rattling guns and guns that spoke thunder. Many would die before a single coup could be counted. He shook his head. It spoke to the low character of men who fought with rattling guns and thunder. They did not fight like men. They did not fight like warriors.

He pushed back off the grassy hill where he lay hidden. He swung up on his pony and wheeled away to the west northwest, circling away from the pony soldier scouts. He rode by the light of the moon that night. The next day, the evening star lit his way by the time he splashed across the shallow creek where the band camped. He loped into the village straight to the lodge of Crazy Horse. Tashunca-uitco rose from his cookfire as Spotted Hawk pulled his pony up and slipped down. The warrior chief read concern in the face of his wolf.

"Pony soldiers come."

Crazy Horse shook his head. He looked off to the new moon rising cold and bright. They won a great victory in Sitting Bull's vision. The medicine was strong. It was not strong enough. The knowing haunted his heart. Now more bluecoats came.

"Where?"

Spotted Hawk pointed southeast. "There."

"How far?"

"Two days. The scouts search there." He swept his arm east and north. "They may not find us."

Crazy Horse shook his head. "They are very close. How many?"

Spotted Hawk met his eyes. "Many. They come with rattling guns and guns that speak thunder."

Crazy Horse knit his brow and looked off to the North Star. "We must move north. We cannot let them find us here."

Spotted Hawk nodded. He took his pony's lead and led him to the picket line. He found Autumn Snow seated before their lodge. She rose to greet him.

"Welcome my husband. I did not think you would be back so soon."

"Pony soldiers come."

A dark shadow crossed her eyes in a flicker of firelight. She let her head rest on his chest. He took her in his arms and held her for a time.

"Crazy Horse says we move north in the morning."

"Come sit by the fire. You must be tired and hungry. I have a corn cake and some pemmican."

He smiled. She always had a corn cake when he returned. She would make one for him each evening he was away. If he did not return, she ate it in the morning only to begin the ritual anew the next night. She believed this simple act would bring him back to their lodge. It did. Each time he knew he'd found his way home.

She brought him his meal and sat beside him. Somewhere nearby the mellow notes of a flute rode a crisp evening breeze. It foretold the coming winter.

"Will the snow stop the bluecoats?"

Spotted Hawk shrugged. "When winter is hard no one can move. When spring comes, so will the bluecoats."

"The bluecoats will fight until they force us onto their reservations. Then the people will no longer belong to the land."

"We will fight. Crazy Horse will lead us." His words blustered over the vision, long bluecoat lines, rattling guns, clouds of thunder smoke.

Snow held her counsel. He did not see the fork in their path. He was not ready to hear her vision. He would not accept it until Tashunca-uitco faced this fork. Then he would see. Then Crazy Horse would decide to live or to die. Spotted Hawk would follow him. Only then would she ask if he made this choice for his son. She would accept his answer. She prayed he would choose life.

"Come, take me to our robes." She took his hand and led him into the tipi. She stepped into the pool of soft light beneath the smoke hole. She drew the hem of her buckskin dress over her head. She turned to the dark figure beyond the pool of starlight. Light and shadow splashed her willowy body swollen with life. She held out her hands, her eyes dark and moist. He came to her. She felt his warmth against her skin as she untied the thong that held his bone breastplate. He drew her to him, holding her fast in his arms. He gathered her in his arms, knelt and settled her gently in the buffalo robes. She gave herself up in the old way to the trill of flute song.

In the morning white frost lay on the ground around the lodges. The women struck camp with practiced efficiency. By midmorning the tipi, clothing, and utensils were secured to the travois pulled by the women's ponies. Wolves returned to report the way north clear for travel. The long slow trek north began.

Crazy Horse led the way. The people trailed out behind in a long loose procession. Children ran with the dogs or rode with their mothers. Warriors ranged far and wide forming a defensive perimeter. Young boys brought up the rear driving the pony herd.

By midday frost melted and a pale sun warmed the afternoon. Autumn Snow rode with the women of her clan. Children laughed and played unaware of the mood of their elders. A muted pall hung over the women, dampening their usual merry chatter. This move did not follow the buffalo herds. This move led to winter camp. Not their usual winter camp. This move would find a winter camp safe from the bluecoats. So they hoped. The danger of the pony soldier presence followed them like a long dark shadow.

Autumn Snow wondered again how long this might last. The question haunted her thoughts accompanied by the echoes of flute song. Her vision felt strong in her heart. She did not have the gift of seeing, but in this she knew she saw far and true.

When the time came, she must make Spotted Hawk see the truth of her wisdom. *Great One Above,* she prayed. *Give me words.*

Yellowstone River
Montana Territory
October 1876

Crook sat at a small camp desk in his tent, wreathed in cigar smoke. The sooty halo of a single oil lamp created the illusion of warmth. Chill night breeze ruffled the tent canvas. The map spread before him showed little by way of topographical features between their current position north of the Little Bighorn and the northerly stretches of the Missouri. He knit his brow and massaged the bridge of his nose. The vast sea of rolling hills and plains suggested a child's game of hide and seek. The tribes left their summer camp killing ground and scattered to the winds in small bands. They'd run. They continued to run. The scouts saw sign from time to time, but nothing fresh. It was as though the land had swallowed them up. The red devils could be anywhere.

Boots crunched out of the darkness beyond the tent flap. "Come in," Crook ordered without waiting for the caller to announce himself. Chief of scouts Caleb Forrester pulled back the flap and stepped in.

"Evenin', General."

Crook sat back in his chair, glanced around the tent, and gestured to his trunk. "Have a seat, Mr. Forrester." Forrester folded his bent frame onto the trunk lid. "I take it your scouts have returned."

"They have, sir."

He fished a cigar out of his breast pocket and offered it to the scout. "Care for a smoke?"

"Got my own, General." He drew a pipe from his vest pocket

and filled it from a small sack.

The scout scratched a match and puffed his smoke to light.

Crook relit his cigar and blew out the match just beyond the tip of his finger. He sat back behind a long easy draw. "Well out with it, man, what do they have to report?"

Forrester blew a cloud of fragrant smoke. "They found sign of a village two days west and north of here. Pretty good sized it was."

"Was?"

"Yes, sir. The Indians was gone. Moved north by the look of it."

"How long ago?"

"Few days, maybe a week. Hard to say for sure."

Crook furrowed his brows in thought, weighing the possibility of pursuit. "What do you make of it, Caleb?"

"Well, sir, my guess is they know we're here. They went north to winter. Left to their old ways, they'd do just the opposite."

"You think we can catch 'em?"

Forrester let the question hang in the air for emphasis. "Maybe. Then again, winter out here can hit pretty hard and fast. They's plenty of snow in the mountains already. You wouldn't want to get caught out here on the wrong side of winter, General. Get caught in a big storm and you might not get out 'til spring." He paused. "If you get out at all, that is."

Damn it! Crook fumed.

"We pretty well know where they're headed. Properly provisioned for an early march in spring we should be able to catch up with 'em before they break winter camp. If we take a westerly line of march and they do break camp early, chances are they'll come right to us."

Like it or not, the scout had the right of it. He didn't like the notion of giving up. He didn't want to report they'd withdrawn to Sheridan. It would make for a damn long winter's wait. They hadn't accomplished much by way of avenging the Little Bighorn fight. The newspapers and public sentiment still yapped about it being his fault. Now he'd have to listen to it for another five or six months before he could take the field again. *Why'd the dumb son of a bitch have to go and get himself killed anyway? Because Custer was Custer, that's why.* Now there was nothing else for it, but to put up with the noise until spring.

"Thank you, Caleb. Ask Major Carpenter to come see me, will you? We'll start back to Fort Laramie in the morning."

CHAPTER FORTY-EIGHT

Missouri River Camp
Montana Territory
February 1877

Tashunca-uitco stared into the embers of his lodge fire, searching for wisdom. His breath rose in thin steamy wisps. Outside icy wind whipped the tipi skins. Winter hurt. The people suffered. This winter hurt more than most. It started with a poor summer hunt. The herds grew smaller with each passing summer. Many times they were forced to move, stopping the hunt to avoid the bluecoats. They arrived in winter camp with too little food stores. Even fuel for the lodge fires was in short supply. Women and children went hungry. The little ones' cries haunted the village on howling winds. The old and the weak became sick. Everywhere the people suffered. The weakest among them died, their bodies bundled against the winter, waited fitting burial in the spring.

Spring would come again in two maybe three moons. The bluecoats would come with it. Would his warriors have the strength to fight? He could fight. His heart was strong. A warrior's death held no fear for him. He knew this death song. The medicine in Sitting Bull's vision weakened after Greasy Grass. Wakan Tanka gave them a great victory. Crazy Horse no longer saw it for a great war. They could hope for a new vision in the spring. Would they make it to the summer dances? If Crazy Horse were a bluecoat, he would not let them. The yellow hair was foolish. The bluecoat Crook was not. His warriors had the better of him on the Rosebud until the rattling guns spoke. Now he came with many rattling guns and guns that spoke thunder. It would be a hard fight with him. Many would die from these guns. Crook would fight behind these guns. He would not run this time. In his heart Crazy Horse knew. They could not win. The bluecoats were too many. Their guns too strong.

Somewhere in the darkness a child cried. What of the old, the sick, the women, the children? What would more fighting do to them? The people would spend another summer running when they should hunt to lay up stores for the next winter. The vision stretched before him. Another poor hunt, another long winter. He saw more sickness, more death. His thoughts were lost in the howl of the wind.

Montana Territory
March 1877
Spotted Hawk lay in the rocks below the crest of a ridge with his brother wolves. He wore a buckskin shirt and buffalo coat against the cold. Tashuncauitco sent his wolves to search for the bluecoat General Miles the runner said was coming. The pony soldier pursuit of the past summer and fall echoed in the arrival of the bluecoat soldiers here before the winter snows passed. Winter had been hard. Stores ran low. Game was scarce. The people were weak. Many too weak to run. Already the pony soldiers followed close. It promised another summer running away from the hunt.

Spotted Hawk squinted against the gray light. The bluecoats camped on a plain below the ridge where he and his brothers hid. Gray canvas tents mingled with fading patches of dirty snow, brown winter grass, and red rock. Cookfire smoke rose in thin wisps. His empty belly hurt with the thought of cooked food. Smoke flattened in the wind and swept away against clouds that smelled of new snow. How long before their scouts found the village? Not long, not long enough.

Spotted Hawk and Stone Heart locked eyes. Spotted Hawk nodded. The wolves pulled back from the crest of the ridge. They climbed down to the pony string waiting in the ravine below with Young Otter. The wolves swung up on their ponies and picked their way to the mouth of the ravine. Spotted Hawk wheeled his pony northwest, putting heel to flank. The bluecoats were coming. The people must flee. It meant more suffering for the sick, the weak, and the hungry. He thought of his Autumn Snow great with child. His heart hurt for her. His heart hurt for their son.

Missouri River Camp
March 1877

The warriors sat in the circle of the council fire. Dancing flames popped and cracked, sending sparks and wood smoke to the chill blanket of night sky. Few elders were among them. Most had followed Sitting Bull north into Grandmother's land to avoid the pony soldiers. Tashunca-uitco sat at council, his features etched in firelight and shadow. He listened to Spotted Hawk and his wolves report what they'd seen. The pony soldier chief Miles was coming. Further south the bluecoat Crook was said to come again. They must move before the threat of snow passed. Winter was their enemy. They fought the cold for food. Snow slowed the pony soldiers hunting them. Winter was their friend.

He thought of moving again. Twice before they moved when there was danger of winter snow. It was hard for the women and children. He thought of the hardships the weak ones suffered in the cold. The snows would end soon. Then what would they do? Crazy Horse steeled his heart to the knowing. He could fight. He could flee. Others could not. They looked to him to lead them. He could not decide this path for himself. He must decide it for those who followed him.

"The people have run many moons because of these pony soldiers. The women and children are tired and hungry. Tashunca-uitco will not make them run again. I will send word to the pony soldier chief. In the next moon I will go to the reservation."

The warriors broke into a low murmur. They looked to Crazy Horse as their war leader. His words hurt their ears. Spotted Hawk spoke for the young warriors.

"Call our brothers to the dances in the moon of making fat. Let the pony soldiers find us there. Together we will defeat them the way we defeated the yellow hair."

Crazy Horse shook his head sadly. "Already the wasichu send many more soldiers. They come with rattling guns and guns that speak thunder. You have seen them yourself. They are too many to fight. Tatanka Iyotanka has taken his people to hide in Grandmother's land. Some of you may choose to join him. Tashunca-uitco will stay in the land of the people." Crazy Horse stood and left the council for his lodge.

Bighorn Foothills
Powder River Country
Winter passed in the high country with the next moon. They broke winter camp and set out for the rising sun. Crazy Horse led them down the mountain toward their home on the plains. They wound their way along a narrow rocky trail, strung out at great length. Snow still clotted the low rocky places they passed. Snowmelt spilled in crystal rivulets and plunged down the mountainside, twisting and racing a white rush of foam. Spring dressed the aspens in buds and new leaves. Green shoots promised summer grass. Earth Mother roused herself from

slumber, swollen with the possibilities of new life.

Autumn Snow sat her pony uneasy, her belly about to burst forth in new life. She bore more than discomfort. She carried a heart heavy for their purpose. This trail led to the white man's reservation. The path held hollow promise for her son. New life should offer more. Still it offered life. Wakan Tanka answered her prayer. Crazy Horse chose the path of life for the people. He chose it for those too tired and sick to fight more. Spotted Hawk too feared for their son. He rode with his head down. His broad shoulders bowed by the weight of worry. She feared for her husband and her son.

She prayed for a vision. She prayed this path might lead to a better life for her husband and son. She saw none. She saw only a distant dark cloud. It spread across the land, covering Earth Mother like a blanket. It crawled toward them like smoke from a prairie fire, rising to the sky. It darkened Brother Sun. Her people rode on, drawn to it.

> They came from the land of the Great Father, as many as grasshoppers in summer. With them, the spirits of the people were driven from the land.
> —Autumn Snow, Tsitsistas (Cheyenne)

AUTHOR'S NOTE

While most of the characters and events recounted here have a basis in historical fact, the author has taken creative license in characterizing the individuals and events to suit the story. The author has also used certain fictional elements in a manner consistent with the overall context of the events and motives of the participants. Spotted Hawk and Autumn Snow are fictional characters as are both Indian Agents and Senator Carswell. Custer did take a woman captive at the Washita, though the Crow Scout Curly's part in her escape is fiction. Curly did escape the Little Bighorn in a blanket provided by one of the attackers. Eli Parker's role has been expanded to suit the story. Parker, a member of the Seneca tribe, served as Grant's Commissioner of Indian Affairs. His 'Buffalo Bill' legislation is fiction.

The suggestion of conspiracy between the general staff and railroad interests is speculation. The general staff plot to confirm discovery of gold in the Black Hills is also speculation. It is consistent with the thinking and public statements of both Sherman and Sheridan. Custer, according to his custom, was accompanied on his survey expedition by reporters. Siting a fort doesn't strike one as being particularly newsworthy. Confirming a rich gold discovery does. It also assures the discovery will be quickly and widely reported, resulting in the ensuing gold rush. That is precisely what the Custer expedition accomplished. Coincidence? Perhaps; but it neatly fits the motives of those

Author's Note

involved. The Black Hills gold discovery effectively broke the Fort Laramie Treaty.

The author's attempt to portray tribal views along with the attitudes and beliefs of leaders like Red Cloud, Crazy Horse, and Sitting Bull is inherently flawed. To borrow the old cliché, it is not possible for a white author to walk in those moccasins. Research reveals little more than broad outlines and snippets of insight. While every effort has been made to understand the cultural implications of the circumstances and events that make up this part of the story, in the final analysis one can only speculate respectfully in what is undoubtedly a superficial understanding.

History is itself a lens through which the past is interpreted by those who record it. Such is undoubtedly the case with this story. The heroic luster of Custer's image as history records it is largely attributable to his adoring wife, Libbie, and her own later writings. Similarly, history's shabby accounts of the Grant presidency reflect the nineteenth century "talking points" of his political adversaries, the newspaper editors who supported Horace Greeley's failed presidential candidacy in the election of 1872. Grant won that election with nearly sixty percent of the popular vote, hardly the reward for an administration whose record is based solely on graft and corruption.

Researching historical events invariably uncovers inconsistencies. By certain accounts, for example, Custer was among the first to fall at the Little Bighorn. By most popular accounts he was among the last to die. For purposes of this story the author has chosen the later account. Where there is conflict between historical fact and the author's interpretation of characters or events, it is the author's intent to present a fictional account for the enjoyment of the reader.

Paul Colt

ABOUT THE AUTHOR

Paul Colt's critically acclaimed historical fiction crackles with authenticity. His analytical insight, investigative research, and genuine horse sense bring history to life. His characters walk off the pages of history in a style that blends Jeff Shaara's historical dramatizations with Robert B. Parker's gritty dialogue. Paul Colt history entertains and informs. *Grasshoppers in Summer* received finalist recognition in the Western Writers of America Spur Awards. *Boots and Saddles: A Call to Glory* received the Marilyn Brown Novel Award, presented by Utah Valley University. Readers say, *"Pick up a Paul Colt book. You can't put it down."* To learn more visit Facebook @paulcoltauthor.

The employees of Five Star Publishing hope you have enjoyed this book.

Our Five Star novels explore little-known chapters from America's history, stories told from unique perspectives that will entertain a broad range of readers.

Other Five Star books are available at your local library, bookstore, all major book distributors, and directly from Five Star/Gale.

Connect with Five Star Publishing

Visit us on Facebook:
https://www.facebook.com/FiveStarCengage

Email:
FiveStar@cengage.com

For information about titles and placing orders:
(800) 223-1244
gale.orders@cengage.com

To share your comments, write to us:
Five Star Publishing
Attn: Publisher
10 Water St., Suite 310
Waterville, ME 04901